CANDY CORN MURDER

This Large Print Book carries the
Seal of Approval of N.A.V.H.

A LUCY STONE MYSTERY

CANDY CORN MURDER

LESLIE MEIER

THORNDIKE PRESS
A part of Gale, Cengage Learning

GALE
CENGAGE Learning·

Farmington Hills, Mich • San Francisco • New York • Waterville, Maine
Meriden, Conn • Mason, Ohio • Chicago

GALE
CENGAGE Learning®

LIBRARY OF CONGRESS CATALOGING-IN-PUBLICATION DATA

Meier, Leslie.
    Candy corn murder : a Lucy Stone mystery / by Leslie Meier. — Large print
edition.
      pages cm. — (Thorndike Press large print mystery)
      ISBN 978-1-4104-8391-1 (hardcover) — ISBN 1-4104-8391-6 (hardcover)
      1. Stone, Lucy (Fictitious character)—Fiction. 2. Large type books. I. Title.
    PS3563.E3455C36 2015
    813'.54—dc23   2015029761

Published in 2015 by arrangement with Kensington Books, an imprint
of Kensington Publishing Corp.

Printed in Mexico
1 2 3 4 5 6 7 19 18 17 16 15

In fond remembrance of Helen Bang,
and for Mary Levitt
and Stephen Bang.

Halloween, 1979

"Where do you think you're going?"

She froze. She'd almost made it. She'd been watching and waiting for months, and it had finally happened: he'd heard the jangly bell that announced a customer, and in his hurry he'd forgotten to lock the door that connected the family's living quarters to the old country store. The old witch was out, too, getting a tooth filled and no doubt skipping the Novocain, insisting that using any sort of painkiller revealed a lack of moral fortitude. "You've made your bed, and you must lie in it." That was the horrid old woman's motto.

She knew she might never have this opportunity again, so she hurried, creeping up the stairs, quiet as a mouse, and grabbing the bag she had hidden under the bed. Holding it tight against her chest, she tiptoed down the crooked, cramped back staircase. Taking a deep breath, she reached for the thick connecting door and pulled; she could hardly believe it when it swung open.

Still on tiptoes, careful to duck behind racks of merchandise, she made her way through the cluttered store. She could hear him talking to the customer; with any luck she'd be able to dash past while he was occupied with writing up a sale. She made it past the Woolrich pants and the Hanes socks, she crept through the narrow aisle between the shelves of canned vegetables and the bread rack, and then she could see the front door, with its narrow panes of glass and green roller shades.

She took a deep breath and dashed for it just as the customer, a rather large older woman with frizzy, obviously dyed red hair, turned to leave and blocked her path. Momentum carried her forward, and she stumbled into the woman.

"My goodness," the woman chided in a schoolmarmish voice. "You're certainly in a hurry."

"No, she's not," he said in that flat voice of his. "She wants to apologize. I hope you're not hurt, Mrs. Clapp."

"No, I'm not hurt," said Mrs. Clapp. "Just a bit shaken."

"That's fortunate," he said, "but at the very least you're due an apology."

She bowed her head. "I'm sorry."

Mrs. Clapp glanced at him, then at her, sensing something wasn't quite right. "No harm done," she said quickly. She was a kind woman and feared she was making more of the incident than was necessary. Suddenly, quite irrationally, she felt she had to get out of that cluttered store and into the fresh air. "Good day," she said, yanking the door open and stepping through.

The door swung closed behind Mrs. Clapp, the pull on the shade arced and fell against the glass with a tap, and the latch clicked. She stared at the scuffed wood floor, unwilling to look at him.

"Just where do you think you're going?" he asked, repeating the question. She could handle this, she told herself. The trick was to soothe him, calm him, and tamp down the seething anger, which frequently flared into violence.

"Just out to get some air," she whispered.

"With a duffel bag!" It wasn't a question; it was an accusation.

She felt as if she were drowning, her mind were slowing, and she reached desperately for something, for any plausible reason. "Just taking some old clothes to the thrift shop."

"Liar!" he bellowed, grabbing the first thing that came to hand, a glass canister filled with penny candy. He threw it at her, and the last thing she saw before the impact that felled her was a golden shower of yellow candy corn.

CHAPTER ONE

Tinker's Cove Chamber of Commerce

Press Release

For Immediate Release

Announcing the First Annual Giant Pumpkin Fest, a Fun-Filled Fall Event That Will Extend the Post–Labor Day Shoulder Season and Will Attract Thousands of Visitors to Our Beautiful Seaside Town!

Halloween already? It seemed to Lucy Stone that summer was hardly over. Even the trees had only just begun to turn in these last sultry days of September. Well, she admitted to herself, a few maples had blazed into bright displays of yellow, but the hills around Tinker's Cove, Maine, were still mostly green. Nevertheless, the cut-glass canister full of candy corn that had appeared in Country Cousins, the coastal town's general store, was a sure predictor of the coming holiday. The canister appeared every year, and shoppers were invited to guess how many pieces of candy corn it contained. The winner got a $250.00 gift certificate.

"Can I have some candy, Nana?" Lucy smiled down at her grandson, who was standing in front of the penny candy display, gazing longingly at the jars full of colorful treats. Patrick was four years old, and Lucy was taking care of him while his parents were overseas, in Haiti. Lucy's son, Toby, who was pursuing a business degree, had received a fellowship to study fish farming there.

"But Haiti?" she'd asked when he announced the project. "Isn't that awfully dangerous?"

"It's a terrific opportunity," Toby had replied.

Lucy had turned to Molly, her daughter-in-law. "Are you in favor of this?" she asked.

"Toby's right. It would be a shame to pass it up."

Lucy thought of the photos she'd seen of the slums in Haiti, the ramshackle structures that served as homes, and the faces of sick and hungry children, often with flies crawl-

12

ing on their skin. "But what about Patrick? You're certainly not planning to take him to Haiti, are you?"

"That's where you come in," said Toby. "We're hoping Patrick can stay with you and Dad while we're gone."

Lucy didn't hesitate, not for one fleeting nanosecond. "Of course! I'd be delighted!" She adored Patrick, her only grandchild, and treasured every moment spent with him.

"We'll be gone for about four months," said Molly.

"Not a problem," said Lucy, unable to restrain herself from smiling. Four months of bliss baking chocolate chip cookies together, popping corn and watching animated DVDs, and reading favorite children's books, like *Make Way for Ducklings* and *Blueberries for Sal*.

Molly and Toby shared a glance. "We know how much you love Patrick . . . ," began Toby.

"But you do tend to spoil him," said Molly.

"Which is understandable, and fine, if it's only for a few hours," said Toby.

"But he can't have unlimited sweets and TV and McDonald's for four months," warned Molly.

"I wouldn't dream of . . . ," began Lucy, sputtering. "I raised Toby, you know, and I think he would agree that Bill and I were rather strict parents."

"That's true," agreed Toby as a smile crept across his face. "You were strict parents, but you two are not strict grandparents."

"He can't have sweets — absolutely no candy, no sugary drinks, and no ice cream," began Molly.

Lucy wanted to protest that a wee bit of sugar and carbonation never hurt anyone and that ice cream was made from calcium-rich milk, but bit her tongue.

"No TV except for an hour or two on the weekend," continued Molly. "And no fast food, ever."

"Lots of fruits and vegetables . . . ," said Toby.

"But no fruit juice — it's full of sugar!" cautioned Molly. "And only fat-free milk."

"And he needs plenty of exercise," advised Toby.

"That will be Bill's department," said Lucy. "He'll love tossing a football with Patrick."

Molly's eyebrows shot up. "No TV sports. I don't want him sitting on a couch for hours, watching grown men in helmets brutally attacking each other."

"But Bill loves the Patriots," said Lucy, wishing she could suck the words right back into her mouth.

"Dad could watch at a friend's house, right?" suggested Toby.

"Sure," said Lucy, knowing full well that was not going to happen. On Sunday afternoons Bill liked to be close to his own TV and beer fridge. "So when do we start?" she asked.

Now, almost three weeks had passed since Patrick made the move from nearby Prudence Path to Bill and Lucy's old farmhouse on Red Top Road, bringing a big suitcase of small size-four clothes and his favorite stuffed toy, Jack the Jaguar. She and Bill had made a real effort to stick to the routines that Toby and Molly had established, and Patrick had slipped easily into the household, pleased to be sleeping in his father's old room, with its antique spool bed and faded *Star Wars* posters.

"Nana?" Patrick tugged at her arm. "Can I please have some candy?"

Lucy looked at the tempting display of treats, penny candy in name only. Nowadays each sugary piece, even a tiny little Tootsie Roll, cost at least twenty cents, sometimes more. Her glance traveled toward the counter, landing on a jar of pretzel rods, also twenty cents apiece. Surely Molly couldn't object to a pretzel or two?

"Let's get a pretzel," she suggested, leading Patrick away from the candy and handing him one of the salty sticks. "And while we're here, let's enter the contest. How many pieces of candy corn do you think are in the jar?"

"A million," said Patrick, biting the pretzel.

"Okay, I think that's a bit high, but we'll go for it. Can you write a one and six zeros?"

Lucy helped Patrick fill out the entry form, enjoying the quaint atmosphere of the country store while he laboriously drew all six zeros with a stubby pencil clasped in his plump little fingers. Country Cousins had managed to maintain the appearance of an old-fashioned general store that stocked everything anybody could possibly need, if anybody happened to be living in 1900. It was masterfully done, thought Lucy, and if you were a tourist buying a half pound of cheddar, which had to be cut with a wire from a giant wheel of cheese, you'd never guess that the true heart of Country Cousins was a massive complex of steel buildings on a back road behind Jonah's Pond. Despite its size, Country Cousins was still a family business owned by the Millers, who had craftily taken advantage of the Internet boom to transform a regional catalog retailer into an international merchandising giant.

Patrick put down his pencil and picked up the remains of his pretzel.

"Good job," said Lucy, folding the entry and giving it to him to stuff into the box. "This means Halloween is coming," she said, taking Patrick's hand. "Do you know what you want to be?"

Patrick certainly did. "A ninja," he said.

"A ninja. Good idea," said Lucy, noticing the rack of costumes in the corner, which featured plenty of ninjas, as well as princesses, mermaids, and superheroes. Whatever happened to pirates and gypsies? she wondered as she reached for the brass doorknob, with its elaborate design almost worn away by generations of customers' hands.

Stepping outside, Lucy noticed a woman walking past with shocking orange hair that blazed in the sunshine. This was not a salon dye job, unless it had gone horribly wrong. It was one of those garish colors you sometimes saw on teens. But this woman wasn't a teenager, not unless teens had suddenly decided to adopt tailored beige business clothes.

"Look at that lady!" exclaimed Patrick in

his piercing childish voice, and Lucy quickly changed the subject.

"Why do you want to be a ninja?" she asked, leading him to the car, which was parked just a short distance down the street.

Hearing Lucy's voice, the woman suddenly turned, doing an about-face, and walked directly toward them. Lucy was quite surprised to recognize her friend Corney Clark and wondered why she'd exchanged her expensive blond highlights for this bright orange.

"Hi, Lucy!" exclaimed Corney. "Fine day, isn't it?"

"It sure is," said Lucy, unable to pull her eyes away from Corney's hairdo, and desperately hoping Patrick wouldn't say anything about it.

But Patrick piped right up. "Why is your hair orange?" he asked.

"Patrick! Apologize right this minute. It's not polite to comment on a person's appearance."

"Never mind, Lucy," said Corney, smiling at Patrick. "I want people to notice my hair. That's why I dyed it."

"It's that spray stuff you can wash out, isn't it?" asked Lucy, noticing that Corney's carefully applied lipstick exactly matched her hair color.

"I sure hope so," said Corney, who was an attractive woman well into her forties and was always perfectly coiffed and conservatively dressed. "I don't want to be stuck like this. It's a publicity stunt for the Giant Pumpkin Fest. I'm in charge, and I want to get folks excited about the big weekend. Halloween is big business, you know, second only to Christmas, and Tinker's Cove has been missing out because we haven't had any sort of fall festival to attract shoulder-season tourists to our town."

"I think everybody's excited," said Lucy. "I see the banners up everywhere."

It was true. All the stores on Main Street were flying colorful banners picturing plump pumpkins and announcing the festival.

"Sticking up a flag is one thing," grumbled Corney, "but actually committing to taking on any responsibility is something else."

"Isn't the business community cooperating?" asked Lucy, resisting Patrick's tug on her hand. She was a reporter for the local newspaper, the *Pennysaver,* and sensed a possible story.

"Not as much as I'd like," said Corney, with a sigh. "Of course they're all busy with their own problems. It's not easy being in business these days." She paused. "The truth is, I may have underestimated how

19

much time the festival would take and overextended myself just a bit."

"Take a deep breath . . . ," advised Lucy as Patrick gave her arm another yank. It was time she got a move on. Patrick was surely bored by this grown-up conversation and most certainly hungry, as it was almost time for lunch.

"No time for deep breathing," laughed Corney. "Actually, you could help."

"Oh, no. I'm sorry, but I've got plenty on my hands these days, what with Mr. Impatient here."

"Let's see how many times you can hop on one foot, Patrick," suggested Corney.

Patrick thought that was a great idea, and began hopping, still hanging on to Lucy's arm, of course.

"What I have in mind," began Corney, "is a story for the newspaper about the new leadership at Country Cousins. That's my other job, you know. Buck Miller . . . Well, you knew him as little Sam Miller, but now he's come back. He's all grown up now, with a new name and a brand-new degree from the London School of Economics, and he's the VP in charge of marketing. He's got big plans for the company, and I think it would make a great story for the *Pennysaver*. Kind of a modern prodigal son,

20

something like that."

"He wasn't much older than Patrick when he left Tinker's Cove, was he?" asked Lucy, noticing that Patrick had got to nine hops.

"That's right. He left with his mother after all that. . . ."

"Not really a G-rated topic," warned Lucy, indicating Patrick. He was now up to twelve hops, and her arm was beginning to ache.

"Oh, right," said Corney. "Well, you were around then. You know what happened. It's not surprising that his mother didn't want to stick around. She made a new life in Europe. She even started calling little Sam by his middle name, Buckingham. I don't think she wanted to be reminded of her husband every time she called her little boy by name."

"Marcia did what she thought best," said Lucy. "But all that was a long time ago."

"And now Buck is back, and the family is grooming him to take over. He's a great guy. He'll make a great story." She smiled. "And he's very photogenic."

Lucy chuckled, knowing that Corney had a keen appreciation for handsome young men, and ruffled Patrick's hair. He had finally stopped hopping and was leaning against her. "I'll run it by Ted," she said, naming her boss at the *Pennysaver,* Ted Stillings. "But now we have to get home for some mac and cheese."

Patrick was a big fan of mac and cheese, so he clambered eagerly into the car and climbed into his booster seat, barely squirming while Lucy strapped him in. Raffi was singing about a baby beluga and Lucy's mind was wandering as she drove the familiar route to Red Top Road and home. She appreciated the logic behind the Giant Pumpkin Fest. She really did. It was a smart plan to lure tourists to town, where they would presumably spend money, boosting the town's economy. That was all well and good, but she really didn't approve of some of the planned activities, which seemed silly in the extreme.

It was one thing, she thought, to have a giant pumpkin–growing contest, but quite another to encourage people to transform their giant pumpkins into extremely unstable watercraft for a foolish and dangerous race across the cove. And worst of all, she thought, turning into her driveway and spying the enormous wooden structure that was taking shape in her backyard, was the pumpkin hurl, featuring homemade catapults.

She really couldn't understand why her

husband thought he had to compete in this ridiculous contest to see whose machine could toss a pumpkin the farthest. To her mind, it was a senseless waste of time, energy, and money, since lumber certainly didn't come cheap these days.

He never would have gotten involved, she thought, if he hadn't fallen under the influence of Evan Wickes. Ev was a great guy. Everybody said so. He was ready for any challenge. *Any challenge except taking a shower,* thought Lucy. It was Ev who had convinced Bill to build the catapult and enter the contest, and it was Ev who was always around the house, making frequent trips to the beer fridge. "Can't run on empty," he'd say, tracking mud and dried leaves and bits of grass through the kitchen. "Man or machine, you gotta have gas if you wanna keep on keeping on."

Privately, Lucy wished Ev would keep on going, taking his smelly self out of the house and out of their lives. But Bill was having a great time building the catapult and was convinced he and Ev would win the pumpkin-hurling contest. "Of course, it's not really just about winning," he had told her as he unloaded yet another expensive wood beam from his pickup truck. "It's about the process, taking on the challenge and working to build something. . . ." Here he had paused, looking for just the right word, and had grinned broadly when he found it. "Something absolutely freaking fantastic!"

CHAPTER TWO

Tinker's Cove Chamber of Commerce

Press Release

For Immediate Release

Free Pumpkin Seedling Giveaway!
Now That the Growing Season Is upon Us, the Chamber Is Giving Away Over One Thousand Giant Pumpkin Seedlings in Preparation for the Upcoming Giant Pumpkin Fest in October. These Seedlings Are Certified Healthy and Guaranteed to Grow. Don't Miss Out on the Fun. Grow Some Giant Pumpkins for the Fest. Limit Five Seedlings per Family.

Next morning, the scent of Bill's breakfast bacon was still lingering in the kitchen when Lucy went looking for her husband. A glance out the window revealed that his truck was still in the drive, so he hadn't left yet, but he certainly wasn't in the house. His egg-smeared plate and the pan he'd cooked it in were on the kitchen counter, so she slipped them in the dishwasher before stepping outside and onto the porch.

It was funny how people thought September was the beginning of fall, she thought, when it was really the tail end of summer. She always felt badly for the kids whose moms sent them off dressed in back-to-school sweaters and jeans on the first day of school; she knew from experience as a parent volunteer that the classrooms that faced south in Tinker's Cove Elementary School became solar ovens in June and September due to their large windows. Today was no exception. The sun was bright, even though it was lower in the sky, and it looked to be a scorcher. The only hint that summer had truly ended was the lengthening shadows cast by the trees.

And there was Bill, as she'd suspected, out in the garden, checking on his giant pumpkin, Priscilla. He was on his knees, measuring her girth with a carpenter's tape, rather like an anxious midwife checking a pregnant woman's progress.

"How's she doing?" she asked, crossing the patch of grass they called the lawn, now scorched and brown.

"She's grown four more inches," he said with a grin, letting the flexible steel tape re-roll with a snap. He stood up, and even after twenty-plus years of marriage, Lucy's heart skipped a beat. He was still the handsome guy she fell in love with in college, tall and lean, but now his beard was touched with gray.

"That's good, right?" asked Lucy. "How much do you think she weighs?"

"A lot," said Bill. "But it's hard to tell. Hundreds of pounds, anyway."

"What's the record?"

"I think the biggest so far was well over two thousand pounds." He cast a critical eye on Priscilla. "I don't think our girl's in that category, but I'm only guessing. We've got over four more weeks before the weigh in."

"And to think, last May she was just a little sprout." Lucy remembered the day the pumpkin seedlings were distributed at the local nursery. Back then each tiny peat pot contained little more than a swollen seed with a few roots and a couple of baby leaves on an arched stem.

"It's the horse manure," said Bill. "Every time I top-dress her, she goes on a growth spurt."

"Is it time for more?" asked Lucy.

Bill shook his head. "I can't get any. I've been calling all over, and nobody's got any."

"It's in high demand," said Lucy. "Everyone who's growing a giant pumpkin wants the stuff."

"That's just about everybody in town," said Bill.

Lucy knew that was true. The entire population of Tinker's Cove had turned out for the seedling giveaway, and almost everyone was planning to enter at least one of the Giant Pumpkin Fest events. It seemed there was no end to the uses for giant pumpkins. There was the pumpkin weigh in for the biggest pumpkins, and the pumpkin boat regatta, and the pumpkin-decorating contest. Smaller pumpkins could be included in the display of pumpkin people on the town green, and the weirdly misshapen and stunted ones would be smashed to bits in the catapult hurl.

"Nana!" Lucy looked up and saw Patrick, still in his Power Rangers pajamas, standing on the porch. "I want breakfast!"

"I'm coming," she said, heading back to the house.

When she got to the kitchen, she found her youngest daughter, Zoe, sitting at the round golden oak table with Patrick. Zoe, now in high school, was working on a container of yogurt and had given Patrick a bowl of Cheerios.

"Do you want a banana with your cereal?" Lucy asked, but Patrick shook his head no.

"I'll take one, if you're giving them out," said Sara, who was coming down the back stairway. "I've got to eat on the run." Sara was a sophomore at nearby Winchester College and was suffering this semester with an eight o'clock class, which was required for her major. Today she was rather dressed up and was wearing a skirt instead of her usual yoga pants, and she had blow-dried and styled her blond hair, rather than tying it back in a ponytail.

Lucy was sympathetic and busied herself filling a commuter cup with coffee for her daughter. "You look very nice this morning," she said, handing it over. She was thinking that when Sara pulled herself together, she looked a lot like her chic older sister, Elizabeth, who lived in Paris, where she worked for the posh Cavendish Hotel chain.

"Thanks, Mom," said Sara, taking a long drink and heading for the door, then pausing in the middle of the kitchen. "I've got to go to town hall today, and I want to make a good impression."

Lucy was puzzled. "What business do you have at the town hall?"

"It's for the scuba club. We need to get on the agenda for the next meeting of the Conservation Commission." She paused. "What are the commissioners like, anyway? Are they sticklers for the rules?"

Lucy often covered the commission's meetings for the *Pennysaver* and knew all the members. "They can be tough," she said with a shrug, recalling some rather contentious meetings. "Why does the club need to go to the meeting?"

"The scuba club wants to hold an underwater pumpkin-carving contest at Jonah's Pond, and we have to get permission from the commission. It's part of the town's conservation land."

"They're pretty conservative," said Lucy. "Pun intended."

Zoe and even Patrick joined Sara in a groan.

"Make sure you're well prepared. They'll have lots of questions, for sure, and they don't like anything that hasn't been done before." Lucy snapped a banana off the bunch and gave it to Sara. "But the whole town seems to be caught up in this pumpkin craziness, and a contest like this will draw attention to the pond and the conservation area. It's really beautiful, and it's not used very much. I don't think most people know that it's really public land, since it's so close to the Country Cousins headquarters."

"Good point, Mom. Thanks," said Sara, hoisting her book bag on her shoulder and giving Patrick a quick peck on the cheek as she left.

"Eeuw," groaned Patrick, rubbing at the offended spot.

"You love it. You know you do," teased Zoe, tickling his ribs. Zoe was no longer the skinny kid she'd been only a few months before. Now she was filling out her Forever 21 shirt quite nicely. She had also refused to go to the budget hair salon, insisting on a trip to an expensive place in Gilead, which she'd paid for herself out of the earnings from her summer job at Fern's Famous Fudge Shoppe.

Patrick scrunched his little body up on the chair, enjoying a good tickle before jumping down and running off into the family room.

"Are you done?" asked Lucy, noticing that he'd eaten only half of his cereal.

"All done!" he yelled back.

She heard the TV come on and speculated that little boys were born with a natural ability to use the remote control. That must be it, because she certainly hadn't taught him, and she knew that his parents didn't allow him to watch TV at all, which reminded her that she'd promised to adhere to their policies on child care, which included a strict ban on weekday TV. "I really shouldn't let him watch TV in the morning," she said.

Zoe was gathering up her school texts and notebooks, stuffing them into her Country Cousins backpack, to the accompaniment of a steady stream of pows, whams, and bangs. "You'll need your superpowers to get him away from the TV, Mom," she said before leaving the house.

Lucy knew it was true. Once Patrick got started watching cartoons, it was almost impossible to get him to stop. She checked the clock, calculating that the show would end in twenty minutes. That was time she could use to tidy up the house and start the Crock-Pot before she had to leave the house for her job and Patrick's day care. "Twenty minutes, Patrick," she yelled, pulling some carrots out of the fridge. "Twenty minutes!"

Lucy was already guiltily aware that she was not the ideal caregiver for Patrick, at least not by his parents' rather rigid standards, when she pulled up outside Little Prodigies in her SUV and was met by his teacher, Heidi Bloom.

"A word, Mrs. Stone," called Heidi, holding a finger in the air as she hurried down the sidewalk. Lucy's friend Sue Finch, who was a part owner of Little Prodigies, as well as its director, was terribly impressed by Heidi's credentials, which included a master's degree in early childhood education, and had recently named her head teacher.

Lucy had climbed out of the car and was unlatching Patrick's seat belt, preparing to help him out of his booster seat. "No problem," she said, setting Patrick down and giving him a kiss and a shove in the direction of the preschool's door, just a short distance from the car.

"Well, actually, there is a problem," said Heidi, adopting a serious expression. Unlike the other teachers, who were breezily casual, Heidi had a buttoned-up quality, reinforced by the long-sleeved and high-collared shirts she wore over baggy-bottomed slacks. Her blond hair was pulled back tightly into a perfect French twist.

Lucy braced herself. She knew Patrick's behavior wasn't always ideal, but she chalked it up to his parents' absence. "I know Patrick can be difficult," she began.

"Oh, no. It's not Patrick," said Heidi. "I'm sorry to say it's you, Mrs. Stone."

"Me?" Lucy was sure there was some

33

mistake. "I paid the bill. I'm quite sure I did." In fact, Lucy had been shocked by the high cost of day care, which Toby had fretted about, confessing that his graduate stipend wouldn't begin to cover it while he and Molly were away. She and Bill, eager to help the young family, had quickly offered to assume the expense, but she was now regretting that promise, as it was taking a big chunk out of their monthly budget.

"It's not that," said Heidi. "It's our drop-off policy. You need to walk Patrick into the school. You can't just let him out of the car. He must be escorted by the hand, and you need to sign him in on the sign-in sheet."

Lucy gauged the distance from the curb to the door with the Little Prodigies sign and decided it was probably less than twenty feet. "Are you kidding me? Patrick is perfectly capable of walking twenty feet, and I always watch to make sure he goes inside."

"That sort of irresponsibility is simply unacceptable," said Heidi. "You may not realize this, but the sign-in sheet is one of the tools we use to ensure the safety of our precious little ones here at Little Prodigies."

Lucy didn't appreciate being scolded, especially since she was the one paying the exorbitant bill, but she figured there was no way she was going to win an argument with

Heidi. "Point taken. In future I will make sure to sign him in," she promised, checking her watch. "Can you do it for me today, though? I'm running late."

"Why don't you just come with me and I'll show you the sign-in sheet procedure?" said Heidi.

Lucy knew when she was beaten. *Sign-in sheet procedure? Wouldn't a scribble do? Apparently not,* she thought, inwardly seething as she followed Heidi up the walk — the very short walk, which she covered in five paces. She knew because she counted.

"You're late," said Phyllis when Lucy arrived at the *Pennysaver* office on Main Street. The office was a relic from the days when the local weekly was printed in the back room, and still smelled faintly of the hot lead of the Linotype machine the typesetter used back then. Now, of course, the entire paper was formatted on computer and sent electronically to a printer in the nearby town of Gilead. But the antique regulator clock still hung on the wall, the plate-glass windows were covered with ancient venetian blinds that rattled, and a little bell on the door jangled whenever anybody came or went.

"I had to learn the proper sign-in procedure at Little Prodigies," said Lucy. "Where's Ted?" she asked, naming her boss, Ted Stillings. Ted was the publisher, editor in chief, and star reporter for the weekly, the former *Courier and Advertiser,* which he'd inherited from his grandfather, a famous New England journalist.

Phyllis patted her strawberry blond hair with a hand sporting glittery nail polish and peered at Lucy over her harlequin reading glasses. She was wearing a shirt decorated with a scattering of embroidered autumn leaves and had a string of orange beads around her neck. Phyllis's closet was stocked with clothing appropriate to every season, and she was working her way through her autumn collection. "Covering a murder," she said, answering Lucy's question.

"A murder?" Lucy couldn't believe it. Tinker's Cove was a small town where people routinely left their doors unlocked and even left their car keys in the ignition when they ran into the Quik-Stop for a gallon of milk or a lottery ticket. "Who was killed?"

"Buzz Bresnahan's pumpkin," said Phyllis, with a nod that set her double chin quivering.

"Oh, dear," said Lucy, somewhat doubtfully. "Are they sure it's murder? Maybe it's vine borers or mildew?"

"Nope. Buzz is a master gardener. He'd know how to deal with bugs and diseases, believe me, and his pumpkin was a favorite to win the weigh in. If you ask me, somebody's eliminating the competition."

"With an ax," said Ted as the bell on the door jangled, announcing his entry. "That pumpkin was smashed to bits." He paused. "Buzz took it pretty hard. It's like losing a member of the family, really, when you consider how he raised the little sprout and watered it and fertilized it. That pumpkin had real potential."

"An ax!" exclaimed Lucy as the horror of the situation dawned on her. What if a pumpkin killer was on the loose, putting everyone's giant pumpkins at risk, including Priscilla? What would happen to the festival then? Even worse, how would Bill cope with the loss of his beautiful golden gourd?

"I better let Wilf know," said Phyllis, reaching for the phone. Her husband also had a promising pumpkin growing in their garden. "He was talking about setting up a motion detector and some lights. I thought it was crazy, but now maybe it's a good idea."

"He should add a siren," advised Ted. "That oughta scare off any pumpkin killer.

And if he adds one of those closed-circuit TV cameras, he could get a photo of this psychopath."

"Good idea," said Phyllis.

"I think you've gone a little mad," said Lucy. "It's just a pumpkin, after all."

Ted and Phyllis looked at her as if she were the one who'd gone completely off her rocker.

"Wilf loves his pumpkin," said Phyllis. "He'd be devastated if anything happened to her."

"Look at this," said Ted, handing over his digital camera, which was displaying a photo of the mauled pumpkin. The giant gourd had been hacked open, and its fleshy interior, loaded with seeds, was spilling out.

Lucy found herself wincing at the gruesome sight, and hoping that Priscilla would never be subjected to such a fate. "Terrible, just terrible," she said.

"I'm going to put this on the front page so everyone can see what this maniac did," promised Ted.

"Are you sure? Publicity like that might encourage the culprit," said Lucy.

Ted nodded gravely, considering the matter. "There's always that possibility," he said, "but I think we have a responsibility to show people what happened. We can't hide it. We need to get this out there, no matter how troubling some people might find it."

"It's a family paper," cautioned Phyllis. "It might be too upsetting for kids."

"That's a risk we have to take," said Ted. "People need to know so they can take steps to protect their pumpkins. It's more than pumpkins, you know. It's a way of life, and we have to protect it."

"We can't have a Giant Pumpkin Fest without giant pumpkins," said Phyllis. "The whole town is counting on this event. A lot of people are still hurting from the great recession."

"Businesses especially," said Ted.

"That reminds me," said Lucy. "Corney Clark wants me to do a profile of Buck Miller. He's Sam Miller's kid, and he's come back to work at Country Cousins. He's got a fancy business degree, and they're grooming him to take over, but for now he's got some ambitious new marketing plan."

"Sounds good," said Ted, who was scrolling through his pumpkin photos. "Go ahead and set up an interview, but first, I need you to call the police chief and ask him if he's got any leads, any suspects. Press him hard, and ask if we've got a serial pumpkin killer on the loose."

CHAPTER THREE

Tinker's Cove Chamber of Commerce

Press Release

For Immediate Release

The Event Schedule for the First Annual Giant Pumpkin Fest Now Includes a Catapult Hurl. Contestants Are Encouraged to Construct Catapults Designed to Hurl Pumpkins, and to Compete in Accuracy and Distance Contests. The Catapult Hurl Will Take Place at Earl Johnson's Hay Field, Overlooking Jonah's Pond, at Noon, Saturday, Oct. 29. Spectators Are Encouraged to Bring Picnics and to Enjoy Live Music by Local Bands. Beer and Soft Drinks Will Be Available.

When Lucy got home that evening with Patrick in tow, she found Bill and Ev out in the garden, by the pumpkin patch, deep in conversation. Patrick made a beeline for his grandfather, who gave him a big hug.

"How was school, big guy?"

"Okay," said Patrick. "Can we play ball?" Patrick loved to play catch with his grandfather.

"Later," said Bill. "Mr. Wickes and I are busy right now."

"What's up?" asked Lucy, joining them. Patrick was kicking at the ground, disappointed that his grandfather wouldn't play with him. "Why don't you let the dog out and throw a tennis ball for her?" she suggested.

"Okay," he agreed, then ran off.

"I guess you heard about Buzz Bresnahan's pumpkin," she said after he'd gone. News, especially bad news, traveled fast.

"Brutal," said Bill. "Who would do something like that?"

"A maniac," said Ev, taking a long pull on the bottle of beer he was holding. As usual, he had a three or four days' growth of bristly beard and was wearing the same plaid flannel shirt and jeans he'd worn for at least a week. Lucy made a point of positioning herself upwind of him.

"Nobody's safe," said Bill, with a wave of his hand, which also contained a beer bottle.

"We're wide open here. The house is empty most of the day. Anybody could come in and . . ." He paused, seeking strength from the bottle. "Well, just look at her." He nodded at Priscilla, golden on her bed of straw. "She's absolutely defenseless."

"We could put the dog out. That might discourage any trespasser," suggested Lucy, who was pulling up a black, withered tomato vine.

"Our dog, Libby?" Bill's eyebrows shot up. "She's not exactly a watchdog."

The black Lab was yipping and jumping with excitement, her tail wagging as she waited for Patrick to throw the ball. Finally deciding he was taking too long, she leaped up and licked his face, causing the little boy to fall to the ground, where the two rolled around together.

Lucy smiled, watching them, and then headed for the compost pile with her dead tomato vine.

"And we'd have to tie her up, so she wouldn't wander off," continued Bill.

"You don't want to put that thing in the compost," warned Ev, adding a burp for emphasis. "You need to burn it. Tomato blight."

"Oh," said Lucy, studying the remaining tomato plants, which were a sorry sight. "So that's the problem. Tomato blight. I never heard of it."

"It's everywhere this year. The only way to stop it is to burn the affected vines. If you put them in the compost, the blight organisms will winter over and emerge in the spring to attack your new plants."

"What if I put it in the trash?" asked Lucy, who really didn't want to start a bonfire.

"Bag it up," Ev advised, then took a swallow of beer and turned to Bill. "You know," he continued, thoughtfully scratching his whiskery chin, "what you need, Billy boy, is a security system. Lights and cameras, sirens, too, all activated by a motion sensor."

"Wouldn't that be awfully expensive?" asked Lucy, still holding the tainted tomato vine.

"Consider the alternative," said Bill, growing a bit red in the face. "Sometimes, Lucy, I don't think you really care about Priscilla."

Ev burped and nodded sagely. "It's understandable. You don't want to share your man's affection."

Lucy glared at Ev. "I am not in competition with a pumpkin," she said.

" 'Course not," said Ev with a smirk.

"We have a lot of expenses right now, Bill," she said. "Day care for Patrick, Sara's

43

tuition, and" — she turned to stare at the hulking wooden catapult the two men were building, which stood between the garden and the drive — "you've spent quite a lot on that thing."

Ev stared at the ground, and Bill's face grew even redder. "Hands off the catapult, Lucy," warned Bill. "It's something I've always wanted to do."

"Okay." Lucy threw up her hands in defeat, waving the defunct vine. "You obviously won't listen to the voice of reason. Do what you want."

She turned to go, but Ev interrupted her. "Hang on," he said. "I can get you some security stuff for free."

"You can?" Bill had finished his beer and was headed for the nearby cooler to get another. "Want another beer?" he asked Ev.

Lucy rolled her eyes but judged it wiser to keep quiet.

"Yes, on both counts. Yeah," he said, accepting a fresh bottle and carefully handing Bill his empty. "I did some work for Country Cousins a while ago, replacing their security cameras, and I kept the old stuff. They said it was okay. The stuff worked fine. It was just big, you know, and they wanted a less obvious system. I could dust it off, see if it still works."

"Gee, that'd be great," said Bill, tossing Ev's empty bottle and his own into a nearby fish box, where they clinked against the others that were awaiting a trip to the recycling center.

The many others, thought Lucy as the tennis ball rolled her way. She picked it up and gave it a toss, getting a big doggy grin and an enthusiastic woof. At least somebody appreciated her, she thought as she headed into the house. Once inside, she stuffed the blighted tomato vine into a plastic bag and tied it securely, then tossed it in the trash, wondering when Ev Wickes became such an expert gardener.

Later that evening, as they got ready for bed, Lucy raised the subject once again with Bill. "You know, Bill," she said, trying to be as tactful as possible, "I really appreciate Ev's generosity about the security cameras and stuff, but I'm not sure it's a good idea to be beholden to him. That stuff must be awfully valuable. . . ."

"I wouldn't worry about it. He's not like that," said Bill, who was sitting on the edge of the bed and pulling off a sock.

"But what if he wasn't really supposed to have the stuff?" said Lucy. "Then we'd be accessories after the fact, wouldn't we?"

"Whoa," said Bill, standing up, stripped down to his briefs, with one sock on and one off. "What are you saying? That Ev's a thief?"

"Not at all." Lucy slipped her flannel nightie over her head. "Just that he's . . . Well, I think he has kind of an old-timey view of things. You know, flotsam and jetsam and all that. Finders keepers."

"Lucy, there have not been any mooncussers around here for at least a hundred years."

"Not traditional ones," said Lucy, referring to early settlers who had scavenged the shore for storm-tossed valuables and had sometimes even lured ships onto the rocky coast and seized their cargo. "But there's plenty of people who'll help themselves to anything that isn't tied down. It's happened to you, with the tools and supplies from your work sites that have disappeared."

"Well," he said, puffing out his chest, "that's a terrible thing to say about Ev. And while we're on the subject, I don't appreciate you telling him about our personal, private family finances."

"Our finances?" Lucy was puzzled.

"Yeah, all that about how we can't afford day care and college . . . ."

"I never said we couldn't afford them. I

said they're expensive, and I don't think that's exactly news, not even to Ev."

"Well," he said, hopping on one foot and yanking off the sock, "I think you should be more careful about what you say."

"Okay," she said, climbing into bed and opening her book and wondering how being responsible and expressing her legitimate concerns had somehow been twisted around until she was the one in the wrong. How did this happen?

That night Lucy had a hard time getting to sleep, finally dozing off in the wee hours of the morning. She didn't hear the alarm, and when she did wake, alone in the bed, she discovered she'd overslept. Then it was a big rush to get herself dressed and out of the house, leaving Patrick in Bill's care since it was Saturday and Little Prodigies was closed. She really hadn't appreciated how difficult things were for working parents who didn't have regular nine-to-five Monday through Friday schedules, she thought as she drove a bit too fast to the Hat and Mitten Fund meeting at her friend Sue Finch's house. After that she wasn't done: she had an appointment to interview Buck Miller.

Sue, whose house was immaculate and who always looked as if she'd stepped out of the pages of *Harper's Bazaar,* was pouring coffee for the women gathered at the fruitwood table in her Country French kitchen. "Sit right down, Lucy," she invited. "I made your favorite coffee cake."

Lucy helped herself to a piece of apple-cinnamon cake, plopping it on a dish with a rooster design, and wrapped her hands around the matching mug of coffee. "I didn't have time for breakfast," she said before taking a big slurp of coffee.

"Now that we're all here, I think we should get down to business," said Sue. The Hat and Mitten Fund was founded by a group of longtime friends that included Lucy and Sue, as well as Rachel Goodman and Pam Stillings, who met every Thursday morning for breakfast. Pam was married to Lucy's boss, Ted Stillings; and Rachel's husband, Bob, was a busy local lawyer. Sue's husband, Sid, had a successful business installing custom closet systems and often worked on remodeling projects with Bill, who was a restoration carpenter.

The four friends originally established the fund to provide warm winter clothing for the town's less fortunate children, but it had evolved through the years, and now the fund's holiday parties were a local tradition. Today, in addition to the original four friends, the planning committee for this year's Halloween party included the town's former librarian, Julia Ward Howe Tilley (Miss Tilley to everyone but her dearest, oldest friends, most of whom were now deceased); local herbalist Rebecca Wardwell; and Heidi Bloom, Patrick's teacher at Little Prodigies. Even though it was her day off, Heidi was dressed as usual in a rather long black skirt and a long-sleeved white blouse buttoned tight at the neck.

"I think we've got things pretty well in hand," said Pam. "It isn't like we haven't done this before."

"Right," agreed Rachel. "Sue is handling refreshments. . . ." She began working her way down a list, ticking off each item as she spoke. "Pam is planning games, Rebecca will tell fortunes, Miss Tilley will organize the costume judging, Lucy's going after donations for the treat bags, and I've got the face painting." She turned to Heidi. "What about you? This is your first year. Do you want to help with the games?"

Lucy helped herself to a second piece of cake and refilled her coffee mug, noticing that Heidi was limiting herself to a weak brew of green tea. "You must have lots of good ideas," she said, hoping to encourage Heidi, who was the youngest in the group, and a newcomer, as well. "After all, you're a professional with a degree in early childhood education."

"Well, since you've asked, I do have some ideas," said Heidi. "It seems to me, and forgive me for saying this, because I know how hard you all work, but this sounds to me like a rather old-fashioned party."

"Old-fashioned?" Sue's finely plucked eyebrows rose in surprise. "I don't know what you mean."

"Well, judging costumes is not the sort of thing we want to encourage, because it might stifle creativity."

"I don't see that at all," said Miss Tilley, with a sniff. She was sitting with her back to the window, and the sunshine backlit her abundant curly white hair, making her look a bit like an angel, an impression that Lucy knew was extremely misleading. "I make sure that everyone gets a prize."

"Well, then, why have judging?" asked Heidi. "You're establishing a hypocritical system that isn't actually judging at all."

Miss Tilley was rubbing her arthritic knuckles and had pursed her lips. "I match the prizes to the qualities of each costume," she said, carefully enunciating each word. "There is a prize for most colorful, for example, and scariest, and most imaginative, and so on. I must say, the children seem to enjoy it."

"They certainly do," said Rebecca, defending her friend. She had long, flowing gray hair and favored loose, colorful garments. Today she had an antique orange-and-black paisley shawl draped over her shoulders.

"As they enjoy the fortune-telling," said Miss Tilley, returning the favor.

"I think my reputation helps," said Rebecca with a sly smile. Some people in town thought she was a white witch, a notion she encouraged with the herbal potions she sold and the little owl she kept as a pet.

"Oh, dear," said Heidi, with a sigh. "I really don't think you want to get involved with the supernatural. It could have negative effects on their fragile young minds."

"I'm very careful. I limit myself to positive predictions," said Rebecca, narrowing her eyes. " 'You will do well on your next spelling test if you study,' that sort of thing."

"I know you mean well," said Heidi, primly folding her hands in her lap and adopting an instructive tone of voice, "but there's a very real danger you might produce anxiety about the test, instead of instilling a confident attitude — and we all know how important confidence and self-esteem are to success."

Lucy was beginning to wonder why she ever thought Heidi needed encouragement to express her views, and was noticing a definite increase in tension among the group. "Well, what do you suggest?" she asked, hoping to forestall Heidi's critique.

"Well, instead of these rather dated activities, why not hire a DJ?"

"Like for a wedding?" asked Pam.

"Trust me, the kids will love it. I'm actually good friends with a DJ who does kids' parties, and I bet we could get him. Believe me, there's lots of popular music that kids love."

"The electric slide?" asked Pam.

"Never heard of it," said Heidi. "Kids today like rap and . . ."

"Rap?" Miss Tilley was curious.

"It's modern, dear," said Rebecca, patting Miss Tilley's gnarled hand. "Like hip-hop."

"If there's loud music, how will we have games?" asked Rachel.

"No games. The kids will dance," said Heidi. "So much easier for you all, and there's none of that winner versus loser stuff," she continued. "Let a pro handle the entertainment, and you'll have a party the kids will really enjoy." She paused. "And there's one other thing. You really shouldn't offer sugary refreshments."

"It's Halloween," said Lucy, who had already arranged to have Country Cousins provide treat bags. "There's got to be candy."

"Tooth decay, behavior, allergies, so many reasons to avoid candy. And there are such good alternatives — popcorn, apples, cheese sticks."

"But what am I going to tell Glory?" asked Lucy. Glory Miller was married to Country Cousins' CEO Tom Miller and was a faithful supporter of the Hat and Mitten Fund. "I can't tell her, 'Thanks but no thanks for the candy you are so generously donating.'"

"I'm sure you can come up with a tactful approach," said Heidi, still speaking in her teacher tone of voice. "What do you say, ladies? Shall we have a really cool twenty-first-century party for the kids?"

Afterward, as she headed over to Country Cousins to interview Buck Miller, Lucy decided it had been a big mistake to under-estimate Heidi Bloom. The woman had amazing persuasive powers, which she would have to have, considering her profession. How else did she manage to convince a dozen contrary preschoolers to wash their hands and take naps and walk in line? She never would have thought it possible, but somehow Heidi had convinced the committee to scrap their tried-and-true plans and instead hire a DJ for the party. Now Lucy was back to square one and would have to renegotiate the treat bags with Glory, a job she wasn't looking forward to.

Meanwhile, she thought, entering the old-time general store, she might as well pick up that ninja costume for Patrick. She remembered the rack of costumes in the front corner of the store, near the window, but it seemed to have been moved. She went in search, roaming the aisles, working her way past shelves of canned goods and racks of sturdy winter gear, past fishing lures and jars of cold cream, ending up by the greeting card display, but finding no sign of the costumes.

"May I help you?" asked a clerk, a gray-haired woman wearing the Country Cousins uniform, a generous calico apron with ruffled shoulder straps. Her name, Alice, was embroidered on the bib of the apron.

"I'm looking for the Halloween costumes," confessed Lucy.

"All sold out, I'm afraid," said Alice in a sympathetic tone. She cast anxious eyes at an oil painting of an extremely unattractive gentleman, which was displayed high on the wall behind the enormous wooden counter, and lowered her voice to a whisper. "I think they still have some at the dollar store."

"It's still weeks until Halloween!" exclaimed Lucy, who had never noticed the portrait before.

"I think it's because of the pumpkin festival. Everything Halloween is selling out fast."

"Thanks for your help," said Lucy, still wondering about the portrait, which showed a rather mean-looking old guy with beady eyes set too close together, thin lips, and hollow cheeks, dressed in a somber black jacket and a starched white shirt with a high collar. A massive gold watch chain could be glimpsed beneath the jacket, fastened to his vest, and he was clutching an account book and a sharp-nibbed pen with his rather unnaturally elongated fingers. Studying the painting, Lucy wasn't sure whether those grasping fingers accurately represented the subject's hands or the artist's lack of skill. "Has that always been here? Is it a Halloween decoration?"

"Heavens no!" exclaimed Alice, stifling a giggle. "That's Old Sam, Samuel Buckingham Miller, Tom Miller's father."

"Really?" mused Lucy, thinking Old Sam looked to be an old skinflint. "You'd think they'd find a more flattering image, wouldn't you?"

Alice's eyes had widened at the approach of Glory Miller, the boss's wife, and she gave a little snort before hurrying off to help another customer. Glory, still vibrant though well into her sixties and sporting close-fitting clothes that emphasized her curvy figure, was wearing an amused expression.

"I told Buck that Old Sam's portrait would scare the customers away, but he insists it's a vital part of his old-fashioned values ad campaign. It's supposed to inspire confidence in Country Cousins' integrity and value for consumers." Glory paused. "I guess we're all going to have to get used to seeing the old miser's sour puss all over town. Buck's having it painted on the trucks, printed on the bags, even put on a billboard out by the highway."

"The younger generation . . . ," said Lucy. "Where do they get their ideas?"

"Well, Buck got his at the London School of Economics," said Glory with a shrug. "What do I know? My reaction is undoubtedly colored by my memories of Old Sam." She gave an exaggerated shudder. "I knew him and can truthfully say I never liked the old cheapskate."

"I guess we're officially old fogies," said Lucy. "I'm just from a Hat and Mitten

Fund meeting, where I learned my ideas are hopelessly out of date."

"How so?" asked Glory, raising her expertly waxed and shaped brows.

"It's the treat bags for the Halloween party," said Lucy. "There is a concern that too much candy isn't good for kids. They want apples and cheese sticks instead."

"Apples!" exclaimed Glory. "The kids will throw them at each other — and us!"

"Definitely a possibility," agreed Lucy, thinking of Patrick's good throwing arm, developed by tossing tennis balls for the dog. "But I've got my instructions."

"Me, too," said Glory, glancing at the portrait and rolling her eyes. "No problem, Lucy. I'll cut down on the candy and get some apples from MacDonald's Farm."

"You're a dear," said Lucy. "You're always so generous."

"It's my pleasure," said Glory. "I didn't grow up with much, you know, so I know how much these little treats can mean to a kid." She turned to go, then whirled around. "Dang it, I will not cut down on candy! I'll give 'em their apples, and the disgusting rubber cheese things, but they're getting double the candy, so there!"

"That'll show 'em," said Lucy, laughing. "Kill 'em with kindness!"

CHAPTER FOUR

Tinker's Cove Chamber of Commerce

Press Release

For Immediate Release

As the First Annual Giant Pumpkin Fest Grows Near, the Planning Committee Still Has Openings in the Schedule of Events. Local Businesses and Organizations Are Encouraged to Sponsor Events That Will Make Our Fest the Best Fest! For More Information, Contact Corney Clark at the Chamber's Office.

Lucy and Glory were still chuckling when Corney Clark joined them. "Good morning, ladies. What's so funny?"

"Kids today," said Glory with a big grin. "They just don't seem to appreciate the benefits of sugar and high-fructose corn syrup."

"I use stevia," replied Corney. "You've got to keep up with the times."

"I'm not so sure about that," said Lucy, who was still feeling disgruntled over the way Heidi hijacked the Hat and Mitten Fund meeting.

"Things are changing so fast," complained Glory. "I finally figured out how to use my new cell phone, and they've just come out with a new, improved model."

Corney gave a polite chuckle and took Lucy by the elbow, leading her toward the stairs. "Well, I'd love to spend the morning chatting, Glory, but Lucy and I have a meeting with Buck, and we don't want to keep him waiting."

"Of course," said Glory, with a touch of sarcasm in her voice. "You mustn't keep Buck waiting."

Lucy allowed Corney to lead the way, wondering as they wove their way through the crowded and cluttered store if Buck's involvement in the family business was causing some resentment. It wouldn't be surprising, she thought, if the young man's new ideas were upsetting to the older generation. After all, Tom had been running Country Cousins single-handedly since his brother's murder more than twenty years ago.

"I thought it would be cozier if we met here," said Corney, opening a door to a storeroom and leading the way through to a staircase. "This used to be living quarters in the old days, but it's been converted to office space. It's really used only by the store manager, since the corporate offices are out by Jonah's Pond. But there is a nice meeting room that they use for staff meetings here at the store."

She found herself feeling rather anxious as she climbed the stairway, which was dark and cramped, and she breathed a sigh of relief when they reached the meeting room, which was surprisingly large and airy, with windows overlooking Main Street. Buck, who was seated at a repurposed dining table and was studying his smartphone, stood up to greet them. He was an attractive young man in his midtwenties, with an engaging smile, and his light brown hair was gelled and combed straight up in the current style. He was dressed, appropriately, in Country Cousins classics: a light blue oxford button-down shirt, a brown sweater with a short zipper at the neck, and tan chino pants. Lucy noticed with amusement that his shoes reflected his European upbringing, as he was sporting a pair of sleek Italian slip-ons rather than the sturdy boots and brogues the store carried.

"Good morning," he said, extending his hand in greeting. "Sit down. Make yourselves comfortable." Once they were seated, he asked, "Can I get you something? Tea, coffee, juice, water . . . we've got it all."

Lucy followed his gaze and noticed that the next room was a kitchen, and found her mind wandering, attempting to reconstruct the apartment that once housed Buck's ancestors. What would it have been like, she wondered, to live above the store? Handy, she guessed, if you happened to need a fresh pack of tighty whities or a pound of cheddar cheese.

"Nothing for me," said Corney, breaking into Lucy's thoughts. She was leaning forward, resting her arms on the table in a way that provided a generous display of bosom edged with black lace.

"Me neither," said Lucy, pulling a pen and notebook out of her bag and flipping it open. "So tell me, Buck, why did you decide to come back to Tinker's Cove and the family business?"

"It's in my blood. What can I say?" he began, with a winning smile, speaking in lightly accented English. "I grew up in

61

Europe, in France and England, but somehow I always knew that this is where I really belong. I'm American through and through, and I found I really like business, which isn't surprising, since I come from a long line of shopkeepers. That's one reason why I chose to use the portrait of my grandfather for this new ad campaign focusing on Country Cousins long tradition of quality and value. I think —"

Lucy interrupted, raising her pen. "But wasn't it hard to come back here, considering everything that happened?"

"Lucy!" chided Corney. "I think you're getting off the track here." She patted Buck's hand in a comforting, protective way. "That was a very difficult time for Buck."

"Not at all," said Buck, shaking his head and removing his hand. "I don't mind. I was only five, just a little kid. All I knew was what my mother told me, that my father had died and we were going to fly away in an airplane and start a new life. I found out later that he'd actually been murdered. I was so young when he died that it never really affected me. I know that sounds terrible, but it's true. I don't really have any memories of him. I don't think he was home much, I guess he was always working." He paused, tenting his fingers. "And that's all I want to say about that. I agree with Corney that there's no sense rehashing the past."

"I just want to say, Lucy, that Buck is being terribly brave about his loss, which we know must have affected him deeply," said Corney. "I don't think we want to remind people about the murder and, um, all that unfortunate business. I think we'll keep Buck's last statement off the record. Okay?"

"I am sorry, but I did have to ask," said Lucy, fearful of scuttling the interview. "I have to include a mention of the past tragedy, but I'll be tactful. After all, it's the one question our readers will all want answered."

"Those who are old enough to remember," said Corney, making a wisecrack.

"Which, I'm sorry to say, is most of the *Pennysaver*'s readers," said Lucy with a rueful grin.

"Well, now that Buck is back home, where he belongs, right here at Country Cousins," said Corney, rising from her chair and standing behind him, with her hands on his shoulders, "the focus is on the future."

"That's right," agreed Buck, slipping out from her grasp and standing beside a motivational flip chart. "We're moving forward, but we want people to know that our values haven't changed. The merchandise may change, the mix of products will definitely change, but the company's slogan hasn't changed, and it's not going to change." He lifted a page of the chart and pointed to the motto printed there: *We're not happy unless you are.*

Just in case Lucy's eyes had failed her, Corney read the motto aloud. "We're not happy unless you are."

"So, Buck," continued Lucy, "what new products do you have in mind?"

"Oh, that would be telling. Besides, we're still in discussions. Nothing has been finalized."

"And the product mix? What would you like to see there?"

"Well, again, we're analyzing sales patterns and revenue flow, gathering data. In the future the company will be largely driven by data. There's no sense making moccasins, for example, if nobody's buying them."

"You're giving up moccasins?" asked Lucy, a note of alarm in her voice. Country Cousins' moccasins were a wardrobe staple in Tinker's Cove. This was news the *Pennysaver*'s readers would definitely want to know.

"Just an example . . . No decisions have been made," cautioned Buck.

"That is absolutely off the record, Lucy," said Corney. "I don't want to see any reference to moccasins in the story."

"Okay," agreed Lucy, with the uncomfortable feeling that she was losing control of the interview. All she'd gotten so far was the fact that young Buck, who was apparently a rather callous fellow, had come back with big plans, plans that he was not about to divulge.

"I suppose your uncle, Tom Miller, must be pleased to have you join the company," said Lucy, unable to resist probing a bit. "It will take some of the pressure off him as CEO, right?"

"Well, um —" began Buck, only to be cut off by Corney.

"My goodness!" she exclaimed, making a big show of checking her watch. "Is this the time? I'm afraid we have to wrap this up."

"Okay," said Lucy, who knew when she was beat. "Thanks for meeting with me. Just one more thing, a photo. How about you standing right there, next to the company motto?"

"Great," enthused Corney. "That would be fabulous, just fabulous. And don't forget to mention the portrait of Old Sam, which is going to be the focus of the old-fashioned value campaign."

"Old-fashioned values, with an *s*," said Buck, correcting her. "We don't have one single product that's a good value. All our products are great values. That's the point we want to make."

"Absolutely," said Lucy, dropping her notebook and pen into her bag and preparing to leave. "Great to meet you."

Buck extended his hand for a parting handshake, and she noticed his fingers were very long, just like Old Sam's. So, she thought, the artist had been true to his subject.

"Just one last thing," she began, voicing a question that had been bothering her, especially since Buck was so keen on exploiting the company's heritage in his new ad campaign. "Why not be called Sam, after your father, grandfather, and even your great-grandfather? Why did you change to Buck?"

"It was Mom," he replied. "She decided to go with my middle name, Buckingham, when we moved to France, and I liked it a lot better than Sam." He gave her a somewhat embarrassed grin. "I thought Sam sounded too much like an old man, and Buck was more masculine, more dynamic."

"That makes sense," agreed Lucy as he opened the door for her. "Thanks again."

"No problem," he said with a grin. "Have a nice day."

Amazing, thought Lucy as she wandered through the store once again, making her way to the Main Street entrance. Buck had been in the United States for only a few weeks, and he'd already caught the "Have a nice day" infection. Well, next up on her agenda was the Conservation Commission meeting, but she had nearly an hour before it was scheduled to begin. Since it was a fine day, she decided to treat herself to a lobster roll lunch, the last of the season, as the Lobster Pool was soon due to close for the winter. She deserved it, she told herself, since she had to work on this gorgeous Saturday instead of relaxing with her family.

"I'm going to miss these," Lucy told the girl at the takeout window. The roll, which had been grilled in butter, was loaded with chunks of lobster meat lightly tossed in mayonnaise and was accompanied by a generous serving of crispy fries and a diminutive paper cup of cole slaw. *You wouldn't want to spoil this meal with anything remotely healthy,* she thought, taking her plastic utensils and plate over to one of the wooden picnic tables that overlooked the cove.

As she sat there, gazing out at the boats

bobbing in the harbor and at the hillside beyond, dotted with neat houses and lots of green, pointy pine trees, along with an occasional golden maple, she savored the moment. Days like this, with crisp air and a cloudless sky, were rare by the coast, where clouds and humidity dominated the weather. She could see the Quissett Point lighthouse on the opposite side of the cove, where it was perched on a rocky promontory that was constantly battered by the waves, even on a calm day like this, and her thoughts turned to the interview with Buck.

She speared a chunk of tail meat with her plastic fork and chewed it, chuckling as she recalled Corney's obvious flirting with Buck. That woman simply could not resist an attractive man, no matter his age or suitability. *Well,* thought Lucy, *more power to her.* If she hadn't been married to Bill for what seemed like forever, maybe she'd be a predatory cougar, too.

She remembered Buck as a little boy, when everyone knew him as Sam. He had been in kindergarten when his father was killed. It had happened around Christmastime, when she had been working at Country Cousins, taking orders over the phone on the night shift during the holiday rush. She had actually discovered Sam Miller's body when she'd stepped outside on her break for a breath of fresh air. She'd found him in his car, a sporty BMW, poisoned by carbon monoxide. His death was first thought to be a suicide, and the fact that it was a murder wasn't discovered until later, after Sam's wife, Marcia, had left town with her little son.

Chewing steadily, Lucy had worked her way down to the bun, which still contained plenty of lobster, and she lifted the sandwich to her mouth and took a bite. This was her favorite part, where the buttery roll and the succulent lobster combined in exquisite deliciousness. She sighed, experiencing bliss. There was no food better than this in the world, she decided, and certainly not when the sun was warming your back and a light ocean breeze was ruffling your hair.

Oh, to be in Maine, she thought, *eating a lobster roll on a sunny day.* Perhaps this was what heaven was like. She hoped so, and she felt a sudden tug at her heartstrings, thinking of her absent children. She thought of Elizabeth, who was presumably having the time of her life in Paris, and wondered if and when her oldest daughter would decide to settle down, marry, and produce a grandchild. And then there were Toby and Molly in Haiti, which was geographically closer to Maine than Paris but somehow seemed even farther away. She wished they were back in Maine, where they belonged, and she suspected that Patrick missed his parents more than he let on. He was a little trooper, but she'd noticed he'd become a bit more difficult lately and even a bit weepy at bedtime. It was only natural that he'd miss his mom and dad and that the missing would intensify the longer they were separated.

She was down to the last bite, but she was full and decided to leave it, sort of as a promise to herself that there would be more lobster rolls next summer. She tossed it out onto the rocks that edged the cove, and a couple of seagulls swooped down to claim it. One succeeded, and the other followed it in flight, complaining loudly.

Well, she decided, standing up and wiping her hands on the little foil-wrapped towelette that came with her sandwich, Buck seemed to be quite the sophisticated, competent businessman, but she suspected that at bottom he wasn't very different from Patrick. They were both little boys whose orderly, secure worlds had suddenly been turned upside down. The difference was that Buck had lost his father for good, but Patrick would be reunited with his parents at Christmas.

Back in the car she headed over to town hall, where the Conservation Commission's monthly hearing would take place in the basement meeting room. She saw no sign of Sara's Civic in the parking lot, but there was a big pickup truck with a scuba bumper sticker, and Lucy guessed she had caught a ride with another club member. She had intended to sit with her daughter, to offer moral support, but when she entered the meeting room, she found Sara sitting with a very good-looking young man. *Better to give her free rein,* she decided, choosing a seat on the opposite side of the room.

Several of the commission members were already seated at the row of tables on the raised dais provided for town officials. She recognized Caleb Coffin and Tom Miller, as well as Millicent Hayes. Fred Witherspoon and Tony Marzetti were last to join the panel, strolling in together, engaged in conversation. The meeting, with only a few routine items on the agenda, hadn't drawn much of a crowd, and only a few retirees were in attendance, apart from Sara and the young man, and the commission's secretary, Lucille Whipple.

"I'm calling this meeting to order," announced the chairman, Caleb Coffin, with a

71

polite tap of his gavel. Caleb, a former bank president, was in his sixties, and he was dressed in the usual uniform of a prosperous Tinker's Cove retiree, a plaid flannel shirt and khaki pants. "As usual, I think we will dispense with the reading of the minutes?" He checked with the other members, receiving nods of agreement. "The minutes will be posted for anyone who is interested," he continued, with a nod in Lucy's direction. Caleb was scrupulous about following the state's open meeting law and wanted to make sure Lucy knew there was no attempt to avoid public scrutiny.

She smiled in return, and he referred to his agenda. "First off, we have a request from the scuba club at Winchester College, which wants permission to use Jonah's Pond for an underwater pumpkin-carving contest." Caleb glanced at the audience over his half-glasses, settling on Sara and her companion. "I presume you are here to represent the club?"

The young man stood up. "Yes. My name is Hank DeVries, and I am the president of the scuba club." Lucy thought he was quite well spoken, and he was neatly dressed in clean jeans and a T-shirt with a dive club logo. "We want to take part in the Giant Pumpkin Fest, and the underwater pumpkin carving was a natural choice for us. These contests are quite popular. I have printouts describing contests held in other towns, such as Key West and, much closer to us here in Maine, Damariscotta." He waved a sheaf of papers, offering it to the committee for examination.

Caleb accepted the printouts and passed them to the other committee members, who studied them carefully, leafing slowly through the pages.

"If you have any questions, I'm happy to answer them," said Hank.

"Jonah's Pond is a pristine body of water, one of the few truly unspoiled ponds in the state," said Millicent. "What will happen with the detritus, the stuff from the inside of the pumpkins?"

"Each contestant will be provided with a mesh bag for the innards," said Hank, "but there will inevitably be some spillage. It's completely natural vegetable material, much like leaves and seeds that fall into the pond from surrounding trees, and I imagine some of it will be eaten by native fauna."

Millicent nodded, apparently satisfied by his response, but Tom Miller was frowning over the papers. "How many people do you think this contest will attract?" he asked, furrowing his brow.

He was a pleasant-looking man, thought Lucy, noticing his tanned face, clear blue eyes, and the touch of gray at his temples. He and Glory certainly made a handsome couple, even if he did have the same weirdly long Miller fingers she'd noticed in the portrait of Old Sam. He was dressed rather more formally than the others, wearing a crisply starched white dress shirt with a tie, a blazer, and gray pants.

"We are planning on limiting the number of contestants to twelve," said Hank, "so it's a relatively small number. There will be spectators, of course, but frankly, there isn't much to see, since the action takes place underwater. It's really all about giving divers a way to take part in the festival. We will have underwater cams, of course, but . . ."

"Cameras?" demanded Tom, seizing on the point.

"Yeah, to make sure there's no cheating. Nobody substituting an already carved pumpkin, for example."

"How many cameras?"

"At least six, one for every two carving stations," said Hank. "And there'll be monitors set up on the shore." He paused, then added quickly, "No big screens or anything like that."

"No JumboTron?" asked Tony with a grin.

"No, that's definitely not in the club budget," said Hank, smiling.

"Will there be prizes?" asked Millicent.

"The Five Cents Savings Bank is providing the prizes. They're American Express cash cards. I don't know the exact . . ."

Sara stood up. "I have that information," she said. "I'm Sara Stone, and I'm the club treasurer," she said, introducing herself. "The cash cards are for twenty-five, fifty, and one hundred dollars." Getting a dismissive nod from Caleb, she sat down.

"This seems like a nice event," said Fred Witherspoon. "I used to dive myself, back when I was younger, and this is a good way to draw attention to the sport."

"It will also draw attention to the pond, which very few people realize is town-owned conservation land, open to all for walking and bird-watching," said Tony. He received nods of agreement from several board members.

But not, however, from Tom Miller, who was frowning. "At the best of times scuba diving is pretty dangerous, isn't it?" he asked. "Are you going to have medics on standby, in case there's an emergency?"

"Well, we weren't planning to," said Hank. "The pond isn't very deep, and we'll do a safety check on everyone's equipment. I don't foresee any problems."

"Well, that's how it is with accidents, isn't it?" demanded Tom, shooting his cuffs, which were fastened with gold cuff links shaped like little gold anchors. "You don't foresee them. And if something unfortunate were to happen, well, who would be liable? Would it be this committee? The town? I don't know if we're willing to assume that responsibility. We could be sued for half a million, a million dollars, even more, if somebody loses their life."

"I don't think that's realistic," said Hank, looking rather anxious. "There have been plenty of underwater pumpkin-carving contests, and I know of no problems related to them."

"Well, as for me, I can't say I think this is a good idea," said Tom.

"Let's call a vote," said Caleb. "Is there further discussion?"

The committee members shook their heads, and Hank sat down nervously on the edge of his seat.

"All in favor?" asked Caleb, and Millicent, Tony, and Fred raised their hands.

"Opposed?"

Tom Miller was the lone opponent.

"As for me, I'm sorry Tom, but I'm in favor, too," said Caleb. "You're outvoted this time."

Tom shrugged. "Just to be on the safe side, I'm going to consult my lawyer about the committee's potential liability, and I'm going to check with the state's natural resources people."

"Do what you have to do," said Caleb in a resigned voice. "In the meantime, young man, you've got your permission. Good luck with the contest."

"Thank you," said Hank, gathering up his papers. As he turned to go, he took Sara by the arm.

Interesting, thought Lucy, catching her daughter's eye as Hank took her heavy book bag and slung it over his shoulder, carrying it for her. Sara had never mentioned Hank, and Lucy wondered if a romantic relationship was in the works. Or maybe Hank was just a polite young man, she thought, then turned her attention to the next item under discussion, the replacement of a culvert under Main Street Extension.

The meeting dragged on, and when it finally ended, Lucy hurried home, eager to see what Bill and Patrick had gotten up to in her absence. She had no sooner pulled into the driveway and braked when a very loud siren began to wail. She clapped her hands over her ears, attempting to block the ear-piercing sound, and got out of the car. Looking toward the garden, she saw Ev, along with Bill, who was on his hands and knees, apparently attempting to cut off the siren. Patrick was jumping up and down in excitement, adding a few hops even after the noise stopped.

Bill stood up and was clapped on his back by Ev. "It worked, Billy boy! It worked!" he yelled. "It went off when she drove in. That used motion detector still works."

"What was that awful noise?" asked Lucy, whose heart was thumping in her chest.

"Pumpkin alarm," said Bill with a satisfied smile. "We just finished installing it."

"I hope it's not going to do that every time I use the car," said Lucy.

"This was just a test," said Bill. "I'll set it only at night and when nobody's home."

"But what about animals? Won't raccoons and deer set it off?"

"Yeah," volunteered Ev. "And that's a good thing. Nobody and no thing is going to mess with this pumpkin. No way."

"Not if they value their hearing," muttered Lucy, climbing the porch steps.

"Can you do it again, Grandpa?" asked Patrick.

"Sure thing!" exclaimed Ev as the siren sounded once again.

Time to buy earplugs, thought Lucy, wondering if she'd ever get a good night's sleep again.

Spring, 1979

She was in the kitchen, looking out the window while she stirred the oatmeal, which was bubbling thickly in the chipped white enamel pot set on the gas stove. Outside, she could see wands of yellow forsythia swaying in the breeze. In the kitchen, the air was thick with the cloying, heavy scent of oatmeal porridge.

It was the only thing he ever ate for breakfast, and it had to be just right, not too thick and not too thin. Waiting every morning for the rattle of keys that announced his arrival, she had become an expert at cooking oatmeal.

This morning he was right on time; she heard the keys at exactly 7:36 a.m. and scooped the porridge into the white bowl with roses on the bottom, which he preferred. The pattern was called Virginia Rose — the name was printed right on the underside — and every day, when she washed it, she imagined being in a green garden in Virginia, a garden with a brick wall that was covered with fragrant pink roses. A secret garden that was very far away and where he wouldn't be able to find her.

The latch clicked, and the door opened. He entered the kitchen and turned, then carefully locked the door behind him. It was crazy, she thought. She had never known anybody like him, anyone who locked every door in their house, but he did. It was some sort of compulsion, some weird habit. It often occurred to her that all these locked doors would be a problem if the house ever caught on fire, and sometimes, when she was especially tired, she imagined him locked in a burning room and unable to get the lock to work. She found that thought particularly comforting.

"Cream," he said, sitting down in his usual place at the table, and she quickly snatched the pitcher from the counter, where she had forgotten it after she filled it, and set it before him. He grunted and picked up the linen napkin, starched and ironed within an inch of its life by that old witch Emily, and arranged it on his lap while she filled his oversize cup with coffee.

He usually ate alone, which was fine with her, because she didn't like watching him eat the oatmeal, slurping and smacking his lips. But today she had a request, something she wanted to ask him, so she asked for permission to join him at the table.

"May I sit?" she asked in the breathy, childish voice he preferred, and received a nod in return.

Slipping into the chair, making sure not to scrape the legs on the floor, and carefully lowering her eyes, she explained that she wanted to go out today, to the library, and needed him to unlock the door for her.

"The library?" he asked, furrowing his bristly, untrimmed eyebrows.

"Miss Tilley called and especially asked for me to help shelve some books for her. She says she got behind. The library was very busy during school vacation week." She paused, studying his expression and trying to gauge his reaction. "I could pick up some books for you, if you'd like."

"No need," he said, and her heart sank.

"There might be a new Louis L'Amour," she said, hoping to tempt him.

"Hmmm," he said, and some oatmeal dribbled down his chin, which he blotted with his napkin. "What time do you want to go?" he asked.

"Two o'clock," she said, hardly believing her luck.

After placing the heavy silver spoon in the bowl, he pulled a slim notebook out of his vest pocket and opened it, then drew the tiny pencil out of its leather loop and jotted down the time. It was now official; the doors would be

81

unlocked at two o'clock.

"Thank you," she said, hopping up and refilling his coffee cup. "I'll be sure to ask about the book for you."

He took a big slurp of coffee, and she could hear him swallow, a sound that usually turned her stomach. But not today. Today she was going to the library, and she wasn't going to shelve books. She was going to the first meeting of a women's liberation group.

CHAPTER FIVE

Tinker's Cove Chamber of Commerce

Press Release

For Immediate Release

Only Days to Go until the First Annual Giant Pumpkin Fest Kicks Off on Saturday! Excitement Is Building in Tinker's Cove as Businesses Prepare for Increased Customer Traffic during the Weeklong Autumn Celebration, Which Is Packed with Fun-Filled Events. Local Restaurants and Innkeepers Are Already Reporting a Substantial Increase in Reservations over Last Year.

Where had the month gone? wondered Lucy, staring at the calendar on the kitchen wall. Only a little more than a week until Halloween and she still hadn't found a ninja costume for Patrick. It wasn't for the lack of trying: she had dutifully scoured every possible source in the area and had come up empty. She considered trying the Internet but feared she'd left it too late and the costume wouldn't come in time. She could pay for overnight shipping, of course, but something held her back, some little puritanical vestige that wouldn't allow her to spend a lot of money on anything as frivolous as a Halloween costume.

No, she decided, she would make the ninja costume. She used to sew all the time when her own four kids were young, and had turned out quite credible gypsies and pirates, even a slinky cat. Unfortunately, she realized, the sewing machine she'd used back then was gone, the victim of a household purge in which she'd followed the advice of an organizing guru and foolishly tossed everything she hadn't used in a year. She did, however, have some black bedsheets left over from Elizabeth's Goth phase, and a couple of old sewing patterns had escaped the purge, including one for children's pajamas, which she'd recently found stuffed in her sewing basket. And she was pretty sure that Miss Tilley had a sewing machine, an old treadle model to be sure, but a genuine Singer.

When she arrived at Miss Tilley's little Cape Cod–style house, she was admitted by Rachel, who was actually Miss Tilley's home-care aide but maintained the fiction that she was just a helpful friend. Miss Tilley herself was seated at the dining room table, bent over an elaborate cut-glass canister.

"What are you doing?" Lucy asked, setting the pattern and fabric down on the lovely old pine table, which glowed from its weekly rubdown with lemon oil.

Miss Tilley looked up from the pad of paper where she was scrawling numbers with a fine new pencil. "We're computing the volume of this canister."

"And why exactly is it important?" she asked, taking a seat.

"Because if I know the volume, then I can figure out how many pieces of candy corn it can hold."

Light was beginning to dawn over Marble-head, as Lucy remembered a very similar canister that was presently sitting in Country Cousins, filled with candy corn.

"You want to win the contest?" she asked.

"I surely do," said Miss Tilley with a snap of her head. "I have entered it every year for sixty or more years, and I have yet to win. And this year I happen to need a new winter coat, and I am quite taken with those ultralight down models they've just come out with at Country Cousins."

"They cost two hundred twenty-nine dollars," said Rachel, who was filling a cup measure with candy corn, counting the pieces one by one.

"Pricey," said Lucy.

"Indeed, but it's quite probably the last winter coat I will ever need," said Miss Tilley with a dramatic sigh.

"I'm pretty sure you'll outlive both of us," said Rachel, adding an exclamation. "Darn! Now I lost count. Again."

She poured the candy corn out and started over.

"I was hoping to use your sewing machine," said Lucy, patting the pattern. "I want to adapt this pajama pattern to make a ninja costume for Patrick."

"You'll need to add a hood," said Rachel, studying the picture on the pattern front. It showed a boy and a girl, clearly fresh from their evening baths, clutching teddy bears as they headed off to bed in their homemade pajamas with no trace of Disney princesses or Marvel superheroes.

"Pretty simple, I think," said Lucy, sketching a design on one of Miss Tilley's discarded sheets of paper covered with numbers and formulas. "I think you've got this wrong. Volume isn't two pi r. It's pi r squared h."

"That does ring a bell," said Miss Tilley, applying herself with fresh energy to her computations.

"And pi is three point one four, not three point one six."

"Aha!" exclaimed Miss Tilley, whose white hair was now springing out around her head in the fashion of Albert Einstein.

"I'm so impressed," said Rachel. "I never knew you were a mathematical genius."

"Neither did I," said Lucy. "I guess there are some things you never forget, like how to ride a bicycle."

"I managed to forget," said Rachel, dumping out the candy corn and starting to count all over again. "I can't seem to remember anything these days."

"Your brain gets stuffed, so you have to prioritize," said Miss Tilley. "The longer you live, the more experiences you have to remember. You have to decide to forget what's not important, because it takes up too much room."

"At what age do we begin to store memories?" asked Lucy, wondering if Patrick would remember the months he spent with his grandparents while his parents were gone.

"My earliest memory is a piece of chocolate my grandmother gave me," said Rachel. "It was wrapped in blue and silver foil and looked like a little purse."

"How old were you?" asked Lucy.

"Maybe three or four. I'm not sure," said Rachel.

Lucy turned to Miss Tilley. "What about you?"

"I remember my mother burning her hand on the coal stove in the kitchen," she said. "I might have been two."

"You're just trying to one-up me," said Rachel. "I don't believe you remember anything that happened when you were two."

"Me, either," said Lucy. "My first memory was playing with my father. He pretended to be a bear and chased me, and it always ended with a big bear hug."

"Sweet," cooed Rachel. "How old do you think you were?"

"Probably three."

"I think that's about right. I think that's when memories begin to stick," said Rachel. "Why do you ask?"

"Well, yesterday I interviewed Buck Miller. He's called Buck now, but we remember him as Sam Miller's son, little Sam. He's come back to Tinker's Cove to work in the family business. He's got all sorts of big ideas."

"That's nice," said Rachel.

"So the prodigal son returns," said Miss Tilley.

"But the funny thing is, when I asked him if it was difficult to come back to the place where his father died, he said he didn't really remember his father."

"Impossible," said Miss Tilley. "He was in kindergarten when his father was murdered. He would certainly have some recollection of his father."

"He said his father was distant, always working. . . ."

"Well, that's a memory, isn't it?" asked Rachel. "And besides, Sam's death was followed by a traumatic event. His mother snatched him out of school and dragged him off to Europe, didn't she?"

"Paris," said Miss Tilley. "Marcia went to Paris. As I recall, she couldn't leave town fast enough. I don't think she even stayed for the funeral."

"Well, she was probably terrified," said Lucy.

"Traumatized, certainly," said Rachel. "Fight or flight is a powerful instinctive reaction. It's not rational."

Lucy turned to Miss Tilley. "You were

friends with Emily Miller, weren't you?" she asked, naming Tom and Sam's mother. "It must have been a terrible time for her, losing her son like that."

"She never said," replied Miss Tilley. "She never spoke about Sam, or her husband, Old Sam, or even her grandson. I thought it was a trifle odd even then, when people were much more reserved than they are now."

"Families have different ways of dealing with grief," said Rachel, who was a psych major in college and had never got over it. "In some families emotions are never expressed. Everything is just stuffed down tight inside."

"Let's see that pattern of yours, Lucy," said Miss Tilley, shoving her calculations aside and deftly changing the subject. "I oiled the Singer last week, when I mended a pillowcase, and it ran just fine." She clucked her tongue. "They sure don't make things like they used to."

Later that afternoon, when Lucy picked up Patrick at Little Prodigies, she was bursting with her big news. "Patrick!" she exclaimed, helping him put on his Windbreaker, "I'm making you a ninja costume for Halloween, and it's almost finished. You can try it on when we get home."

Patrick stamped his foot and tossed his backpack on the floor. "You can't make a ninja costume!"

"Sure you can," said Lucy, retrieving the backpack and taking him by the hand. "You'll see."

"I don't want a homemade costume!" he yelled, yanking his hand away.

"But, Patrick," she began, bending down so they were face-to-face, "the stores are sold out. I can't buy a ninja costume, but I can make one. It's going to be really great."

Patrick wasn't convinced. "Homemade costumes stink!" he snarled, marching to the door.

Lucy ran after him and grabbed him by the shoulders. "You have to wait for me to sign out," she reminded him.

"I don't want to! I'm going!"

Lucy was horribly aware that Patrick's tantrum had drawn the attention of Heidi Bloom and another teacher, as well as a couple of parents, who were all watching the mini-drama. Action was definitely called for.

"No, you're not," said Lucy, snatching him up and hugging the squirming child close. "Please sign out for me," she panted in Heidi's direction as she hurried out the door to the car, carrying forty-odd pounds of wriggling boy.

After dumping him in his booster seat with perhaps a bit too much force, Lucy snapped the seat belt in place. "That's quite enough of that, young man," she said. "And if you don't want a homemade costume, you'll have no costume at all!"

She slammed the door and was reaching for the handle of the driver-side door when she realized Heidi had run out of the building after her.

"Um, Mrs. Stone, this is the schedule for the next two weeks," she said, proffering an orange sheet of paper. "Halloween and all," she added.

"Oh," said Lucy, exhaling and straightening her jacket, which had become twisted. "Thank you."

"And, Mrs. Stone, I just want to mention that you really shouldn't threaten Patrick. He's much too young to understand cause and effect, so threats and bribes are really meaningless to children his age. It's preferable to explain a situation and let him know the sort of positive behavior you expect."

From inside the car Lucy heard Patrick crying.

"Thanks for the advice. I'll keep it in mind," she said, sliding behind the wheel.

She switched on the ignition and pulled away from the curb, determined to get home as fast as possible.

"It's okay, Patrick," she said, glancing in the rearview mirror and seeing her grandson's face, red and wet with tears. "Everything's going to be okay."

Patrick clearly wasn't convinced; he cried all the way home and stopped only when Libby bounded up to greet him and licked his face.

"Hi, fella," said Bill, joining them in the driveway. "What's the trouble?"

Patrick was half crying and half laughing and was trying to both hug the dog and push her away.

"One of those days," said Lucy by way of explanation. "It started over his Halloween costume, but I think he's really beginning to miss . . ."

"Right," agreed Bill with a nod. "Come on, buddy. Let's check on Priscilla and see how much she's grown."

Patrick sniffed and rubbed his eyes with his hands. "Can I measure her?"

"Sure," said Bill. "And we'll give her a drink of water, too."

He and Patrick went off in the direction of the garden, and Lucy gathered up Patrick's things, his backpack and jacket and the day's art project, as well as the sewing and the groceries she'd bought and her purse, and went inside. She was putting the groceries in the fridge when she heard the crunch of gravel in the driveway that announced somebody's arrival. She looked out and recognized the same pickup truck she'd seen at the Conservation Commission hearing, the one with a scuba bumper sticker. She assumed Sara had gotten a ride home with Hank, and when several minutes passed with no sign of the passenger door opening, she assumed her daughter was apparently in no hurry to say good-bye.

Lucy had hung up the jackets, emptied Patrick's lunch box and backpack, turned on the oven, and put the half-sewn ninja costume away before Sara came inside, her cheeks quite flushed. Bill was right behind, demanding, "Who was in that truck with you?"

"Just Hank," she said, then disappeared up the back stairway.

"Who is this Hank?" he demanded, yelling up the stairs.

"He's the president of the scuba club," said Lucy, taking a package of ground beef out of the fridge. "Meat loaf for supper," she added, naming his favorite dish.

"Have you met him?" he asked, taking a

seat at the round golden oak table.

"Not exactly," said Lucy. "But I saw him at the Conservation Commission meeting a few weeks ago. He seems very nice, well spoken, and polite."

The door opened, and Patrick came in, along with Libby. "I'm hungry," he said, and Lucy, who was mixing up the meat and egg and bread crumbs with her hands, asked Bill to give him some mini carrots. Soon he was also seated at the table, under the watchful eye of Libby, who adored carrots and was hoping one or two might come her way.

"He drives too fast," said Bill. "Did you see him peel out of the driveway?"

"I missed that," said Lucy, who hadn't heard a thing and was pretty sure Hank had made a careful exit.

"And I don't like this scuba stuff," continued Bill. "It's ridiculous, going in the water this time of year. . . ."

"They wear wet suits," said Lucy.

"It's still dangerous," said Bill. "And what do they wear under those wet suits? Where do they change?"

"I have no idea, Bill," said Lucy, turning the meat into a pan and patting it into shape. "I think you're just being an overprotective father." She slipped the meat loaf into the oven. "Look, I don't know this guy, but you've got to admit, he's probably better for Sara than that Seth Lesinski she was so hot on last spring. Remember him? The campus agitator and radical, the guy who got her arrested at a demonstration?"

"Oh, him," snorted Bill, getting up and pulling a bottle of beer out of the fridge and unscrewing the cap.

"Have some faith in your daughter's good sense," she urged, resolving to take her own advice.

"C'mon, Patrick," said Bill, reaching for his cap. "Let's make sure the pumpkin security system is up and running."

"The siren, too?" asked Patrick, hopping down from his chair.

"Absolutely," agreed Bill. "We've got to make sure the siren works."

Lucy sighed and got busy scrubbing some potatoes. She was putting them in the oven, beside the meat loaf, when she discovered that the siren on the security system was working just fine.

CHAPTER SIX

Tinker's Cove Chamber of Commerce

Press Release

For Immediate Release

The Wait Is Over! The First Annual Giant Pumpkin Fest Will Kick Off at 11:00 a.m., Saturday, Oct. 22, When Local Officials Will Join Chamber Executive Director Corney Clark in a Ribbon-Cutting Ceremony Opening a Harvest Figure Display on the Town Green. The Display Features More Than Twenty Life-Size Dioramas Created by Local Businesses and Organizations, Utilizing Figures with Pumpkin Heads and Clothing Stuffed with Straw. See if Your Favorite Wins a Prize!

That evening, when Lucy had finished loading the dishwasher and was giving the kitchen counters a final wipe, the doorbell rang. When Lucy opened the door, she was surprised to encounter the bearded, smiling face of Seth Lesinski. He was dressed in the army jacket she remembered, and was holding a box of copy paper.

"Hi!" he said. "I'm dropping off some stuff for Sara."

"Oh," said Lucy. "She didn't say you were coming." Lucy was wishing she hadn't spoken earlier; her confident claim that Sara was no longer involved with Seth had obviously jinxed the situation.

"Sorry, Mom," said Sara, appearing in the kitchen. "I forgot."

Lucy had her doubts about that, noticing Sara had swapped the baggy sweatshirt she had been wearing for a clingy sweater and was wearing fresh lipstick.

"No problem," said Lucy. "Your friends are always welcome."

"I'm not staying," said Seth, indicating the box of copy paper. "These are just the posters for the Take Back the Night March, fresh from the copy shop."

"Right," said Sara with a dazzling smile. "I'll distribute them tomorrow."

"What march is this?" asked Lucy, wondering if it was a possible story for the *Pennysaver.*

"We do it every year, the first Sunday night after daylight savings ends and it's dark at four in the afternoon," said Seth. "It's to raise awareness of violence against women."

"Every year?" asked Lucy, wondering how she'd missed this annual event.

"On the campus, Mom," said Sara. "It's just a college thing. At least it was. This year we're bringing it into town because of Mary Winslow."

"The woman who was nearly killed by that TV guy?" asked Zoe, who had come downstairs, wondering who was at the door.

Lucy had followed the story, which had filled the newspapers for weeks. Mary Winslow's lover and attacker, popular cable news weatherman Brian Mitchell, had been accused of abusive behavior by several girlfriends but had always gotten off with a warning, despite the fact that the incidents had become increasingly violent. The attack on Mary Winslow hadn't been so easy to brush aside. For one thing, it had been particularly brutal, leaving her paralyzed and unable to use her legs, but perhaps the biggest factor in bringing the case to public attention was the fact that Mary's father was a powerful aide to the governor. Mitchell was now in jail, facing charges of attempted murder, and serious questions were also being asked as to how he had been able to avoid justice for so long.

"We want to draw attention to the fact that the cops and the courts are too lenient when it comes to violence against women," said Seth.

"Especially if the perpetrator is popular and well connected," added Sara, flipping her hair.

"We want to make sure that Mary Winslow gets justice," said Seth.

"If you give me some more information, I can put it in the *Pennysaver*," said Lucy. "Why don't you sit down and I'll get my notebook?"

"Good idea," said Sara enthusiastically.

"Actually," said Seth, glancing rather furtively at the regulator clock that hung on the wall, "I've got a, um, previous engagement. But, Sara, you can fill your mom in on the details, right?"

"Sure," said Sara, smiling rather too brightly.

"See ya when I see ya," said Seth, backing out the doorway.

"Yeah," said Sara, opening the box and extracting a couple of posters.

"Okay," said Lucy, sensing her daughter's disappointment at Seth's departure, but breathing a sigh of relief that he did not seem interested in Sara romantically. She sat down next to Sara and flipped open her notebook. "What's the story?" she asked.

"I bet he's taking Callie Obermeyer to the sea chantey concert tonight," said Zoe, who was looking in the fridge for a snack.

"You just ate," said Lucy in a disapproving tone. "Supper was less than an hour ago."

"Why do you think he's dating Callie?" Sara asked Zoe.

"I saw them at Jake's the other day," said Zoe, who had found a container of yogurt. "She had cappuccino, and he had regular coffee."

"That's the last one, and I was planning on having it for breakfast," said Lucy, plucking the pot of yogurt from Zoe's hand and replacing it in the fridge. "Have an apple."

"I bet she got that froth on her lip and was licking it . . . ," speculated Sara.

"Actually, he used his finger," said Zoe, choosing an apple from the bowl on the counter. "And then he put that finger in his mouth."

"Disgusting!" cried Sara.

"We were talking about the march . . . ," prompted Lucy, bringing her daughter back to the matter at hand.

"All the information is on this poster," began Sara.

"Tell me why it's important to you," said Lucy, who needed more for a story.

"And not because you want Seth to notice you," teased Zoe, biting into the apple.

"It's important to me," said Sara, "because men are scum and they get away with everything!"

"Yeah, Mom," said Zoe. "You always let Toby eat whatever he wanted."

"I'm sure that's not true," said Lucy, defending herself at the same time she wondered if her daughter was right. Had she treated Toby differently from the girls? Had she given him preferential treatment? "Anyway, boys are different. They need more food."

"And they don't have to watch their figures," said Sara. "How unfair is that?"

Saturday morning, Lucy was back at Miss Tilley's, finishing up Patrick's ninja costume. She was putting a zipper in the back, using the treadle sewing machine, which stitched along at a stately pace as she rocked her feet back and forth.

"This machine is fun to use and so good for your legs," she said, pausing to snip the thread. "I used to be a little afraid of my electric one."

"I remember a girl in my home ec class who sewed her hand," said Rachel with a grimace. "Ouch."

"Do they still have sewing and cooking classes in high school?" inquired Miss Tilley. "I remember boys used to have wood shop and girls got home economics."

"Not so much," said Lucy. "They have more choices now, so the academically challenged students end up taking classes like that and the college bound take advanced placement."

"And they say there's no child left behind," scoffed Rachel.

"Actually," said Lucy, "Zoe's taking wood shop — it was the only class that fit into her schedule — and she's loving it. I think she's her father's daughter."

"Good for her," said Miss Tilley. "Are there many girls in the class?"

"I didn't think to ask," admitted Lucy, checking that the zipper worked smoothly. "I guess we girls have come a long way."

"I don't know," said Rachel, who was watering the African violets that were flourishing on Miss Tilley's windowsill. "Take that Brian Mitchell. I used to enjoy watching him give the weather report, and all that time he was beating up his girlfriends and getting away with it."

"A stormy personality," said Miss Tilley, who was seated in her Boston rocker, with her beautiful Siamese cat, Cleopatra, on her lap.

"Sara and some other kids at Winchester College are holding a Take Back the Night March a week from Sunday," said Lucy. "It's been an annual event at the college, but this year they're taking it to Main Street. It's going to be a candlelight vigil for Mary Winslow."

"Good for them," said Rachel. "I'll go."

"Me, too," said Miss Tilley, surprising her friends. "If you'll give me a strong arm to lean on."

"Absolutely," said Rachel.

"You can count on me, too," said Lucy, snapping the last thread on the costume and giving it a shake. She laid the black costume out on the dining table and began folding it. "But the march will be tiring, and it might be chilly. Are you sure you want to risk catching cold?"

"Lucy, I'm surprised at you," chided Miss Tilley. "You can't catch a cold from the cold."

"I know," said Lucy. "But if you get chilled and tired, it puts a strain on your immune system, doesn't it?"

"She's right," said Rachel. "Remember how long it took you last winter to get over the flu?"

"Flu, shmoo," scoffed Miss Tilley. "You may not realize it, but I was a feminist pioneer here in Tinker's Cove. I started one of the first women's liberation groups in the state, right here at the library, back in nineteen seventy-nine."

"I had no idea," said Lucy, impressed.

"I'm not surprised," said Rachel. "You've always been a bit of a rebel."

"And back then, we really made a difference. If this Mary Winslow had come to us, we could have got her away from that Brian Mitchell. We had safe houses, a whole underground system to help battered women escape from dangerous situations."

"That would make a great story," said Lucy.

"Sure," said Miss Tilley with a shrug. "I remember one woman in particular. She was practically a prisoner in her own home, but we got her away."

"Who was she? Can I interview her?" asked Lucy.

Miss Tilley shook her head, and Cleopatra leaped lightly off her lap, then stretched in a perfect cat's pose, one that the most lithe yogi could only hope to imitate. "We never heard from her again, but that was the way it worked. It was like the witness protection program. The woman had to cut off all ties in order to be safe. Otherwise, there was always the risk that the husband or boyfriend or father — whoever the abuser was — could track her down."

"What happened to the group?" asked Rachel.

"Oh, you know how those things are," said Miss Tilley, with a flap of her big, clawlike hand. "I think our little group was a victim of its own success. The members went back to school and got degrees and jobs, some of the very unhappy ones got divorces, a few moved away, and after a while nobody was coming to meetings anymore."

Lucy nodded, seeing a parallel to her own life. When the kids were small and she was home caring for them, she had time for club meetings and volunteer jobs, like being a Cub Scout den mother. As they grew older, however, and she began to work outside the home as a reporter for the *Pennysaver,* she found she had less free time for such activities. All of a sudden the days were too short for everything she had to do, the shopping, cooking, cleaning, the chauffeuring, and the interviews, the writing, and the deadlines.

"I'm glad they're having the march," said

Rachel. "It's overdue."

"Quite frankly, I think women are losing ground," said Miss Tilley. "They're losing control of their own bodies."

"I heard that in some states they're arresting women who have miscarriages, charging them with child endangerment or some such thing," said Rachel.

"How can that be?" asked Lucy.

"I don't know," she admitted. "It is something Bob told me. I guess the presumption is that the mother was taking drugs or drinking alcohol or misbehaving in some way that caused the miscarriage."

"That's a scary thought," said Lucy, thinking of her three daughters, who were all of childbearing age. She certainly didn't want them to become prisoners of their biology; she wanted them to have the freedom to determine their futures. "I guess I'm going to be marching, too."

"But I'm not burning my bra," said Miss Tilley with a wicked grin. "Those days are over."

"Did you ever?" asked Lucy.

"Off the record, yes," she said as the grandfather clock in the corner began to chime eleven o'clock.

"Oh, my goodness," said Lucy, hopping up. "I'm late. I'm supposed to cover the opening of the Harvest Figure Display. Corney's going to kill me!"

Lucy stuffed the costume in her tote bag and grabbed her jacket off the hook. At the same time Rachel retrieved her handbag from the chair where it was resting and handed it to her. Then Lucy was out the door with a wave, dashing down Miss Tilley's steps, where a gray and blue salt-glazed crock held a gorgeous bronze chrysanthemum, and hopping into her car.

Fortunately, it was only a couple of blocks to the town common, the big, open space in the center of town, which had once been used by residents to pasture their cattle. Now it was a park, with a bandstand and a grassy lawn, dotted with bright yellow-leaved maple trees. Lucy arrived just as things were getting started, and found Corney Clark and several town officials gathered beneath a Giant Pumpkin Fest banner that was hanging from the bandstand. The town band played the last notes of "America the Beautiful," and Corney stepped forward, microphone in hand.

"Thank you so much. That was our talented town band, led by Norm Philpott."

A handful of citizens who had gathered for the event, mostly seniors and a few moms with small children, gave a little burst of applause.

"Now I'd like to introduce Roger Wilcox, chairman of our board of selectmen, who has a few words."

Roger Wilcox, a distinguished man in his sixties, who had swapped his usual half-zip sweater for a camel hair blazer in honor of the occasion, stepped forward. "Well, this is indeed an honor, to open this, our very first Giant Pumpkin Fest in Tinker's Cove. A lot of people have put a great deal of effort into this event, and I am sure it will be a great success for our town, this year and hopefully for many more years in the future. So, without further ado, I hereby announce that the Giant Pumpkin Fest has now officially begun." He cut an orange ribbon that had been stretched from the bandstand to a nearby tree, and everybody clapped again.

Lucy was able to snap a photo of the ribbon cutting and joined the group of people following Corney and Roger to view the displays of pumpkin people that had been erected by various local businesses.

They trooped along to the first display, created by Marzetti's IGA, which featured a family of pumpkin-headed figures, their vintage clothing stuffed with straw. The figures were seated at a 1950s chrome and vinyl dining set, preparing to eat an apple pie. Lucy noticed that one of the figures, the mother, looked a bit like Dot Kirwan, the cashier at the IGA, and she snapped a picture.

"Terrific, terrific," murmured Corney.

"So clever," agreed Roger. "I like the dad's plaid shirt and the mother's shirtwaist dress."

"And the kids have striped T-shirts right out of *Leave It to Beaver*," said Lucy, snapping a photo.

The next display, from the Cut 'n' Curl salon, showed a well-endowed figure seated in a salon chair, its pumpkin head stuffed inside the plastic hood of a hair dryer. The figure was a bit askew, as if the wind had blown it over, and its skirt had risen, revealing the stuffed panty hose, now spilling straw from its torn crotch, that served as the figure's legs.

"Oh, dear!" exclaimed an embarrassed Ann Briggs, who owned the shop. "Just let me fix this." She straightened the figure and replaced the skirt so it covered the rather lewd damage, and everybody clapped in approval.

When they viewed the following display, a wedding scene created by Orange Blossom Bridal, it was clear that the wind hadn't done the damage. Here the bride had been thrown on her back, her straw-filled stomach had been ripped open, and her pumpkin head smashed. The pumpkin groom's mouth had been carved into a leer, and his stuffed gloved fingers arranged in an obscene gesture.

"Come away, Jessica," said one of the mothers, leading her daughter away from the display. Other parents followed with their children, leaving a handful of puzzled observers.

"Who would do this?" asked one gentleman, leaning on his cane.

"What a shame," tutted his wife, shaking her neatly clipped head. "So much work."

"This is an outrage," said Corney, looking ahead to other displays, which had been similarly vandalized. The grass was strewn with smashed pumpkins, overturned furniture, and ripped costumes that flapped in the breeze. "What are we going to do?"

"First off, we close the exhibit," said Roger, taking charge of the situation. "Then we call the police."

"How can we do the judging?" fretted Corney. "We promised prizes to the entrants, but now the judges can't possibly see what the displays were originally like."

"They can rebuild," suggested Lucy. "It's only pumpkins and old clothes and straw."

"Some are too far gone," said Corney sadly.

"We'll give honorable mentions to the folks who don't want to rebuild. How about that?" suggested Roger.

"That's not fair," protested Ann Briggs. "I'm not going to get a prize, because my display wasn't vandalized enough? That stinks! I worked really hard on this, you know?"

"It was just an idea," said Roger as a police cruiser arrived, siren blaring. "We haven't come to a final decision. We'll certainly keep your comments in mind."

"What's the trouble here?" asked Officer Barney Culpepper, shifting his heavy belt as he joined the group. Barney was an old friend of Lucy's, and she gave him a little smile.

"The displays have been vandalized," said Corney, waving her arm at the destruction.

Barney planted his feet firmly, removed his cap and ran his hand over his gray brush cut before replacing it, and studied the situation.

Lucy knew that Barney had seen a lot of things he wished he hadn't in his thirty or more years on the Tinker's Cove police force, and this certainly wasn't in the same category as a tractor-trailer crash on

Route 1. Nevertheless, observing the way his jowls were quivering, she understood that he found the scene troubling.

Following his gaze, she noticed that the figures that had been most severely damaged were all representations of females, and they'd been attacked viciously. There was the disemboweled bride, a witch slashed to ribbons, a grandma whose wire-rimmed glasses dangled from a completely smashed head, and a chorus girl whose fishnet-stocking legs were splayed wide open and whose torso was split from her crotch right up to her neck.

"This is a crime scene," he said, his tone flat. "Everybody out."

"But what about the Giant Pumpkin Fest?" demanded Corney, practically in tears.

"Sorry," said Barney. "I don't have a choice. This here is a hate crime, and I've got to call in the state police."

"It was probably just kids," protested Corney, turning to Roger for support. "Don't you think it was just kids?"

"Probably," agreed Roger.

"Mebbe you're right," said Barney. "But if these were kids, they were a bunch of sick bastards."

"Can I quote you?" asked Lucy, who had

been writing it all down.

Barney stretched out his arms and gestured for everyone to leave. "Move along," he said. "Clear the area. Nothing to see here."

On the contrary, thought Lucy, there was plenty to see, and if she was right, it was evidence of a severely troubled personality. Whoever did this, she decided, really hated women. She only hoped he would stick to pumpkin-head figures and would not take his anger out on real flesh-and-blood women.

CHAPTER SEVEN

Tinker's Cove Chamber of Commerce

Press Release

For Immediate Release

Giant Pumpkin Fest in Full Swing! Don't Miss the Awesome and Imaginative Display of Jack-o'-Lanterns on Main Street, While Enjoying Sidewalk Sales and Free Refreshments Offered by Local Retailers. Be Sure to Stop in at Country Cousins to Enter the Candy Corn Contest and Guess How Many Pieces of Candy Are in the Canister!

Sometimes, thought Lucy as she yanked the *Pennysaver* door open on Monday morning and heard the jangling bell announce her arrival, it was a relief to go to work. She suspected this was a secret that men had kept from women for years, leaving their wives home to cope with all the messy little disasters of daily life while they were free to concentrate on the more straightforward demands of their jobs. While it was true that the workday sometimes posed difficult challenges, she was always able to walk away at the end of the day, while problems at home just seemed to simmer on and on, like one of those big pots of split pea soup that you never thought you'd ever get to the bottom of.

Truth be told, she was sick and tired of having Ev Wickes around the house all the time. There was the matter of his questionable hygiene, for one thing, and the fact that he drank beer all day long. Bill was joining in, somehow feeling it was rude to let him drink alone, and the pair of them were a very bad influence on little Patrick. She was counting the days to the pumpkin hurl, figuring that once the catapult was built, Ev wouldn't be hanging around, but this morning Bill had mentioned something about having him help with some repairs on the garden shed.

"Everything okay?" asked Phyllis, peering at Lucy over her half-glasses. She was seated at her desk behind the reception counter, the bulwark from which she handled reader queries, subscriptions, ads, classified ads, and accounts payable.

"It's been a tough morning. I never thought I'd pry Patrick away from Ev Wickes and get him fed and dressed and off to day care," said Lucy. "Is there any coffee?"

"I made a big pot this morning," said Phyllis, lifting her favorite mug, printed with perky French poodles. "I didn't get much sleep last night, because Wilf installed lights for his pumpkin. They're triggered by a motion sensor, and apparently, there's a lot more motion in the backyard than he thought. Every time a cat or raccoon went through, the lights flashed on." She took a big swallow of coffee. "I didn't get much sleep."

"With Bill, it's the siren," said Lucy. "Patrick loves setting it off, and every time the darn thing sounds, I jump out of my socks. My nerves are shot," she said, adding some milk to her mug of coffee. "If you ask me, it's a lot of fuss over a vegetable."

"Actually, pumpkins are fruits," said Ted, emerging from the morgue, where old copies of the *Pennysaver* were stored. He was carrying several of the oversize volumes containing copies of the papers dating from the early 1900s. "They have seeds, so they're fruits."

"I don't care. I don't like pumpkins, and I don't like Halloween. I want it to be over," said Lucy, plunking herself down at her desk and powering up her PC.

"It's not over till it's over," said Ted, grinning broadly and setting the big books down on the rolltop desk he inherited from his grandfather. "And I'm happy to say we've sold all the ad space in the Giant Pumpkin Fest special supplement."

Lucy noticed he looked a lot more relaxed than he had in weeks, and attributed his improved attitude to the increased ad revenue. These days it was a challenge to keep a small town weekly newspaper afloat, and Lucy knew Ted and Pam sometimes had to resort to using their home equity line to pay the bills.

"And, even better, Country Cousins has signed a contract to run a full-page ad every week until Christmas," he continued, leaning back in his swivel chair. "So if either of you has some free time, I'd like you to look through these old papers for graphic elements. They want old-fashioned illustrations for the ads."

"And just when do you think I'll have this free time?" asked Phyllis, her thinly plucked eyebrows rising above her reading glasses.

"That goes double for me," said Lucy. "I've got this big story about the vandalism at the Harvest Figure Display, on top of everything else."

Normally, these protests would earn a sharp rebuke from Ted, but today he replied only, "We'll work it out." He turned his attention to the door, where the bell was tinkling, as Corney Clark breezed in. "Hi, Corney!" he exclaimed. "What have you got for us today?"

Despite her dyed orange hair, Corney was not in a holiday mood. "Oh, Ted," she moaned, sinking into a chair and clutching her tote bag in her lap. "I really think someone's out to ruin the Pumpkin Fest."

"Probably just kids," said Ted. "Kids can't resist smashing pumpkins."

"I don't know," said Lucy, remembering the female harvest figure slit from crotch to neck. "From what I saw, I don't think it was kids."

"Probably kids, but who knows?" said Corney, rummaging in her bag and producing an envelope, which she passed to Ted. "It's a letter to the editor, thanking the Harvest Figure Display contestants for their participation, and also the Rotary Club. The club members came out big-time yesterday afternoon and repaired the damage. The

119

display is better than ever."

"That's great," said Lucy.

"See?" said Ted, opening the envelope and unfolding the note. "Sometimes things just work out."

"But if this keeps up, I don't know how we're going to manage," fretted Corney. "Chief Kirwan said he'd make sure the night patrols cruise by the display, but he doesn't have enough manpower to do anything more. There's only so many times you can ask people for help. First, it was Buzz Bresnahan's pumpkin, and then it was the Harvest Figure Display. What's next?"

"Better look on the bright side," offered Ted, causing Lucy and Phyllis to exchange worried glances. This was not the boss they knew.

"I'm trying," admitted Corney, "but I can't help but worry."

"I'm sure everything will be fine," said Ted. "There's no sense fretting about stuff that might never happen."

"Easy to say, hard to do," murmured Corney, standing up and swinging her bag over her shoulder as she made her way out the door.

"She worries too much," said Ted, who was leafing through the old papers, chuckling from time to time at the antiquated prose.

But as Lucy wrote up her account of the vandalism at the Harvest Figure Display, she was more than ever convinced that Corney was right to worry. She tried to give the story a positive spin, beginning with the Rotary Club's restoration of the display, but the fact remained that somebody had put a lot of energy into an act of wanton destruction.

"I just can't imagine why anyone would do such a thing," said Tony Marzetti, an energetic volunteer who was not only a member of the Conservation Commission but was also president of the Rotary Club, when Lucy called him for a quote. "It's really hard to understand destruction like that, and I'm glad we were able to help."

The obvious question, and the one that Lucy put to police chief Jim Kirwan, was how the police were going to prevent future acts of vandalism.

"It's a problem. I'm not going to pretend it's not a challenge for our department," he replied. "Preventing crime is a big challenge for us, since we can't be everywhere at once, but I am asking my officers to be extra vigilant. And, of course, the one thing we've got going in our favor is the fact that the more times this perpetrator acts, the easier it becomes for us to catch him." He paused, then added, "Or her."

"How so?" asked Lucy.

"The evidence begins to pile up. Every crime scene gives us a piece of the puzzle, and sooner or later it will come together. Take this latest incident . . ."

"The Harvest Figure Display?"

"Oh, no. This second giant pumpkin slashing."

"A second giant pumpkin?" asked Lucy, fearing for Priscilla. Well, not so much for the giant gourd, but for Bill. He would be awfully upset if anything happened to Priscilla.

"Yeah, at Sukie Evans's place. A really big one. She's got a couple of horses, you know, so she had plenty of manure."

Lucy breathed a sigh of relief, then reminded herself that even if Priscilla was safe, the pumpkin killer was still at large. "Any leads?" asked Lucy.

"I'm not at liberty to say," said the chief, "but I will say that my department is taking these attacks very seriously and we will catch whoever is doing this and we will prosecute to the full extent of the law."

"What exactly is the penalty?" asked Lucy.

"Could be jail time," he responded. "Like

I said, this goes beyond a prank. This is systematic and purposeful destruction of property, and I am committed to using the full resources of this department to preserve our way of life here in Tinker's Cove."

Lucy dutifully jotted down this rather grand quote, aware that the full resources of the department were extremely limited due to recent budget cuts. It sounded good, she supposed, but it was just so much hot air. She had just started to write the story when her phone rang again. This time it was Hank DeVries from the scuba club.

"I have an update for you about the underwater pumpkin-carving contest," he began.

"Great," said Lucy, expecting him to announce some new prizes.

"Not great," said Hank. "I've just been informed that the state's environmental protection department wants to review the plans for the contest."

"That's understandable," said Lucy. "How is it a problem?"

"I don't have plans," said Hank. "That's the problem. I haven't studied inflow and outflow at the pond, I don't know the chemical content of the water, except that I'm pretty sure there's two hydrogen atoms for every one oxygen, and I don't know about fertilizer runoff and nitrogen loading. We were just gonna throw some concrete blocks in there and invite people who enjoy diving to try their hands at carving pumpkins."

"Oh," said Lucy. "I get your point."

"And what I think," continued Hank, "is that the guy who voted against the contest at the Conservation Commission meeting . . ."

"Tom Miller?"

"Yeah, him. I think he ratted us out to the DEP because he doesn't want us to have the contest. He got outvoted, so this is how he thinks he can stop us."

"Maybe it's just routine," said Lucy. "Maybe the committee always checks with the DEP when waterways are involved."

"Maybe," admitted Hank, "but I doubt it. Anyway, I thought there might be a story there."

"Thanks for the call," said Lucy.

She flipped through her Rolodex and then put in a call to the committee chairman, Caleb Coffin. He wasn't home, but his wife said she'd be sure to pass along the message. Lucy's next call was to the state DEP, where she had a contact, but her call went straight to voice mail. She glanced at the clock, discovering it was almost noon, which meant she had forty-eight hours until the Wednesday noon deadline to track down this story, which she wasn't sure was a story. *Not a lot of time,* she thought, scribbling a reminder to follow up on a sticky note and pasting it on her computer screen.

She got up to retrieve her lunch from the office fridge, and when she brought it back to her desk, her phone was already ringing. When she picked up, fire chief Buzz Bresnahan was on the line.

"I'm sorry about your pumpkin," she said, thinking it was only polite to express her condolences.

"Oh, yeah, that was a blow," he said, "but that's not why I'm calling. It's because the Coast Guard just called and informed me that I'm going to have to keep the department's rescue boat on standby during the pumpkin boat regatta."

"Sounds like a sensible precaution," said Lucy, picturing a wide variety of unstable watercraft constructed from giant pumpkins that were likely to capsize in the chilly water of the town cove.

"It may be sensible, but it's not in my budget," said Chief Bresnahan. "If I put the rescue boat out, I've got to man it, and that means overtime, which I do not have funds for. That's why I'm calling you. I've got to go to the selectmen for an emergency appropriation, and I need some support for that request. We gotta have some interested citizens there to speak up, or this whole thing is going down in flames. There isn't much time. The race is next Sunday. That's less than a week away."

"Does the Coast Guard usually get involved in stuff like this?" asked Lucy, thinking she'd never really heard of a similar situation. She had thought the Coasties at the local station had their hands full inspecting fishing boats and enforcing safety regulations.

"Not until now," fumed Bresnahan. "I think somebody musta made a fuss about the regatta, somebody with connections, but that's off the record."

"Got it," responded Lucy, who was beginning to agree with Corney that somebody was out to spoil the Giant Pumpkin Fest. But who? And why? Was it really Tom Miller, like Hank thought? She dismissed the idea, remembering that Tom had been an early supporter of the festival, which, he had argued, would bring lots of business to the town and especially to Country Cousins.

Lucy spent a frustrating afternoon trying to contact sources at the state DEP and the Coast Guard and not getting anywhere.

When her phone finally did ring, it wasn't one of her contacts calling back. It was Heidi Bloom at Little Prodigies.

"I'm sorry to bother you at work," she began, "but Patrick is having a very difficult day, and I'd appreciate it if you'd pick him up."

"Is he sick?" asked Lucy, suddenly anxious for her grandson.

"No. It's a behavioral issue."

Lucy didn't understand. "I'm sorry, but isn't this what you guys do? You're a day-care center, and you take care of kids while their folks are at work. Isn't that what I'm paying you to do?"

"Little Prodigies isn't simply a babysitting service," said Heidi, sounding affronted. "We're a child-care facility, and we take great pride in caring for our little ones and doing what's best for them, not what's most convenient."

"It isn't a question of convenience," said Lucy, picking up on Heidi's attitude. "I have a job to do, and my employer expects me to do it. I can't just leave."

"I'm afraid I must insist," said Heidi, "or we'll have to disenroll Patrick."

Lucy wasn't sure she'd heard correctly. "Disenroll?"

"That's right," said Heidi. "We have a

waiting list of families who would be more than happy to take his place."

"So it's either pick him up this afternoon or lose his spot at the center?"

"I'm afraid so," said Heidi. "It takes a village, you know, and we believe in working together as a team. . . ."

Lucy had heard enough. "I'll be right over," she said, slamming down the phone.

When she arrived at Little Prodigies, she heard childish shouts and laughter but didn't see Patrick among the children who were playing outside, among the swings and slides and sandbox, so she approached the teacher who was supervising.

"Patrick needed a time-out," she explained. "He got in a fight with one of the other children during outdoor play. He's inside."

Lucy stepped inside and found Patrick sitting in the classroom, his dirty face tracked with tears. "What happened?" she asked.

Heidi, who was sitting beside Patrick at the table, writing, looked up. "Oh, Mrs. Stone, I'm just writing up an incident report. It seems that Patrick attacked another little boy."

"He took my truck," said Patrick with a sniffle.

"All the toys here belong to everyone,"

said Heidi. "We have to share."

"I had it first," said Patrick.

"If that happens, and someone takes a toy you are playing with, you must talk to a teacher. We can't hit, ever," insisted Heidi.

"No, you can't hit," agreed Lucy, taking Patrick's hand. "I presume Patrick will be welcome here tomorrow?" she asked, leading him to the cubby where his jacket and lunch bag were stored.

"Absolutely, but Patrick will need to apologize to the group at circle time."

"This place is beginning to sound like Communist China during the Cultural Revolution," muttered Lucy.

"I'm sure we seem a little . . . Well, let's just say that child development is better understood now than it was in your day, Mrs. Stone," said Heidi with a condescending smile. "And one area where we've made great strides is in the area of diet and how foods can affect child behavior. Gluten, for instance, is a real troublemaker, and I've noticed that Patrick's lunch often includes wheat bread and sugary cookies, and a great deal of dairy, which we know many children are sensitive to."

That morning, Lucy had packed the same lunch for Patrick as she had made for herself: a ham and cheese sandwich on multigrain bread, a sippy box of low-fat milk, an apple, and a homemade oatmeal-raisin cookie. "What foods would you suggest?" she asked.

"Kale is fabulous, and there's broccoli and quinoa, and almond milk is preferable to cow's milk. The list goes on and on. I can give you our list of lunch guidelines," said Heidi, pulling open a drawer and producing a sheet of paper.

Lucy glanced at the list, which included many foods she'd never heard of and others she knew from experience that children didn't like. "So how exactly do I give him brussels sprouts?" asked Lucy. "Raw?"

"Oh, no," laughed Heidi. "You steam them and put them in a little plastic container with a little bit of hummus for dipping. They're so cute, like little cabbages, and the kids pretend they're bunnies eating baby cabbages."

Lucy didn't believe the children actually ate brussels sprouts, not for a minute, even if they were accompanied by hummus. "Well, I'll try to do better," she said, intending to add some baby carrots to Patrick's lunch bag tomorrow.

"Whatever you do, no raw carrots," said Heidi. "They're a choking hazard."

"Thanks for telling me," said Lucy, heading for the door.

Once they were outside and walking to the car, she asked Patrick for his side of the story. "Why did you hit that boy?" she asked.

"He took the truck. He said it was his because his daddy drives a truck." Patrick sniffled. "He said I don't have a daddy."

"Oh," said Lucy, beginning to understand the situation. "Of course you have a daddy. Your daddy is in Haiti, but he'll be home soon, and Mommy, too."

"When will they be home?"

"For Christmas," said Lucy, aware that two months was an eternity to a small child. "But you know what? We'll put in a call tonight. How about that?"

"Okay," agreed Patrick, brightening up as she strapped him into the booster seat. "And when we get home, can I make the siren go?"

Lucy sighed, suspecting that Patrick was taking advantage of the situation, and figuring it didn't really matter. "Sure," she said, giving him a hug.

CHAPTER EIGHT

Tinker's Cove Chamber of Commerce

Press Release

For Immediate Release

New Events Have Been Added to the Already Jam-Packed and Fun-Filled Schedule of Giant Pumpkin Fest Events! These Include an Underwater Pumpkin-Carving Contest at Jonah's Pond, Sponsored by the Winchester College Scuba Club, Planned for Saturday, October 29, and an All-You-Can-Eat Pumpkin Pancake Breakfast, Sponsored by the Tinker's Cove Fire Department, on Sunday, October 30, at the Firehouse. Details to Follow.

Patrick was in a better mood the next morning, and Lucy's spirits were lifted, too, when she discovered Heidi was home, sick, and

Sue was filling in for her at Little Prodigies. Sue greeted them both warmly, with a big smile and a hug for Patrick. Lucy had helped Sue out at the center in the past, and she was confident that circle time would feature songs and finger plays, not forced confessions and apologies. *Sometimes,* she thought, giving Patrick a good-bye kiss, *you just got lucky.* Then she was off to the elementary school, where she was covering Officer Barney's annual Halloween safety program.

It had been years since she'd had a child in elementary school, but one whiff of the school's unique scent took her right back to the day she enrolled Toby in kindergarten. What was it exactly? she wondered, trying to identify the source of the scent. Well-worn sneakers, floor wax, childish sweat, chalk dust? *A little bit of each,* she decided, stepping into the front office and signing in.

That was a new procedure, instituted after school shootings became so prevalent. There was a time, she remembered, when such a thing was never thought possible, but that was long ago. She took the temporary pass provided by the school secretary, Tina Simms, and hung it around her neck. "This makes me feel like I'm on my way to the bathroom," she said.

"Better be careful. The sink and toilets are quite low," said Tina with a wink.

"I guess I'll take a pass," said Lucy, making a little play on words. "Is Barney in the multipurpose room?"

"I guess you've done this before," said Tina.

"You betcha," said Lucy, heading out the door and down the long tiled corridor. The multipurpose room, a combination auditorium, gym, and cafeteria, was at the very end. When Lucy opened the door, she was hit with a blast of sound, the result of several hundred high-pitched young voices. Barney was already there, standing in front of the room and chatting with the principal, Paul Nesbitt, and waiting for a class of kindergarteners to seat themselves on the floor in the very front of the room.

"Good morning, children," said Nesbitt, raising his hand for silence.

The children chorused back, "Good morning, Mr. Nesbitt."

"Today we have a special guest, Officer Barney from the police department, who is going to talk about Halloween safety. I expect you all to pay close attention. Officer Barney . . ."

Barney stepped forward, adjusted his heavy belt, and planted his feet, shod in sturdy regulation oxfords, wide apart. His buzz cut was gray now but hadn't thinned a bit, although his round belly had grown an inch or two. He still looked a bit like a bulldog, with jowls and a pug nose.

"Good morning, children," he began, launching once again into the speech he'd given every October for more years than Lucy liked to count. "Who's going trick-or-treating on Halloween?" he asked, getting an enthusiastic response, as every small hand in the room was raised.

"It's very important to carry a flashlight," he said. "And be extra careful when you cross the street. If you wear a mask, it can make it hard to see, so you have to look both ways and then look again, right?"

Many heads were nodding.

"And what about that candy?"

This got a cheer from the kids.

"It's good, isn't it? But you aren't going to eat any until you get home, where your mom or dad will look it over and make sure that it's all wrapped and good for you, right?"

A little girl raised her hand. "My mom says candy isn't good for you."

Barney thought for a minute, clearly struggling to come up with a politically correct reply. "Well," he began, "your mom knows what's best for you. You might get apples or raisins or sugar-free gum, and those are good treats, right?" The little girl nodded. "But just like candy, you need an adult to check every treat before you eat it, okay?"

There were nods all through the room. A little boy raised his hand and, getting a nod from Barney, posed the question all the little boys in the room wanted to ask. "Officer Barney, can we see your gun?"

Barney stood his ground. "This gun is my responsibility, and it's going to stay exactly where it is, which is in my holster."

This was met with a chorus of groans.

"Guns are dangerous, and if you find one, you should not touch it, but tell an adult. This is very important, and I want you to remember it. Never, ever touch a gun, because it might be loaded and hurt someone, maybe even you." He paused, letting this advice sink in. "But I do have *Play It Safe* coloring books and Tootsie Rolls for everyone," he added, concluding his talk. This time he got cheers.

Afterward, as the children were filing out and heading back to their classrooms, Lucy approached her old friend. She and Barney first became acquainted years ago, when they were both on the Cub Scout pack committee. "Great talk, Barney, as always."

"Thanks, Lucy." He rocked back on his heels. "It's one of my favorite duties."

"The Fourth of July fireworks talk is also good," said Lucy.

"Yeah, but that's for the summer rec program. There aren't as many kids."

"I always like it when you explode the watermelon with a firecracker," said Lucy.

Barney smiled at the memory. "Yeah," he said.

"So tell me," continued Lucy, "any progress on the pumpkin murders?"

"Aw, Lucy, you know I can't talk about department stuff. You gotta talk to the chief."

"I did. He says that every time this perpetrator acts, the department gets a little closer to apprehending him."

"Or her," added Barney.

"Right," said Lucy, thinking that when it came to perpetrators, the department was strictly equal opportunity, but not so much when it came to hiring.

"A lot of folks have installed security cameras. It's just a matter of time before we get a photo."

"But no leads so far?" asked Lucy, pressing the matter.

"No comment," said Barney, grinning.

Leaving the school, Lucy got a text from Ted asking her to cover a special emergency meeting of the board of selectmen, which had just been announced. There had not been time for the meeting to be posted in advance, so only a handful of town hall loyalists were sitting in attendance in the town hall basement meeting room, along with the police and fire chiefs. Bob Goodman, who was the town's legal counsel, met her in the doorway.

"This is most unusual, Lucy," he said. "The meeting is taking place under the provisions in the town charter for emergency situations that require action by the board. The board is mindful of the state's open meeting law, and the minutes will be available to any interested citizens." He gave her a copy of the relevant section of the charter. "We don't want any misunderstanding," he said. "I'm counting on you to make it clear in your story that the board is acting in an open manner under the provisions of the town charter."

"Okay. I understand," said Lucy, who knew the taxpayers association was always ready to pounce on any perceived misconduct by town officials. "But what exactly is the emergency?"

"The fire department is asking for an

emergency appropriation to cover unanticipated costs for the Pumpkin Fest," he said as Corney Clark joined them.

"What a mess!" she exclaimed, running her fingers through her orange hair. For once the always perfectly turned out Corney looked rather the worse for wear. Her eye makeup was smudged, as if applied in haste, and her rumpled red jacket clashed with her pumpkin-colored hair. "This festival is going to be the death of me."

"Take a deep breath," counseled Lucy. "Think happy thoughts."

"I'll tell you a happy thought," growled Corney. "I'm miles away from here, on a Caribbean beach, sipping a piña colada, and there are no pumpkins anywhere."

"Can I come?" asked Bob.

"Sorry, Bob, but nobody from Tinker's Cove is allowed in my daydream."

"I understand," he said with a grin. Then he walked to his seat in the front of the room, where he would be available to advise the board members. Moments later the selectmen filed in and took their places at the long table on the dais.

"I'm calling this meeting to order," declared Roger Wilcox, who was the longtime chairman of the board. "This is an emergency session to consider a budget request from the fire department. Chief Bresnahan, you've got the floor."

Lucy and Corney sat down next to each other, and Lucy pulled her notebook from her bag and opened it.

"Thank you, Chairman," said Bresnahan, who was wearing his dress uniform, the one he wore to fire department funerals throughout the Northeast. "I have been informed by the Coast Guard that the department will have to deploy the water rescue craft for the duration of the pumpkin boat regatta. This means additional manpower, to the tune of sixteen hundred dollars."

"That seems high," said Florence Whittaker, the board's newest member, who had campaigned promising to keep a sharp eye on town finances.

"May I speak?" asked Corney, raising her hand.

Roger gave her a nod. "Ms. Clark."

Corney stood up. "As you know, I represent the chamber of commerce, which is sponsoring the Giant Pumpkin Fest. This is the first year for this autumn festival, which we hope will become an annual event. I am happy to report that the event is getting a lot of attention, a lot of notice, and people are enthusiastic and excited. Our members in the hospitality business tell me bookings are up, rooms are filled, and restaurants are turning away requests for reservations. This is not only good for the business community, but the Giant Pumpkin Fest is also an event the whole town can enjoy. It's bringing people together to celebrate our way of life here in Tinker's Cove."

"I don't know about that," muttered Chief Bresnahan. "As far as I can tell, this festival of yours is causing a lot of trouble. I've already committed to the pancake breakfast, and now this. I just don't have the manpower."

"I find I must agree with the chief," said Roger. "I understand that the Pumpkin Fest is something new, but it doesn't seem to me that it's very well planned. There's no excuse for under-budgeting. . . ."

"I have to say that there was no way we could have anticipated the Coast Guard's demand . . . ," began Bresnahan, defending his budgeting.

"You couldn't have made a phone call, asked if there were any special requirements for a pumpkin boat regatta?" asked Florence. "I mean, this so-called regatta involves putting people in unstable watercraft in very chilly weather, but you figured there was no need for extra safety measures?"

"I will take complete responsibility . . . ,"

began Corney, noticing the fire chief was growing rather red under his collar.

"Both the police department and the fire department have been most cooperative," said Angus MacDonald, owner of MacDonald's Farm. "I'm not satisfied that the police department is any better prepared than the fire department."

The police chief, Jim Kirwan, wasn't about to take this sitting down. He rose to his feet and cleared his throat. "I want to assure the board that my department is indeed prepared. I have scheduled extra details for the duration of the festival, and we are bringing in additional manpower, in the form of special details from our neighboring towns. The budget for this has been approved by the finance committee, with the understanding that the chamber will bear the cost for the special details."

"I certainly commend your careful planning and most especially encourage these public-private partnerships," said Florence.

"Yeah, you've got the festival covered, but what about this vandalism?" demanded Bresnahan, who had not come to terms with the loss of his giant pumpkin. "My giant pumpkin . . . Well, it was a terrible sight to see."

Everyone in the room was silent, acknowledging the fire chief's loss.

Finally, the police chief responded. "We're coming closer to making an arrest. Every day we're a little closer."

"That's all well and good," said Bresnahan, whose quavering voice betrayed the depth of his emotion, "but nothing can bring back my pumpkin."

"There's one way we can honor the chief's loss," said Corney, speaking in a reverential tone. "And that's by refusing to give up. We must be strong and not give in to these vandals. I'm asking you for your support, for your vote to provide the necessary funding so the Giant Pumpkin Fest can take place as an example of civic pride and fortitude."

"All in favor?" asked Roger.

The measure passed, four to one, with Florence the only nay vote.

"Boy, that was close," said Corney as she and Lucy walked out to the parking lot.

"Not that close," said Lucy. "There was only one nay vote."

"It could have gone the other way," said Corney, tossing her bag into her car and climbing in after it. "I'm off to the next crisis," she said, checking her smartphone. "Buck needs his hand held. He's getting a lot of blowback from old-timers at the company."

"Change is hard for some people," said Lucy, who was also checking her smartphone and finding a message from Ted. "Photo op at Jonah's Pond, ASAP."

"See ya," called Lucy, giving Corney a little wave before settling herself behind the wheel. Her stomach growled as she started the car, and she thought, *How nice it would be to have some lunch.* Unfortunately, lunch was in the office fridge, so it would have to wait until she got her photos at the pond. It would have been nice of Ted to let her know who and what she was supposed to shoot, but she guessed all would be made clear in time.

When she arrived at the pond, she found Hank's pickup with the scuba bumper sticker in the parking area and pulled alongside it. Hurrying down the path, she found several members of the scuba club, all dressed in wet suits, sitting on the ground and adjusting their gear. Sara was among them and greeted her mother with a wave.

"I texted Ted. I hope it's okay," she said. "I thought this might make a good photo for the paper."

"What exactly is going on?" asked Lucy,

pulling her little camera out of her bag and snapping a photo of the divers.

"We're setting up for the underwater pumpkin-carving contest," said Sara. She pointed to an aluminum rowboat that was riding rather low in the water due to the fact that it contained a couple of cement blocks; there were about a dozen more blocks stacked nearby. "We've got to put these concrete blocks in the water to give the contestants workstations."

"So you got the go-ahead from the DEP?" asked Lucy.

"Not yet," admitted Hank, who was seated on a rock and was pulling on his flippers. "But we haven't got a cease and desist order, either, so we're going ahead with our schedule. If we have to call it off, we'll remove the blocks. There's no way a dozen concrete blocks are going to hurt this pond." He cast his eyes over the smooth expanse of water. "If it's like every other pond in the state, there's all kinds of stuff that people have tossed in there, believe me."

Lucy nodded agreement. She knew that ponds were favored dumping grounds for people who wanted to get rid of stuff, and the ever-increasing fees at the town landfill had only exacerbated the trend. Why spend fifty bucks to get rid of an old TV when you could just chuck it in the pond on a moonless night?

"You better be careful down there," warned Sara. "You don't want to get tangled up in some rusty old garbage."

"I'll be careful," promised Hank, rising to his feet and walking awkwardly toward the water in his flippers. When he was about waist deep, he waited for a couple of club members to launch the boat, and then he swam alongside as they rowed it out until it was about fifty feet from the shore. He then gave a signal and they tossed one of the blocks into the water and he submerged.

"Why's he going down?" she asked Sara.

"He's checking that the block is in a clear area, and if it's okay, he's going to attach a line with a bobbing flag to serve as a marker," she explained. "He should be back up in a minute or two. It's only about ten feet deep out there."

Lucy waited, camera at the ready, but Hank didn't appear. A series of ripples spread across the smooth surface of the water, indicating the spot where the block was dropped, but that was all.

"Isn't this taking a rather long time?" asked Lucy.

"He's got an air tank. He'll be fine," said

Sara. "Maybe he's having a problem with the marker line."

A few more minutes passed, and Sara called out to the guys in the boat. "Is everything okay?"

They were leaning over the side, attempting to peer into the water, when there was a big splash and Hank surfaced, apparently unconscious. He was floating facedown in the water, his arms and legs hanging limply.

"Ohmigod!" exclaimed Sara, diving into the water and swimming out to the boat, looking like a sleek seal in her black wet suit.

Lucy watched, horrified, torn between her concern for her daughter and her duty as a reporter to get the story. She was calling 911 on her smartphone at the same time she was watching the rescue.

The two guys were struggling with Hank's body, trying to haul him out of the water and into the boat, but were having no success. When Sara reached them, she joined in the effort, kicking furiously and pushing from below, and they were finally able to lift Hank. Once he was in the boat, one guy was able to start CPR while the other manned the oars. Sara swam alongside.

Lucy had managed to snap a few photos of the rescue, all the while praying that

Hank would be all right. She was relieved to see that by the time they reached shore, Hank was spitting out water, his chest heaving as he took great gasps of air. They could hear the siren on the town's ambulance, signaling that help was on the way, and Lucy let out a long sigh of relief.

The ambulance arrived, with flashing lights and a few final blasts of its siren, and two EMTs were rushing to Hank's side. He was sitting up and shaking his head, telling them he was fine.

"We're going to take you to the cottage hospital, just to make sure," said one EMT, only to get a vehement no from Hank.

"Really, I'm fine," he insisted. "I musta set my regulator wrong, that's all."

The EMTs shrugged and returned their empty stretcher to the ambulance. They drove off without using either the lights or the siren. It was a rather anticlimactic end to a near tragedy, thought Lucy, finding herself standing all alone. The club members were all gathered around Hank and Sara, who had their heads together as they examined his dive equipment.

"That's funny," she heard Hank say. "The regulator's fine."

"Check your hose," advised one of the guys. "You might have a little tear."

"It's not little," said Sara, pointing to a neat cut in the hose, near the air tank. "But you'd never notice it, it's so close to the tank. . . . And the tank's behind you, on your back."

"My fault. I should have checked all my gear more thoroughly before I went in," said Hank.

"You still could have missed it," said Sara, who was bending the hose. "It wouldn't have shown up until there was pressure on the hose, like this." When the hose was straight, the slice didn't show, but when she bent it, the gap became visible. "I don't think this was from wear and tear. It looks like somebody cut your hose with a knife."

Hank shook his head. "Don't be paranoid," he said. "This stuff is old. I've been planning on asking for some new equipment for Christmas." He checked his clunky dive watch. "We better get a move on if we're going to get those blocks in today. I know I'm not the only one who has a paper due on Monday."

This got a chorus of agreement from the others, who started to prepare to dive once again. Lucy gave Sara a wave and, receiving one in return, headed for her car. When she opened the door, she took one last look back at the beach, where the club members were launching the boat.

Maybe Hank was right and his equipment had simply worn out, and Sara had been too quick to assume that the hose had been cut on purpose. Or maybe, she thought, remembering the eviscerated harvest figures and the smashed pumpkins and the sudden explosion of bureaucratic red tape, maybe the dive equipment had also been damaged by the person who was intent on sabotaging the Giant Pumpkin Fest.

Spring, 1979

What a disappointment! She looked round at the women gathered in the library, wondering what she might possibly have in common with them. They all seemed to know each other, for one thing, and they were all talking noisily about their husbands and kids. They were wearing brightly, you might even say garishly, colored clothes, crocheted vests, and dangling jewelry, even long skirts, and a few had wild hair that curled every which way. She was the only one wearing neatly tailored gray slacks and a matching turtleneck sweater. She felt as if she were in a black-and-white movie and they were all in glorious Technicolor.

They were so outspoken, saying things she'd never dare to mention. They complained that their husbands never helped with housework, which she didn't think was a husband's responsibility at all, and she certainly didn't think a husband was supposed to change the baby's diapers or give the kids their bedtime baths. They seemed plain lazy to her, expecting their husbands to take on household chores and child care after a long day at work.

Honestly, she enjoyed cooking and cleaning. The routine was soothing, and it gave her something to do, something to keep her mind busy so she didn't have to think about the things that, well, the things she didn't like to think about.

She sat quietly, listening, as they ranted about magazines and TV ads, claiming they promoted unrealistic body images, whatever that meant. She rarely ever saw a woman's magazine, but when she did, she enjoyed the bright photos and the recipes. She liked to imagine herself in one of the sparkling kitchens with all the modern conveniences, or sitting on a sofa in one of the beautifully decorated living rooms, all so different from the old-fashioned apartment over the store, where nothing had changed in fifty years. She didn't understand why they bought the magazines and read them if they didn't like the contents. And as for TV, well, she didn't have one, but she did understand that you could just turn it off if you didn't like the shows.

"Let's burn our bras!" declared one woman, who was rather fat and was wearing sandals on her chubby, dirty feet.

Much to her surprise, the other women seemed to think this was a good idea. Why did they want to destroy perfectly good clothing? What was wrong with bras? She didn't have much in that department, but she couldn't imagine going without a bra. Wouldn't it be terribly uncomfortable?

Miss Tilley, the librarian who was running the meeting, seemed to agree with her and was urging the group to "get back on track." Apparently, she wanted them to support something called the Equal Rights Amendment, which would be added to the Constitution and would require that women be treated as equals to men. They would get the same pay for the same job, and laws that discriminated against women would be eliminated. It all sounded like a good idea, and the women at the meeting were all for it, but she didn't see how it would help her. She'd made her bed, as her mother-in-law frequently reminded her, and now she had to lie in it. "Marry in haste, repent at leisure." That was another favorite of Emily's, and she had to admit Emily knew what she was talking about.

The meeting was ending, and the women were standing up and chatting with one another, embracing each other and saying their good-byes. She slipped around the group, heading for the door, but Miss Tilley left the group and caught up with her.

"I'm so glad you came to the meeting," she said. "Did you like it?"

"It was very interesting," she said, checking her watch.

"I suppose you need to get back home."

It was later than she thought, and she knew he'd be upset with her. "I'm late," she said.

"I understand," said Miss Tilley, walking through the children's section with her. "I really do. I grew up in a very restrictive home environment."

She was amazed. How did she know? She looked at this tiny woman, with her piercing blue eyes and aureole of curly gray hair, and was both intrigued and a little bit afraid. "I really have to go."

"Of course," said Miss Tilley. "But I hope you'll come back, because I may be able to help you."

She knew she'd stayed out too long, and she hurried down the street, walking as fast as she could without attracting notice, but somehow feeling almost lighthearted. It was probably nothing — she didn't see how a lady librarian could really help her — but it was the

first hopeful thing that had happened to her in
a very long time.

CHAPTER NINE

Tinker's Cove Chamber of Commerce

Press Release

For Immediate Release

Calling All Ghosts and Goblins, Fairies and Witches! All Children Twelve and Under Are Invited to the Annual Halloween Party Sponsored by the Hat and Mitten Fund, 7:00 p.m., Friday, at the Community Church Fellowship Hall. Fun and Games! Music By DJ Jayzon! Refreshments and Prizes! Come as Your Favorite Character.

This couldn't be right, thought Lucy. The ATM had refused to allow her to withdraw fifty dollars from her account because there was an insufficient balance, which was really weird because she had deposited her monthly paycheck just a few days ago.

Where did the money go? All the way home, as she drove the familiar route from Little Prodigies, she went over the past few days, trying to remember if she'd used her debit card for groceries or gas and forgotten it. But even if she had, she realized, she couldn't have gone through more than a thousand dollars in just a few days. Maybe she was a victim of identity theft, she thought, feeling a bit sick. Or maybe, which was far more likely, Bill had spent the money.

She pulled into the driveway, braked and turned off the engine, then helped Patrick out of the booster seat. He immediately spotted his grandfather and Ev working in the backyard, out by the catapult, and ran to join them just as the machine's arm swung back and released a pumpkin into the air. The pumpkin sailed through the sky in a graceful arc, finally descending to earth in the woods behind their yard.

"Wow!" yelled Ev, prancing about like Rumpelstiltskin. "Did you see that? That baby must've gone some four hundred feet — maybe more!"

"I saw," said Lucy, joining them.

"This baby is going to totally kill that Hyundai! We're gonna win for sure! I think this demands a celebration," said Ev, pulling a can of beer out of the cooler, which he always seemed to keep nearby. "Want one, Bill?"

Lucy gave her husband a warning look. "No, I'll pass," he said.

"I get it," said Ev, snapping the pull tab with a practiced movement, "Little wifey here doesn't want you to drink, right?"

Bill's face darkened. "Not at all," he said. "I just don't want any right now."

"Let's look for the pumpkin," urged Patrick, tugging on Bill's arm. "I bet it's all smashed."

"Good idea," said Bill. He turned to Ev and Lucy. "Want to come?"

"Sure," said Ev, before taking a long swallow of beer.

"I'll pass," said Lucy, who had really had enough of Ev. Thank goodness the catapult was finally finished, and there were only a few more days until the pumpkin hurl at the Giant Pumpkin Fest. Then, she hoped, it would all be nothing more than a bad memory.

She wandered through the garden, gathering a few late salad greens, and then headed for the house, planning to start supper. They had to eat a bit early this Friday night because of the Hat and Mitten Fund Halloween Party, which was scheduled to start at seven. She was washing the lettuce when Bill and Patrick came in; Patrick couldn't wait to tell her that the pumpkin had been thoroughly smashed, with its innards scattered over a large area and even hanging from low branches.

"Fabulous," said Lucy, thinking this whole thing was utterly ridiculous. Imagine two grown men working for weeks to build a huge and cumbersome machine, the only purpose of which was to smash pumpkins. "By the way, Bill, have you cashed any checks lately? I tried to get fifty bucks from the ATM, but it said our account had insufficient funds."

"Oh, yeah," he said, filling glasses of water for himself and Patrick. "I had the bill at the lumberyard, and I paid Ev."

"You what?" demanded Lucy, whirling around to face him. "You paid Ev? Why?"

" 'Cause he was working for me."

"On a remodeling project?"

"No. On the catapult."

Lucy put the knife down very carefully on the cutting board. "You paid him to help build the catapult?"

Bill had drained his glass of water and was refilling it from the tap. "That hike in the woods was thirsty work, hey, Patrick?"

Patrick held out his glass for a refill. "Yup."

Lucy wasn't about to let her husband change the subject. "I thought Ev was volunteering to build the catapult. I didn't think you were paying him."

"Well, I was. Be realistic, Lucy. It was a lot of work, and I couldn't expect him to do it for nothing."

"He wasn't working for nothing. He got gallons of beer, not to mention the sandwiches and pizzas and I don't know what all."

"It was the least I could do, Lucy. I was paying him only fifteen dollars an hour, way less than he usually gets. He was doing me a big favor."

"Taking you for a ride is more like it," muttered Lucy, picking up the knife and dicing the cucumber into very small pieces.

She had tucked the salad in the fridge and was scrubbing potatoes when she heard the crunch of gravel in the driveway that meant the girls were home. A few minutes later they came into the kitchen, chatting excitedly about the Take Back the Night March.

"Do you know women make only seventy-seven cents for every dollar a man makes?" asked Zoe, opening the refrigerator and taking out a bag of mini carrots.

She plumped herself down at the kitchen table and began chomping away, working her way through the bag.

"You'll spoil your dinner," said Lucy, who knew only too well that her earnings had never matched her husband's, not even in the early days of her marriage, before kids, when they lived in New York City and both worked on Wall Street.

"And now there are all these restrictive laws limiting women's health-care choices," added Sara, unscrewing the cap on a bottle of water.

"Those bottles are for lunches and the car," grumbled Lucy, who was cutting up the potatoes. "Fill a glass from the tap, please."

"This tastes better," said Sara before draining half of the bottle.

"They cost a lot more than water from the tap," said Lucy. "So when you finish it, just refill it from the sink, please."

The girls exchanged a look.

"Your friend Miss Tilley was at the meeting," said Zoe.

"And that witchy lady, Rebecca Wardwell," added Sara.

"She's not a witch," said Lucy, putting the cut-up potatoes in a pot and covering them with water. "I'm surprised at you, using an antifeminist term like that."

"The goal is to get past these linguistic

taboos," said Sara, "to get to the point where women are accepted for themselves, for their unique qualities as individuals, and not regarded as inferiors because of their sex."

Lucy set the pot on the stove. "But we've made a lot of strides working together, sisterhood and all that."

"Mom," said Sara in a schoolmarmish tone, "I don't think you realize what's actually going on. In some states it's practically impossible for a woman to get an abortion, even though it's a right protected by the Constitution."

Lucy had started to say she knew about that when Sara continued, "And there was that case in Texas where they kept alive a pregnant woman who was actually brain dead, hooked up to wires and machines, like some sort of human incubator."

"And some states require women who want abortions to submit to vaginal probes," said Zoe, shuddering.

"And violence against women is still a big problem, and women don't get support from the courts . . . ," said Sara.

"Take Mary Winslow," said Zoe. "She begged a judge to refuse bail for her boyfriend after he beat her up, and even after he almost choked her to death, the judge gave her only a restraining order, which the guy promptly violated, and she nearly died as a result. Now her legs are paralyzed, and she's stuck in a wheelchair."

"But," added Sara, a note of excitement in her voice, "Seth knows somebody who knows Mary Winslow, and he thinks she might actually be able to take part in the march. Wouldn't that be great?"

"When is it?" asked Lucy, glancing at the calendar and thinking it was awfully full, with something scribbled in every box. "During the Pumpkin Fest?"

"It's always the first Sunday after daylight savings ends, which this year is November sixth," said Sara. "When it's dark at four in the afternoon, you know? It gets dark early, but we're taking back the night. Get it?"

"Yup," said Lucy, realizing the potatoes were boiling over and using a dish towel to protect her hands as she snatched the pot off the burner. "I got it," she said, reducing the heat and replacing the pot.

Even though daylight savings was still in effect, the days had become noticeably shorter and the sun was setting earlier every day. It was already dark when supper was over and Lucy brought the ninja costume to Patrick, who was playing with Legos in the family room.

"It's time to get ready for the party," she told him.

"I don't want to go," said Patrick, snapping a couple of plastic blocks together.

"Sure you do," coaxed Lucy. "It will be fun."

"It's not a good costume," said Patrick, keeping his head bowed over the pile of Legos.

Lucy bit her tongue. "Why not try it on? You might be surprised."

"I don't want to." Patrick snapped the last piece on to the spacecraft he was making and waved it in the air, making zooming sounds.

"I put a lot of effort into this costume," said Lucy, growing rather irritated. "And I have to go to the party to help out, and I think you should come, because people have gone to a lot of trouble to give you kids a good time."

"Go on, Patrick," said Zoe, who had come into the family room, toting her book bag, intending to do her homework. "It'll be fun."

"Okay," he said with a huge sigh. "But I don't want to wear the costume."

"Yes, you do," said Lucy in her most

authoritative mother voice. "Everyone will be wearing costumes."

"Yeah," said Zoe, holding up the ninja hood. "And this is so cool."

By the time he was dressed in the costume, even Patrick had to admit it was "pretty okay," especially since Lucy had added a store-bought belt and some plastic ninja weapons, which looked like gardening tools to her but which were guaranteed to impress a small boy. He climbed quite happily into the car for the short drive to the community center, where the party was to take place.

In past years Lucy had enjoyed the low-key gathering, which gave the town's children a chance to show off their costumes, play a few games, and enjoy some light refreshments. Everyone got a prize for their costume, and they all went home with a small bag of treats.

But this time, when she parked the car, it wasn't "Monster Mash" that was issuing from the church hall, but loud techno music, with a thumping beat played by DJ Jayzon. When she went inside, she winced at the noise, wishing she'd thought to wear earplugs.

Heidi Bloom was at the doorway, apparently fully recovered from her bout of flu and enthusiastically greeting all comers, and apparently in her element, wearing a police officer costume complete with cap and false badge, brass buttons, and a tightly knotted necktie.

"Fantastic, isn't it?" she asked. At least that was what Lucy thought she had said, since the deafeningly loud music made lipreading and signing the only possible means of communication.

"Can't he turn it down?" asked Lucy, who was holding her hands over her ears.

"Fab DJ!" enthused Heidi. "The kids love it."

The kids were definitely excited, running around the large room in packs, shrieking and screaming. Lucy recognized a few of the kids from Patrick's day-care class and spotted little Pear and Apple, neighbors who lived on Prudence Path. They were dressed as princesses, their tiaras askew and dripping glitter, their faces flushed from running away from the pint-size superheroes that were pursuing them. There were also plenty of ninjas, all with hoods over their faces, and Lucy soon lost track of Patrick.

"This is madness," said Sue, who had just arrived, carrying a tray of popcorn balls.

Arriving together, on Sue's heels, were Miss Tilley and Rebecca Wardwell. They were both dressed as witches, with tall, pointy hats and flowing black clothes. Miss Tilley had added red-striped stockings to her outfit, and Rebecca had her little pet owl perched on her shoulder.

"Oh, my," said Rebecca, stepping backward as the music suddenly increased in pitch. "Owls have very sensitive ears."

"As do I," said Miss Tilley.

With that, the two turned on their heels and left the hall, leaving Lucy momentarily speechless.

"That puts us down two helpers," said Sue, doing a quick count of the adults in the room.

"More parents have stayed, though," said Lucy, taking in the little groups of grown-ups clustered in the corners.

"They're probably afraid to leave their kids alone in this madness," said Sue.

"Tell me about it," said Lucy, who thought she'd spotted Patrick chasing a little fairy dressed in blue with sparkles. She marched across the room, grabbed him, and told him to calm down, only realizing when he pulled off his mask that he wasn't Patrick at all. "Sorry," she said, growing increasingly concerned. Which ninja was Patrick? Why hadn't she made him a pirate costume? And would this horrible music never end? She was getting a headache and could hardly think for the noise.

She was pacing the room, looking for a familiar little ninja figure, and finding none that resembled Patrick. What shoes was he wearing? The work boots? The blue sneakers? She didn't see any footwear that looked like Patrick's, and was growing quite panicked when a tall man appeared in the doorway, holding two ninjas by the hand. One of the ninjas pointed at her, and the man approached, towing his little captives. Just then, praises be, the music ceased.

"I think this ninja may belong to you," he said. He was a nice-looking man, with tousled hair and a friendly grin.

"Patrick?" she asked, lifting his mask and recognizing her grandson. "Thanks," she said, overcome with gratitude. "I've been looking all over. Where did you find him?"

"He was outside, playing with my son."

"Outside!" Lucy was horrified. Anything could have happened outside. He could have fallen and gotten hurt. He could have been kidnapped. He could have wandered too far and become lost. And there were bears and coyotes in the woods. . . .

"We're ninjas," said the other little boy.

"Ninjas hide in the dark," said Patrick.

The music was starting again, and Lucy made an executive decision. "How about some ninja ice cream?" she asked, grabbing Patrick by the hand and leading him to the door.

"But what about the party?" he protested. "I want to stay."

Sue was standing in the doorway. "You're not leaving, are you?" she asked, with panic in her eyes.

"I'm sorry," apologized Lucy, who was struggling against the inevitable sense of guilt. "I would stay except for Patrick here." Lucy was holding him tightly in case he made a dash for freedom. "The party was a mistake."

"You can say that again," agreed Sue. "We never should have given in and let Heidi bring in her boyfriend."

"The DJ is her boyfriend?" asked Lucy, thinking they were an unlikely pair. He with his studs and tattoos, and she with her high-necked, tightly buttoned blouses.

Sue nodded, her expression grim.

"We're going to get some ice cream and take it home and watch the Peanuts TV special about the Great Pumpkin," said Lucy. She could already hear the tinkling piano music in her head. So calming. So relaxing. And considering the way things were going all wrong this Halloween, she

definitely needed some rest and recupera-
tion.

"What kind of ice cream?" asked Patrick
suspiciously. "Not that nut kind."

"No maple walnut," promised Lucy, recalling a recent ice cream choice that hadn't
gone over well with the family. "You can
choose whatever flavor you want."

"Monster marshmallow whirl," he said
promptly as they made their way out to the
parking lot.

Where did that come from? she wondered
as she buckled his seat belt. And she added
a little prayer. *Please let there be monster
marshmallow whirl at the IGA.*

CHAPTER TEN

Tinker's Cove Chamber of Commerce

Press Release

For Immediate Release

The Giant Pumpkin Fest Swings into High Gear on Saturday! The Event Anxious Pumpkin Growers Have Been Waiting For, the Giant Pumpkin Weigh-In, Is at 9:00 a.m. at MacDonald's Farm Stand. How Big Is Your Pumpkin? The Fun Continues with the Catapult Hurl, Kicking Off at 1:00 p.m. at Foster's Hay Field on Jonah's Pond Road with Live Music by the Claws. Refreshments Will Be Available at Both Events.

Lucy loved the loosey-goosey feel of Saturday mornings, when everybody fended for themselves. There was no need to get the kids up early and rush them through breakfast, making sure they had their lunches in hand before they left the house to catch the school bus. On Saturdays the girls liked to sleep late, and Bill and Patrick, who were early risers, had a special breakfast together, cooked by Grandpa Bill. That left Lucy free to enjoy a second cup of coffee in peace and quiet. At least, that was usually how it went on Saturday, but this Saturday morning was different.

This morning, Bill was pacing anxiously in the kitchen, pausing every few minutes to peer out the window. Libby knew something was up and was determined to keep him company, pacing beside him, nails clicking on the hardwood floor.

"It's not Christmas, Bill," said Lucy, with a yawn, "and Santa isn't coming."

"I'm not looking for Santa. I'm looking for Ev," said Bill.

"It's not even seven," said Lucy, who was slumped over a mug of coffee at the kitchen table. Bill had asked her to get up early to serve coffee and doughnuts to the catapult crew, and she'd agreed, knowing how much the catapult hurl meant to him. Since he had to be at the catapult hurl all day, she and the girls were taking Priscilla to the weigh-in at MacDonald's farm stand.

"Ev was supposed to be here half an hour ago," grumbled Bill, who was standing at the window and holding the curtain back with his hand so he'd have a clear view of the driveway. Libby had lowered her hindquarters temporarily and was sitting beside him, at the ready. "Tom Mastrangelo will be here any minute with the trailer. It's going to take a while to load the catapult, and we've got to be on-site by nine, or we'll be disqualified." He snorted and walked over to the sink, accompanied by the dog, where he filled a glass with water and drank it down. "I can't imagine what's keeping him."

Lucy could, knowing Ev's penchant for alcohol, but wisely kept that thought to herself. "Have you called him?"

"Several times. All I got was voice mail."

"Maybe you should go over to his place," suggested Lucy. "Maybe he overslept."

"He was so excited about the catapult — and he's an early riser." Bill was standing in the middle of the kitchen, legs apart and hands on hips, staring at the clock that hung on the wall over the stove. Libby was sitting on her haunches, watching him.

"When's the big truck coming?" asked Patrick, coming down the kitchen stairs and getting a lick and a wag of the tail from Libby. He was still in his pajamas, and his hair was tousled. Lucy thought he looked adorable.

"Any minute," said Bill, coming to a decision and pulling out his cell phone. "I don't have time to track down Ev, whatever he's gotten up to. I'm going to call Sid."

"Good idea," said Lucy, who knew that Sue's husband, Sid, was a reliable helper. She filled a bowl with Cheerios, added some milk, and set it on the table, but Patrick had eaten only a few mouthfuls when Tom Mastrangelo arrived in his big dump truck, towing a flatbed trailer. The trailer was normally used to haul heavy earth-moving equipment, but today it was carrying only a small forklift. As soon as Patrick saw the truck, he was out of his chair and heading for the door.

"Hold on," said Lucy. "You're still in your pajamas."

Patrick was up the stairs in a flash, with Lucy following. In a matter of minutes he pulled on jeans and a T-shirt and was wriggling with excitement as Lucy added a sweatshirt against the morning chill. He shoved his feet into his sneakers, without socks, and clattered noisily down the stairs and out the door, just in time to see Sid arrive in the white van he used in his custom closet business.

"Boys and trucks," muttered Lucy, picking his discarded pajamas up off the floor and tucking them under his pillow as she made his bed.

When she got downstairs, the moving operation was in full swing. Going out onto the porch, she saw that Tom Mastrangelo had already loaded Priscilla into Bill's pickup truck and was chugging across the driveway on his forklift, with Patrick on his lap. Patrick was ecstatic, as was Libby, running along beside them, but Lucy was dismayed. She ran down the porch steps and across the yard, intending to stop this dangerous stunt, but by the time she caught up to them, Patrick was safely on the ground.

"That was so dangerous! Don't do that again," she warned Tom, giving Patrick a hug.

"Sorry," Tom muttered, hanging his head to hide a smirk as Patrick wiggled out of her arms.

"Gee, Lucy," complained Bill. "Lighten up a little."

Patrick was already climbing up the ramp that had been lowered off the back of the trailer, eager to inspect the equipment.

She was about to tell him to get down but was stopped by Bill. "Leave him be. He's in no danger."

"I'll keep an eye on him," promised Sid, indicating Bill with a nod of his head and causing Lucy to laugh.

Tom had maneuvered the trailer as close as possible to the catapult, which Bill and Ev had equipped with recycled tractor tires. The plan was to employ a winch and a cable to draw the catapult onto the trailer, but when the cable was attached, the winch was unable to budge the heavy wooden catapult.

Lucy watched, standing to the side, with Patrick held firmly by one hand and Libby by the other, as the winch whined in protest and the cable sang with the strain. When Tom cut the winch motor, the quiet seemed very loud.

"You're gonna have to push," said Tom, then waited for Sid and Bill to get into position before restarting the winch. This time the catapult inched forward and rolled up the ramp and settled into position on the trailer.

"Tom's the best," said Sid, nodding with approval as Bill and Tom chained the catapult in place for the short trip to the pumpkin hurl site on the shore of Jonah's Pond, not far from the Country Cousins complex.

Lucy brought out mugs of coffee and a

plate of doughnuts, and the men stood in a little knot, discussing the finer points of the catapult's construction. Patrick was all ears, consuming a large chocolate doughnut with relish, but when the conversation turned to Ev Wickes, Lucy intervened.

"Patrick, we need to get you dressed properly for the festival," she said, "and you haven't brushed your teeth."

"Right," said Bill, popping the last bit of doughnut into his mouth and draining his coffee mug. "And we need to get this show on the road."

"Can I watch, please?" begged Patrick, so Lucy waited while the men climbed into their various vehicles. Bill led the way in Lucy's SUV, followed by Tom in the big dump truck towing the trailer with the catapult aboard, and Sid followed in his van. When the procession was out of sight, Patrick finally agreed to go inside, accompanied by Libby, who had transferred her tail-wagging allegiance from Bill to Patrick.

"Grandpa's catapult will win, won't it?" Patrick asked as Lucy squeezed toothpaste onto his brush.

"Maybe," agreed Lucy, with a smile, and she meant it. She hadn't really thought the project was a good idea, but now that the catapult was built, she had to admit Bill and Ev's adaptation and construction of this medieval war device was quite an achievement. And who knew? Maybe the silly thing would win the contest. She figured the thousand dollars in prize money would just about cover the cost of constructing the infernal machine.

After Lucy got some socks on Patrick and brushed his hair, she roused the girls. "I'm leaving with Priscilla in fifteen minutes," she told them, purposely fibbing in order to get them moving.

Patrick, however, took her threat seriously. "Hurry up!" he yelled. "You'll miss the contest!"

Half an hour later they were on the road, Lucy and Patrick riding in Bill's pickup, with Priscilla in back, and Sara and Zoe following in Sara's little secondhand Civic. It wasn't far to MacDonald's farm stand, where Halloween was big business. Angus MacDonald had been quick to see the possibilities of the holiday when he took over the family business, which previously had been limited to selling apples, cider, cheddar cheese, and his mother's homemade baked goods. Now the farm stand boasted a corn maze, a huge field of pick-your-own pumpkins, and a small petting zoo of farm animals, in addition to the original products. The change had been a big success, and the parking lot was always full on fall weekends, packed with SUV's displaying BABY ON BOARD decals.

Today, Lucy noticed, both the original parking lot and a nearby field were packed with cars. Linc MacDonald, Angus's teenage son, waved the pickup right on through to the weigh-in, which was taking place in front of the farm stand, but directed Sara to park in the field. Lucy drove carefully along the rutted driveway, mindful of pedestrians and trying not to jostle Priscilla, as she joined the line of contestants' trucks.

At first she kept the engine running, not realizing how long it took to unload each pumpkin and transfer it to the scale, but eventually she turned off the engine. Patrick was just beginning to get restless when Sara and Zoe arrived, having hiked some distance from the field where they parked the car.

"I'll stay with Priscilla," said Lucy, "but you guys can go on ahead and watch the weigh-in."

"Okay, Mom," agreed Sara as Patrick scrambled out of the truck cab.

"Hold his hand," Lucy cautioned, mindful of the crowd.

"We'll keep you posted," promised Zoe as

178

the crowd gathered around the scale gave a round of applause.

"How big?" Lucy asked, calling after them.

"Six hundred and thirty-two pounds," replied Zoe.

The competition was going to be tougher than she'd thought, she realized, deciding to take a look for herself. There was no hurry about moving the truck. The organizers still had to remove the pumpkin from the scale and place it on display before the line of contestants could inch forward. Lucy counted as she followed the kids, and discovered she was ninth in line. As she walked along, she studied the competition, examining each enormous pumpkin and comparing its size against Priscilla's, and decided that Bill's pumpkin had a decent chance of winning. They were just removing the six-hundred-pound pumpkin with a super-big heavy-duty forklift when she joined the kids, and she was surprised to see it seemed smaller than Priscilla.

"I'll go back to the truck, Mom," offered Sara. "You stay here and keep an eye on the competition."

"Thanks," said Lucy, taking Patrick's hand. "What do you think? Do you think Priscilla is bigger than that pumpkin?"

"Priscilla's ginormous," said Patrick, getting chuckles from the people who were standing nearby. "I bet she weighs a million pounds," he added, giving his favorite number.

The contest continued throughout the morning as each pumpkin was lifted by forklift and placed on the scale. Each pumpkin's weight was shown on a giant digital electronic display. Angus MacDonald was an entertaining emcee, offering up plenty of country-style humor while the pumpkins were loaded and unloaded. Everyone was having a good time, enjoying the crisp October weather, but Lucy found she was surprisingly nervous. She really didn't care, she told herself, but her stomach gave a lurch every time a weight was announced.

She watched anxiously as Sara inched the pickup forward through the crowd, realizing with a shock that they were next to last, just in front of Phyllis's husband, Wilf.

"Now, who takes credit for this beauty?" asked Angus as Sara moved the truck into place.

"We do," said Lucy, stepping forward with Patrick.

"Did you grow the pumpkin?" Angus asked, shoving the mike in front of Patrick.

"No. Grandpa did," answered Patrick,

then added, "Her name is Priscilla."

This got a laugh from the audience.

"So tell me, young man, how much do you think Priscilla weighs?"

Patrick didn't hesitate. "A million and one pounds," he replied, getting an even bigger laugh.

"That's a lot," said Angus. "Let's see if you're right."

Lucy held her breath while Priscilla was gently lowered onto the scale and the forklift withdrawn. The display blinked a few times, then registered the pumpkin's weight: 599 pounds. The crowd groaned in unison, as this was well below the current leader's weight of 641.

"Too bad," said Angus, sympathizing. "But Priscilla's probably happy, right? The ladies don't like to weigh too much."

"She's not a lady. She's a pumpkin," said Patrick, scowling.

His reaction tickled the crowd's fancy, and people were laughing and joking as Priscilla was removed from the scale and added to the arrangement of enormous pumpkins that was growing around the farm stand's sign. Lucy looked for Sara and Zoe in the crowd and finally spotted them with a group of friends.

Last up was Wilf's pumpkin, and Lucy

waved to Phyllis, who was standing beside her husband as the gleaming orange gourd was set on the scale. Wilf had taken a great deal of trouble, she realized, and had polished up his pumpkin. As before, the electronic display blinked a bit. Then the numbers appeared: 812!

"Folks, we have a winner," said Angus, clapping Wilf on the back and shaking his hand.

Wilf was grinning broadly, and Phyllis was beaming with pride, her dyed hair a close match to the pumpkin's orange skin.

"Are you willing to share your secret?" asked Angus.

"Massage," confessed Wilf, getting a roar from the crowd. "I massaged the pumpkin every night."

"Wasn't your wife jealous?" joked Angus, causing both Wilf and Phyllis to blush furiously.

"If she was, she didn't say," said Wilf, with a twinkle in his eye.

"Did you mind?" Angus asked Phyllis.

"Nope," said Phyllis. "Because he promised to give the prize money to me!"

"Well, here it is," said Angus, producing a white envelope. "Five hundred dollars."

"Thank you," said Phyllis, plucking the envelope from his hands and giving her husband a kiss.

"Danged shame," muttered Buzz Bresnahan, approaching Lucy. "My pumpkin would've won, you know, if it hadn't been vandalized."

"Any progress on that?" asked Lucy as they walked over to congratulate Wilf and Phyllis.

Bresnahan shook his head. "Nope." He extended his hand to Wilf, who took it and shook it enthusiastically. "Congratulations. Darn fine pumpkin you got there."

"I appreciate your saying so," replied Wilf. "I know you must be disappointed."

"There's always next year," said Bresnahan.

"Right," said Wilf, exhaling a big sigh. "Tell the truth, I don't think I'll enter again. It was a heck of a strain, 'cause of what happened to you. I ended up sleeping outside all last week, in a tent, right next to the pumpkin. Hell of a way to live."

"Is that true?" Lucy asked Phyllis. "You never said."

"I wasn't about to admit my husband was sleeping with a pumpkin instead of with me," muttered Phyllis.

"Oh," said Lucy. "I see your point . . . , but these were extraordinary circumstances."

"Nana, can I have some ice cream?" asked Patrick, tugging on her arm.

Lucy hesitated, thinking of Molly's instructions. "How about an apple?"

Patrick's face fell. "I don't like apples."

"Okay," she said, admitting defeat. "We'll get ice cream."

Going inside, Lucy bought a chocolate cone for Patrick and a pumpkin one for herself. They walked to the truck, licking their ice cream as they went and greeting friends and neighbors.

"Maybe Grandpa's catapult will win," said Patrick as he climbed into his booster seat licked his cone while Lucy buckled him in. She'd already finished hers, savoring every mouthful of the sweet and spicy ice cream.

Lucy expected that the atmosphere would be somewhat rowdier at the pumpkin hurl than it was at the weigh-in, which had attracted lots of families with kids. The Claws rock band was playing, which attracted plenty of young singles, and the refreshment stand sold beer, as well as the usual soft drinks and hot dogs. Contestants at the hurl competed in two categories: distance, to see who could hurl a pumpkin the farthest using a catapult, and accuracy, as they aimed to hit a target, which was always a wrecked car marked with a big red bull's-eye. This year's target was an aged Hyundai that had dropped its transmission on Route 1, causing a giant traffic jam, which Lucy had covered for the *Pennysaver.*

When Lucy arrived, the band was playing, wailing guitars and thumping drums filling the air with oldies she recognized. Patrick picked up on the band's energy, hopping and skipping along beside her, grasping her hand with sticky ice cream fingers. The announcer this time was a woman, DJ Phoebe, from a Portland radio station, and she was informing the crowd that they were in for a special treat, an exhibition by the team that currently held the Guinness World Record for distance pumpkin hurling, which would attempt to break its own record of 5,231 feet.

"That's almost a mile, folks," she said as an ungainly metal contraption resembling a giant grasshopper was rolled into place. "This is the Amazing Thunderbuss, brought all the way from Erie, Pennsylvania, by Dick Turpin and his team, the Amazing Thunderbusters!"

Lucy found Bill, who was standing with Tom and Sid, studying the machine with admiring eyes. "Look at the swing on that thing," said Bill as the catapult's giant arm swung back in a smooth arc and then pivoted forward, releasing its pumpkin missile.

There was a big *aah* from the crowd as the pumpkin sailed off into the distance, right across Jonah's Pond, and landed on the opposite shore.

DJ Phoebe was checking her smartphone for the results, sent from a team of judges on the shore. "Dangerous work," she joked, waiting for the results. "Here we go," she said, raising her arm. "Five thousand two hundred ninety-six. Not a record."

After a few more tries, the Thunderbusters gave up, claiming a stiff headwind was causing resistance, and admitting defeat. Then, the exhibition completed, the accuracy competition featuring local entries began, the first of which was Bill's catapult.

"Any sign of Ev?" asked Lucy.

"No," said Bill, shaking his head. "I'm really surprised."

"Me, too," agreed Lucy, remembering how excited Ev had been about the catapult's prospects the night before. "You wouldn't think he'd want to miss this."

Bill shrugged and ran forward, getting a big round of applause from the crowd. Reaching the catapult and standing beside it, he gave an exaggerated bow. Then he loaded a pumpkin onto the swing arm of the catapult. "Here we go. Stand clear," he yelled, releasing the arm and sending the pumpkin flying directly into the Hyundai, denting the roof. Pumpkin guts oozed down over the windows and slid to the ground.

The crowd roared with approval. This was what they'd come to see. A second pumpkin was loaded onto the catapult. This time it hit the rear window, breaking it.

The crowd loved it. Patrick was jumping up and down with excitement, and Bill was beaming with pride.

"Who would think a pumpkin could do so much damage to a car?" mused Lucy, talking to Sid.

"It's the speed," said Sid as they watched a third pumpkin sail into the sky. "The weight and the speed combine to create a good deal of force."

"I guess so," said Lucy as the pumpkin landed with a thud and the trunk popped open from the impact.

"Wow," crowed DJ Phoebe. "Great work from Team Stone, right here in Tinker's Cove. Three points for accuracy. Next up, Team G from Gideon, but first, while they're setting up, some music from the Claws!"

"I think I'll get a couple of photos for the paper," said Lucy, remembering her responsibilities as a reporter and pulling her camera from her bag. "Will you keep an eye on Patrick for me?"

"No problem," said Sid.

"I'll just be a minute," promised Lucy.

"Okay." Sid had opened a cooler and was pulling out a beer for himself and a soda for Patrick.

Lucy hurried across the field to the car, thinking it was a good thing that Molly didn't know about the ice creams and sodas Patrick was getting, and hoping she never found out, though she wasn't sure how she was going to prevent it. Patrick was sure to tell his mother. She could just hear him saying, "But Nana let me have Coke," the first time Molly told him he couldn't have any. Then she'd be in for it, she thought, reaching the car and raising her camera to her eye. Peering through the viewfinder, she noticed a scrap of cloth. It was in the trunk, spattered with pumpkin gore. Lowering the camera, she stepped forward, realizing she'd seen that plaid before. It was a shirt, a shirt she'd seen every day for weeks on Evan Wickes — and he was still wearing it.

Chapter Eleven

Tinker's Cove Chamber of Commerce

Press Release

For Immediate Release

Don't Miss Any of the Fun! The Giant Pumpkin Fest Continues with the First Annual Giant Pumpkin Fest Noise Parade. Bring a Noisemaker and Scare the Ghosts and Goblins Away as We March Down Main Street to the Town Green, Where the Kiwanis Club Will Build a Giant Bonfire! The Parade Steps Off from the Post Office at 5:00 p.m.

It was all a blur after that. First, Bill ran to see what Lucy was upset about, and then Tinker's Cove police officer Todd Kirwan, who was assigned to patrol the pumpkin hurl, joined them. He called in the discovery, and the rescue squad arrived, but it was clearly too late to do anything for Ev, whose body could not be removed from the trunk, because it had stiffened due to rigor mortis. Then the state police arrived and declared the Hyundai a crime scene. Todd got busy setting up yellow tape around the car, which was left in place for the medical examiner and crime-scene specialists.

Bill took the loss of his friend very hard. "I can't believe we were lobbing pumpkins at him," he said, shaking his head and blinking furiously as his eyes welled with tears he refused to shed.

"You couldn't have known," said Lucy, who was a bit shocked at his reaction. Blinded by her own dislike for the man, she hadn't realized how close Bill had grown to him.

"I was just mad at him this morning, when he didn't show," said Bill, his voice thick.

"That's natural," said Todd. "He was a grown man, able to take care of himself. It wasn't like he was a child who'd gone missing."

Hearing this, Lucy scanned the crowd for Patrick, and found him with Sid among the crowd of gawkers on the other side of the yellow tape. "Can we go?" she asked Todd.

"I'm here with my grandson. He's only four."

The officer nodded his head. "We know who you are and where you live, Lucy." He turned to Bill. "Don't leave town. We'll need a statement from you."

"Fine," said Bill. He grabbed Lucy's hand, and they crossed the stubbly field together and joined Sid and Patrick.

"What happened?" asked Patrick, who was wide eyed with excitement and sugar.

"Mr. Wickes had an accident," said Lucy. "He was in the car."

"The car Grandpa hit with pumpkins?" he asked.

"I'm afraid so," said Lucy, with a glance at Bill. She was afraid that the boy's questions would upset him.

"Was he hurt?" persisted Patrick.

"We don't know what happened or why," she said, attempting to end the discussion.

"Will Mr. Wickes be okay?" asked Patrick, whose little face expressed worry for his friend. "I really like him."

"No," replied Bill, choking up. "He's gone."

"Gone where?" demanded Patrick.

"He's dead, sweetheart," said Lucy, falling to her knees and giving her grandson a hug. "We don't know how it happened or why he was in the car."

"I can't believe it," moaned Bill. "If I only had known he was in there . . ."

Sid clapped an arm around his friend. "Whatever happened to Ev, it wasn't your fault. No way."

"My goldfish died," said Patrick, who was struggling to understand. "It got all stiff and icky, and we buried it in the backyard."

"We'll take good care of Mr. Wickes's body," promised Lucy. "There'll be a funeral, and he'll be buried properly."

"Will he go to heaven?" asked Patrick. "Mommy said my goldfish would go to heaven."

"I'm sure he will," said Lucy, who had her doubts. She knew it was wrong to think ill of the dead, and was struggling with her conscience.

"A heaven where they make catapults and all sorts of cool stuff," said Sid.

"He was a mechanical genius. He truly was," said Bill.

"A real engineer," added Sid.

"Old school," said Bill, coming to a decision. "You go ahead, Lucy. I'm gonna stay until they move his body." He sighed. "I feel like I owe him at least that much."

"Yeah, man," agreed Sid. "We can't leave him, not like this."

Lucy wanted to say what she really thought: that Ev was a drunk and a ne'er-do-well and nobody would really miss him, except his drinking buddies, but instead she took Patrick by the hand. "I'll take Patrick home," she said, getting a nod from Bill. A knot of men was gathering around him, mostly guys who gathered at the roadhouse outside town, stopping for a brewski or three before heading home after work.

"Nana, what does 'old school' mean?" asked Patrick as they stopped by the car and Lucy fumbled in her purse for the keys.

"It's just an expression. It means he had old-fashioned values, like being a good friend."

"He was my friend," said Patrick in his sweet, innocent little boy voice.

"In you go," said Lucy, unlocking the door for him. Suddenly, she found tears welling in her eyes and blinked them away. Once she was sure Patrick was safely buckled in and she had started the car, she let out a big sigh. Okay, she admitted to herself, while she really had had no use for Ev, he was, well, not exactly her friend, but he was definitely part of her world. She started to think she would miss him but changed her mind, realizing that whether she liked it or not, Ev was going to be part of her world for a long time. She knew there was certainly going to be an investigation to figure out how and why he died, and it was most likely going to be lengthy. She hoped desperately that he died from natural causes, but knew it was unlikely, considering he'd been stuffed into the trunk of a car. Maybe, she thought, clutching at straws, he'd been drunk and climbed in the car to sleep it off. It could have happened that way, she thought, trying to convince herself.

When Lucy got home, she found Sara's little Civic parked in the driveway, as well as Hank DeVries's pickup truck with the scuba sticker.

"What's up?" she asked, finding them in the kitchen, sitting at the golden oak table and drinking herb tea.

"The underwater pumpkin-carving contest was canceled," said Sara. "After all that work we did to get DEP approval and all, the cops came and shut us down."

"Yeah," confirmed Hank. "We had everything set up and were ready to go when they started putting up yellow tape and told us to move along."

"They wouldn't tell us why," said Sara.

"It's because of Ev," said Lucy. "He was found dead at the pumpkin hurl."

"What?" demanded Sara.

Lucy glanced down at Patrick, who was standing by her side. "You know what, Patrick? How about I make you some lunch and you can eat and watch a movie, too?"

Patrick sensed he was in an advantageous bargaining position. "*Despicable Me* and peanut butter with potato chips." He paused, considering further options. "And chocolate milk."

"You got it," said Lucy, hustling him into the family room and inserting the DVD into the player. Back in the kitchen, she recounted the morning's events while assembling his lunch. "It was horrible," she began, spreading peanut butter on a piece of whole wheat bread.

"No whole wheat!" called Patrick, pressing his advantage.

"It's all I've got," she called back, getting a mumbled "Okay" in reply.

"It was horrible . . . ," repeated Sara.

"Right. It was at the pumpkin hurl. The catapult worked great, and your dad was hurling pumpkins at this old Hyundai. The trunk popped open, and Ev was inside, dead."

Lucy was shaking some potato chips out of the bag, arranging them alongside Patrick's sandwich.

"How'd they know he was dead?" asked Hank.

"Well, they couldn't get him out, because of rigor mortis," said Lucy, squeezing chocolate syrup into a glass of milk and stirring it with a spoon.

"That is horrible," said Sara, "but I don't understand why they shut down our contest at the conservation area."

"They must have their reasons," said Lucy, setting the food on a tray and carrying it into the family room. When she returned, she picked up the conversation. "They must think it's part of the crime scene."

"They don't even know it's a crime. They don't actually know how Ev died, do they?" demanded Sara, still in an argumentative mood.

"I don't think he crawled into the trunk of a car all by himself," said Hank.

"It might've been a joke, a prank gone wrong," insisted Lucy, seizing on the notion. "He might've thought he'd surprise your father at the hurl."

"Some surprise," said Hank, shaking his head.

"Poor Dad," said Sara, staring into her mug of tea. "He must be so upset."

"He is," said Lucy. "He really is, although

he doesn't want to show it, especially not in front of his friends."

Lucy sat with Sara and Hank while they drank their tea. Then they left for the college, where they planned to get together with other scuba club members to figure out their next move. She made herself a sandwich, and one for Bill, too, expecting him to arrive any moment, but he didn't come, and she finally covered it with plastic wrap. Patrick's movie had ended, and Lucy was considering taking him for a walk along the old logging trails that meandered through the woods behind their house when Bill finally came home.

"It's official," he said. "Ev was murdered."

"How awful," she said, letting the news sink in. Then, deciding she needed to keep Patrick busy, she put some chocolate chip cookies on a plate and took them in to her grandson, who was playing with some Legos in the family room. Returning to the kitchen, she questioned Bill.

"Are they sure?"

"Yeah, the medical examiner took one look and said he was killed by a blow to the head." He paused. "It was obvious, if you looked past the pumpkin gore."

"Who would do that?" she asked, thinking aloud. "He was . . . Well, maybe not everybody loved him, exactly, but he was a local character. A town fixture, somebody everybody knew."

"Well," said Bill, popping open a can of beer he'd taken from the fridge, "they seem to think I had something to do with it."

"You?" Lucy couldn't believe it.

"Yeah, it seems I was the last person to see him alive."

It was then they heard the gravel in the driveway crunch, indicating the arrival of an unmarked police car. As they watched, two detectives in plain clothes got out of the car and walked up to the porch.

Bill opened the door for them. "Come on in," he said.

The two showed their badges.

"For the record," said the first, a tall, thin guy in his forties with a brush cut. "I'm Detective Lieutenant George Ferrick, and this is my partner, Detective Sergeant Paul DeGraw." DeGraw was also tall, but heavier, and he had a dark five o'clock shadow. "Mr. Stone, we have a few questions we'd like to ask you."

"Would you like some tea or coffee?" asked Lucy, indicating the table. She didn't like this at all. She had cultivated a long and cordial professional relationship with another state cop, Detective Lieutenant

Horowitz, but she didn't know these officers at all.

"No, thanks, ma'am," said Ferrick.

"Is it all right if I stay?" she asked as they seated themselves.

"Fine," said Ferrick, who apparently spoke for his partner, too.

"Are you fellows new?" asked Lucy. "Doesn't Detective Lieutenant Horowitz cover this area?"

"Horowitz is on vacation," said Ferrick

Not a good sign, thought Lucy, watching as he pulled out a chair, scraping it noisily on the floor. He sat down heavily, set a leather-covered notebook on the table, and flipped it open.

"Okay," he began. "I believe you told us you saw the decedent, Mr. Evan Wickes, last night, at approximately seven o'clock."

"That's right," said Bill, with a nod of his head. "He was here. We went over the catapult, oiled a few springs, and had a drink for luck."

"How did he seem?" asked DeGraw. "Anxious, angry? Did you have words?"

"No." Bill shook his head. "He was in a good mood, looking forward to the contest today. 'We're gonna show 'em, Billy boy.' That's what he said." Bill's voice thickened. "That was the last thing he said to me."

"So I guess you spent a lot of time together, building this catapult," suggested Ferrick. He had a sharp nose, thought Lucy, and sniffed a lot. Maybe it was allergies, but it made him seem a bit like a mouse. *Or a rat,* she thought uncharitably.

"Yeah. We started a couple of months ago," said Bill. "End of August, I guess."

"Whose idea was it?" asked DeGraw in a challenging tone. "Yours?"

"No," answered Bill. "It was Ev's. I ran into him at the lumberyard, and we started talking, the way you do, you know, and he said it might be fun to enter the pumpkin hurl. Oddly enough, I've always been interested in the Middle Ages, knights and armor and stuff, ever since I was a kid, and I even had a toy catapult. I thought it would be neat to build a big one." He grinned ruefully. "Kinda stupid, I guess. It cost a lot of money and took a lot of time, but it was something I always wanted to do. We wanted to do." He paused, catching Lucy's eye. "And we weren't alone. There were quite a few others who entered the contest."

She put her hand on his and gave it a squeeze.

"And he left here in the Hyundai?" asked Ferrick.

"No. He had a pickup. That's what he

drove. I never saw the Hyundai before the contest."

"You have any idea what his plans were for the evening?" asked DeGraw. He was staring hard at Bill, knitting his thick brows together.

"He didn't say," said Bill.

DeGraw pressed the issue. "Well, what did he usually do? Do you know?"

"Not really," said Bill, with a shrug. "He could've gone home. He has . . . I mean had, a little house out on Bumps River Road. Sometimes he went out to the roadhouse, especially if there was a game. He liked the Bruins and the Patriots."

"Did you owe him money?" asked Ferrick.

"No," said Bill. "I did pay him," he added, glancing at Lucy. "I insisted on it. I knew he didn't have much money, and he was spending a lot of time on the project, but he said he didn't want any money. We finally agreed I'd give him fifteen bucks an hour. That's what I pay a carpenter's helper. He was much more skilled than that, but he wouldn't take any more." Bill rested his hand on Lucy's thigh. "I settled up with him last night, gave him a check for six hundred dollars."

"We didn't find any check," said DeGraw.

"Maybe he cashed it," said Bill.

"Didn't have any cash, either," said De-Graw.

"Well, maybe he spent it," said Bill. "I can show you the carbon in my checkbook, and the bank will have records."

Lucy had been so intent on the conversation that she hadn't noticed Patrick, who suddenly climbed on her lap and pressed a couple of Legos into her hand. "I can't get them to work," he said, studying the cops. "Who are they?"

"These are policemen. They're here about Mr. Wickes's accident," said Lucy.

Bill took the Lego pieces from Lucy and stood up, pressing the plastic pieces together with a snap. "Do you have any more questions?" he asked.

"Not at the moment," said Ferrick, rising and pushing his chair back.

"But we might want to talk to you again," said DeGraw, also rising.

"You know where I live," said Bill, lifting Patrick off Lucy's lap and taking him by the hand. "Let's see if we can make a catapult out of these Legos, okay?"

"Good idea, Grandpa," said Patrick as they went into the family room.

Lucy opened the door for the cops, who weren't in a hurry to leave. DeGraw glanced around the kitchen, as if memorizing the decor, while Ferrick reviewed his notes before finally pocketing the notebook.

"Mind if we look around?" asked Ferrick, standing in the doorway.

"Not at all. We have nothing to hide," said Lucy, whose heart was pounding in her chest, "but my lawyer friend would be very disappointed in me if I didn't insist on a warrant."

DeGraw placed himself squarely in front of her, facing off. "Are you sure you want to play it that way? Because we can make things very unpleasant for people who don't cooperate."

Lucy took a deep breath, willing the flutters in her chest to subside. "It's time for you to leave," she said, hoping she wasn't making a big mistake.

"We'll be back," growled DeGraw, before stepping through the doorway.

When they were both outside, on the porch, Lucy was tempted to slam the door behind them but thought better of it. Instead, with shaking hands, she found the bottle of chardonnay she kept in the fridge and poured herself a glass, which she gulped down.

CHAPTER TWELVE

Tinker's Cove Chamber of Commerce

Press Release

For Immediate Release

The Giant Pumpkin Fest Continues With the Pumpkin Boat Regatta in Our Very Own Cove. The Starting Gun Goes off at Noon, When Our Courageous Contestants Will Attempt to Be the First to Cross the Finish Line in Boats Made of Giant Pumpkins. Don't Miss the Fun. There Are Plenty of Free Viewing Locations around the Cove, and Picnicking Is Encouraged.

That night Lucy didn't sleep well. For one thing, she couldn't erase the image of Ev stuffed in the trunk of the Hyundai and spattered with pumpkin gore that kept popping up every time she closed her eyes. That was bad enough, but even more troubling to her peace of mind was the interview with the state cops, DeGraw and Ferrick. They seemed to have identified Bill as their prime suspect in Ev's death, and she had an uneasy feeling that they wouldn't give up, even if there was no evidence. She'd heard of cases where police had falsified and even manufactured evidence, and she was afraid they might stoop to such behavior rather than admit they were wrong.

It was just plain bad luck that Horowitz was on vacation, she thought with a sigh. He was one cop she respected and trusted. She knew he was a careful and thorough investigator, and although he would have had to include Bill on his initial list of suspects, she was confident he would have promptly eliminated him. Well, she thought as she flipped over onto her other side, maybe he was taking only a short vacation and would be back soon. There was no sense worrying, she told herself, because this was one matter that was out of her hands. This was one situation she could not control. And with that thought, she finally dozed off. Next thing she knew, Patrick was banging on her bedroom door.

"Wake up, Nana! Today's the pumpkin boat race!"

"I'm coming," she answered, throwing back the covers and reaching for her robe. It was early, barely seven o'-clock, and she had a lot to do. She had planned a special day for the family, intending to make pumpkin muffins for breakfast and to pack an elaborate picnic lunch to take along to the pumpkin boat regatta, and she had to get moving.

Hurrying downstairs to the kitchen, she found the girls and Patrick at the table, but there was no sign of Bill.

"Where's your dad?" she asked, noticing they were eating the sour cream apple cake and hard-boiled eggs intended for the picnic basket. "Those were for the picnic lunch," she said in rather a sharp tone.

"Oops," said Sara. "Sorry."

"There's plenty left," added Zoe, with a nod at the half-eaten cake. "And Dad's out in the garden."

Lucy glanced out the window and saw that Bill was clearing out the garden, hacking away at Priscilla's abandoned vine. She was reassured that he was coping, working off his sadness.

She wasn't doing quite so well, she realized, when a glance at the half-eaten cake brought memories of Ev wolfing down leftovers and made her want to cry. She quickly turned around and poured herself a cup of coffee. Cradling the warm mug made her feel a little better. "I was going to make pumpkin muffins for breakfast."

"You still can," said Zoe brightly. "Or even better, Patrick and I will make them for the picnic."

Patrick really liked this idea. "Yeah!" he said.

"Okay," said Lucy, joining them at the table, where she sipped her coffee. "I don't know what came over me. We can take some cheese instead of the eggs."

"Or cookies," suggested Patrick.

Lucy smiled. "And cookies."

Lucy's spirits had improved by the time they left for the regatta, with the revised picnic tucked into the back of the SUV, along with a generous supply of blankets and the family's collection of beach chairs. Plenty of people had gathered to watch the spectacle, which was taking place in the town cove, with judges arranged on the fish pier. Most of the spectators had the same idea as the Stone family and had brought picnics, which they spread out on the grassy hill beside the parking area. It was a classic October day, with a clear blue sky and a nip in the air, so Lucy was glad they'd thought to dress warmly and bring blankets. It was not a day, she thought as she unfolded her chair, in which she would like to risk a dunking in the cold water of the cove.

"Quite a few entrants," said Bill, seating himself beside her.

She took his hand, knowing the effort he was making to keep his emotions from affecting the family's good time.

The contestants were busy unloading their pumpkin watercraft, which varied greatly in design. Some had gone for a catamaran concept, attaching their hollowed-out pumpkins to big blocks of Styrofoam, often carved into a streamlined shape. Another enterprising contestant had cut the front and back off an old canoe and had inserted his pumpkin in the middle, a design that Bill thought had potential. Others had simply gone with the pumpkin itself, often adding decorations and even, in one case, a beach umbrella canopy. Means of locomotion also varied: some attached small trolling motors, while others relied on oars and paddles.

"Wanna make a bet?" asked Ted, plopping himself down on the ground. Pam was with him, struggling to unfold her rusty beach chair.

"I'm not a betting man," said Bill, jumping up. "Let me help you with that."

"No, I can do it. There's a trick," said Pam.

"The trick would be to buy yourself a new one," advised Ted. "They're on sale, now, you know."

"I just like this one," said Pam, finally succeeding in opening the chair, which squeaked in protest. She'd no sooner sat down than she jumped up. "Look. They're going in the water. It's going to start!"

"It's not starting for that guy," said Ted, as one of the pumpkin crafts began sinking the moment it was boarded.

"That poor man," shrieked Pam.

"He's going to get soaked," said Lucy, wrapping her blanket a bit tighter around her legs. She glanced at Patrick, making sure he wasn't chilled, and saw that excitement was keeping him warm. He was hungry, however.

"Nana, when are we going to eat?" he demanded.

"Right now," said Lucy, opening the picnic basket. "Who wants a sandwich? I've got tuna, egg salad, peanut butter. . . ."

"What a feast!" exclaimed Pam.

"I feel a little weird about it," confessed Lucy, whispering in her friend's ear. "About all this, I mean. It seems disrespectful."

"They couldn't cancel the whole festival

because of Ev," replied Pam, whispering Ev's name. "So much work went into it."

"There goes another!" exclaimed Zoe, pointing. Lucy looked up just in time to see one of the pumpkin boats keel over, depositing its sole occupant, a woman dressed as a witch, into the water.

"They used to test witches with water, didn't they?" asked Bill, managing a chuckle. "If they floated, they were witches, right?"

"And if they sank, they weren't witches, but they were dead, anyway," added Sara.

"But they passed the test," said Pam, her eyes widening in horror. "Oh, my gosh!"

The woman in the water was also passing the test, despite struggling to stay afloat, encumbered by her heavy witch costume. Fortunately, a crewman in the Coast Guard boat noticed her distress and tossed her a life ring, which she was able to grab.

"It won't do the festival any good if people keep dying at the events," observed Ted wryly.

Lucy could have strangled him for the callous remark, even though she knew that maintaining a flippant attitude was a professional trick, a way journalists protected themselves from the tragic and disturbing stories they had to cover.

"Ev didn't die at the pumpkin hurl," said Bill in a voice tight with emotion.

"Details, details," replied Ted, getting a warning glance from Lucy. "Doesn't matter, since his body was found there."

"Little pitchers have big ears," she said, with a nod at Patrick, who was happily munching on a chocolate chip cookie.

"Well, I'm glad they're going forward with the festival," said Pam, accepting a glass of cider from Lucy.

"We had to cancel the underwater pumpkin-carving contest," said Sara. "Bummer."

"That's too bad," sympathized Pam.

"Some of the kids in the scuba club knew Ev," said Sara. "They said he sold them pot."

This news stunned them all, except for Patrick, who had finished his cookie and had moved on to a pumpkin muffin.

"Is that true?" demanded Ted, who, Lucy knew, was sensing a scoop for the *Pennysaver.* "Will they talk to me?"

"Not if it's going to get them in trouble," said Sara.

"Talk about trouble!" exclaimed Pam, pointing at the cove, where the wake from the Coast Guard boat had capsized all the remaining contestants. "Look at that!"

"Camera, Lucy!" yelled Ted. "Get a photo!"

After the excitement at the pumpkin boat regatta, Lucy expected the atmosphere would be much calmer at Country Cousins, where the winner of the candy corn contest would be announced. She was surprised when Patrick insisted he wanted to go along with her and Pam, certain that his guess of one million would win.

"But, Patrick," Lucy asked as the three climbed the hill from the cove, "what would you do with a gift certificate?"

"I'll buy something for Mom," he said as they turned onto Main Street.

"What a nice idea," said Pam.

Lucy agreed, pleased by his thoughtfulness. But as they continued along the street, which was filled with day trippers lured by the jack-o'-lanterns displayed outside every business, she began to worry that he might be disappointed when he didn't win. "I don't think you'll win, Patrick. A million is a very great many, more than the canister could possibly hold."

"Well, maybe I'll get a prize, anyway," he said philosophically as they paused to admire a jack-o'-lantern wearing a mail carrier's cap displayed on a hay bale outside the post office, along with a bag filled with mini pumpkins complete with stamps and addresses. "None of the pumpkin boats finished the race, but they all got prizes."

"I'm glad they gave a prize to that poor witch," said Pam. "Wettest, wasn't it?"

Lucy laughed, remembering the ridiculous ceremony. Although none of the ridiculous watercraft had made it to the finish line, the judges had hastily revised their criteria and had awarded prizes for closest to the finish line, most colorful, and wettest.

When they reached Country Cousins, they discovered a crowd had already gathered in front of the old-fashioned shop's front porch, which was roped off. The long deacon's benches, one each for Republicans and Democrats, were sporting clever jack-o'-lantern displays that made Lucy smile. The Republicans had a pumpkin carved to resemble an elephant, with cabbage ears and a long gourd for a trunk, and the Democrats had one like a donkey, with a butternut squash nose and pointy parsnip ears.

A podium equipped with a public address system had been set up, and all was ready for the awarding of the grand prize by Country Cousins CEO Tom Miller. Lucy observed that the candy corn contest had attracted many more local residents than

213

the pumpkin boat regatta; folks in Tinker's Cove were clearly more interested in cash than glory. Miss Tilley and her friend Rebecca Wardwell were there, of course, and Lucy noticed that Miss Tilley was keeping her fingers crossed.

"I thought you were confident that you'd calculated correctly," teased Lucy, stepping beside her. "What's with the crossed fingers?"

"I'm taking no chances," said Miss Tilley, whose gaze was fixed on the temporary podium.

Rebecca was more philosophical. "What will be, will be."

Just then the door opened and Tom Miller stepped out, carrying the glass canister filled with candy corn. He was accompanied by his nephew Buck and Corney Clark. Stepping up to the podium, he raised the canister above his head, causing everyone to gasp. The cut-glass facets of the canister had caught the sunlight, which was bouncing every which way in dazzling rainbow effects.

"Can you see, Patrick?" asked Lucy. "Can you see the rainbows?"

"Yeah," said Patrick, clearly awestruck. "Wow."

"People are acting like it's some sort of holy relic," said Pam, who didn't approve.

"It's nothing but diffraction, you know."

"It's pretty," said Lucy, giving Patrick's hand a squeeze.

"It's crass commercialism, the glorification of consumer goods," insisted Pam, who had been a bit of a hippie in her youth and had retained some of her counterculture views.

"I'd like to welcome everyone here," began Tom, but before he could go any further, Corney stepped up and whispered in his ear. He covered the microphone with his hand and said something in reply, something that caused Corney to shake her head and give his arm a tug.

"As I was saying," continued Tom, speaking into the mike, "it's a great day today in Tinker's Cove, and we here at Country Cousins are very excited —"

He was interrupted by Buck, who had stepped forward and taken Corney's place beside him.

"Oh, in case you haven't heard," said Tom, realizing an introduction was necessary, "this is my nephew Buck Miller, who has recently joined the firm."

"Right," said Buck, coolly plucking the mike from his uncle's hands. "And I'm very pleased today to be able to award this two-hundred-fifty-dollar gift certificate."

Tom's jaw had dropped; he looked completely stunned. "But . . . ," he protested, only to be shushed by Corney and pulled aside.

"Thank you for the introduction," said Buck, smoothly segueing to an explanation of the contest's history and rules.

Behind him, Tom and Corney were deeply involved in a whispered discussion in which, it was obvious to all, there was little agreement.

"So now," said Buck, displaying an oversize orange envelope fastened with a gold seal and a yellow ribbon, "I will announce the winner."

Everybody was quiet, and all eyes were fixed on the envelope.

"The winning guess was one thousand sixty-seven, which is, amazingly, the exact number of pieces of candy corn."

Miss Tilley's face crumpled in disappointment, but Pam was glowing with excitement. "That's me!" she exclaimed.

"The winning entry was submitted by Pam Stillings," said Buck, confirming Pam's win. "Is Pam here?"

"Yes, yes," said Pam, weaving her way through the crowd of onlookers, many of whom were applauding. "I'm coming. I'm right here."

"Congratulations, Pam," said Buck, taking her hand and shaking it. "I don't think we've ever had a winner who got the exact number, have we?" he asked, turning to his uncle, who was walking off the porch.

"No, no, we haven't," growled Tom, who didn't stop but kept right on walking, determined to absent himself from the proceedings.

"What was your secret?" asked Corney, joining Buck at the podium. "Did you have a method?"

"That's what I want to know," declared Miss Tilley with a sniff. "Did she have inside information?"

"Hush," warned Rebecca, patting her friend's hand. "You were very close, weren't you?"

"I was," said Miss Tilley. "Which is why I don't think it could be a lucky guess."

"No inside info," said Lucy, who knew how Pam had arrived at the winning number. "It was all completely aboveboard."

"No method," laughed Pam, gleefully accepting the gift certificate prize. "It's my phone number!"

"Bah!" exclaimed Miss Tilley, clearly disgusted.

When Lucy and Patrick got home that

afternoon, they found Bill out in the pumpkin patch. He was dismantling the security system, which was a great disappointment to Patrick.

"No more siren?" he asked.

"Here goes, one last time," said Bill, smiling as he set the thing off.

Lucy covered her ears, but Patrick was delighted, prancing around the garden, joined by an exuberant Libby. When the wailing stopped, so did they. Picking up a stick, Patrick wandered off to explore the yard, accompanied by the dog.

"Don't go too far," cautioned Lucy, mindful of the woods behind their property.

"I won't," he called back, whipping the stick and decapitating a dandelion.

"Boys," sighed Lucy.

"You know you love having him," said Bill, who was coiling up a length of electrical cord and adding it to the sizable pile of equipment he'd collected.

"That's a lot of stuff," observed Lucy.

"He saved everything that came his way," said Bill. "He'd even pick up stuff that people put out for the garbage collector — and he usually managed to find a use for it."

"How'd he get the job?" asked Lucy. "I mean, you'd think an outfit like Country

Cousins would hire some professional security firm." She was about to add, "Not a local yokel like Ev," but caught herself in time, vowing not to speak ill of the dead.

"What you really mean is, why would they hire a guy like Ev, who, face it, had a bit of a reputation?"

"I was just thinking that a professional outfit would have all the latest bells and whistles, and probably would offer guarantees and warranties . . . ," said Lucy, refusing to be drawn into an argument.

"Ev was probably cheaper," said Bill, picking up the plastic fish box he'd filled with the security equipment.

"But riskier," said Lucy.

"You mean he might have been tempted to share his inside information about the alarms?" asked Bill, getting a bit huffy. "For money? He'd never do that."

"The Millers must have trusted him," said Lucy in a placatory tone. "That's all I mean. They must have had some relationship with him."

"Well, it is a small town," said Bill, carrying the box into the shed, where he dropped it with a thud. "Maybe they just wanted to give employment to local workers."

When he emerged, he found Lucy picking the last of the late salad greens they'd planted in August, when the nights started getting cooler.

"Lucy, I hope you're not thinking of investigating Ev's death yourself," he said, plucking a few leaves of arugula.

"Of course not," said Lucy, who was thinking she really ought to go inside and get something to hold the greens.

"Because I know you think the cops want to pin this on me, and you might think you have to find the killer to protect me," he continued, biting into an arugula leaf.

"You're assuming an awful lot. Maybe I'd like to see you go to jail," teased Lucy. "Sometimes you can be awfully annoying."

He grabbed her by the arms and drew her close, causing her to drop the salad greens as he pressed her against him. "I'm serious," he said. "Whoever killed Ev is not a nice person, and I don't want anything bad to happen to you."

"And I don't want anything bad to happen to you," said Lucy, raising her face for a kiss.

Spring, 1979

It was only to be expected, she decided, watching him close the door and hearing the click of the latch as he turned the lock. She'd felt excited, even elated, when she left that

220

first women's lib meeting at the library. Miss Tilley, the librarian, had seemed to understand her situation and had offered help. But now, as the days passed so slowly, with no end in sight, her spirits had plummeted. She had nothing in common with those women who wanted to burn their bras, nothing at all. She had to face the fact that she was a prisoner in her own home and had only herself to blame. She wasn't like those women at the meeting, who blamed their husbands for all their woes. She knew full well that she had been a fool for love and had jumped into marriage without really knowing her husband and understanding exactly what was expected of her.

And if that wasn't bad enough, her prison had gotten smaller as the store had grown, spreading through the farmhouse like cancer. First, it took over the fancy front parlor, with its lace curtains and big family Bible, then the back parlor, and finally the dining room. Where there once had been horsehair sofas and Persian rugs and a fine oak dining set, there was now a jumble of fishing tackle; rubber boots and waders; newspapers; a refrigerator case filled with packaged cold cuts, milk, and eggs; and racks of sturdy woolen clothing. The counter, with its old-fashioned cash register, remained near the front door and also held jars of penny candy and a machine that ground keys.

He loved locks and keys and used them wherever he could. Of course, he could hardly lock the front door to the store, as Emily had pointed out, adding that rueful little nod of her. Even he understood it was unwise to lock the customers out. But he locked all the other doors, including the extra-solid door that connected the store to the private living quarters, which were now confined to the cramped rooms upstairs that were hunched beneath the sharply angled roof.

It hadn't been quite so bad before, when she had absolutely no hope of escape. But now, when she served him breakfast and lunch, and when she cleaned and did the laundry, and when she cooked dinner, all the waking day long, she kept her eyes on the clock, waiting for her chance during the store's business hours — 6:00 a.m. to 10:00 p.m. She didn't ever think about the other eight hours, the dark hours.

CHAPTER THIRTEEN

Tinker's Cove Chamber of Commerce

Press Release

For Immediate Release

First Annual Giant Pumpkin Fest Deemed a Success! A Survey of Member Businesses Conducted by the Chamber Reveals That October Profits Were Up by More Than 50 Percent across the Board. Retailers Reported Increased Sales, and Restaurants and Hotels Were Fully Booked for the Festival Weekend. Asked if the Festival Should Be Continued Next Year, Over 90 Percent of Respondents Replied with an Enthusiastic Yes!

"What a hoot," said Phyllis, pulling a sheet of paper off the fax machine and handing it to Ted. "Corney says the Pumpkin Fest was a big success."

"Well, there was only one murder," said Lucy, who had just arrived, fifteen minutes late. It was finally Halloween, and Patrick was so excited that the morning routine had taken longer than usual.

"And there's no denying business was up," said Ted. "The town was packed with tourists all weekend."

"So they're going to do it again next year?" asked Lucy, hanging up her jacket.

"Looks like it," said Ted. "I wonder if the cops have made any progress on Ev Wickes. Wanna put in a call for me, Lucy?"

"Better not," said Lucy, taking a deep breath, determined to be open and honest about the situation. "I'm afraid I've got a conflict of interest. The state troopers came to the house on Saturday. They were asking Bill a lot of questions."

"You think they suspect him?" he asked.

"That's crazy!" exclaimed Phyllis.

"I know," agreed Lucy. "But I think maybe I shouldn't be the one covering this story."

"I think you're overreacting," said Ted after a few moments of thought. "They had to question Bill. He was working with Ev on the catapult. I'm sure it was just to gather information. Just because Bill was questioned doesn't make him a suspect."

"If you say so," said Lucy, who didn't share Ted's optimism.

"You're on the story until I say you're not."

"Okay, boss." Lucy was reaching for the phone when Corney herself came in, following up on her press release. Her hair was back to its normal brown, but she hadn't had time to get to the salon for highlights, and there were puffy bags under her eyes.

"What a disaster!" she declared, plopping herself down in the chair Ted kept for visitors, next to his desk.

"We got your press release," said Lucy. "According to you, the festival was a whopping success."

Corney glared at her. "Get real, Lucy. We all know there was a murder. It doesn't get much worse than that." She turned to face Ted. "But I'm confident your coverage of the weekend's events is going to be fair and balanced."

Ted scowled at her. "We strive to report the truth," he said. "Do you have a problem with that?"

"Well, I just think you ought to cover the entire weekend, not just the, uh, regrettable incident at the pumpkin hurl. There were lots of other events, like the fabulous jack-o'-lanterns displayed on Main Street. Those would make great front-page photos. They were very creative and attracted quite a crowd. And there was the pumpkin boat regatta. That was such a lot of fun, right? And don't forget to mention the candy corn contest."

Lucy and Phyllis were all ears, waiting to hear what Ted would say. They weren't disappointed.

"A man was murdered. That is a big story, and it's going on the front page," he said.

"The business community won't like it," said Corney. "They've put a lot of effort into this festival, and they don't want to read anything derogatory about it." She shrugged. "You know how they are — they might even start to pull ads."

That was the wrong thing to say to Ted, and Lucy inhaled sharply, waiting for his riposte.

"Phyllis takes care of the ads," he snapped. "I handle the news, and Ev Wickes's death is news."

"That's right," said Phyllis, with a little nod that jiggled her double chin. "And for your information, our ads are up."

"Because of the festival," said Corney. "That's why your ads are up, and that's why you'd be smart to let everybody know that the festival was a big success. Ev Wickes's death was unfortunate, but it had nothing to do with the festival."

"Well, his body was discovered at the pumpkin hurl," said Ted. "I think there may be a teeny little connection there."

"Whatever Ev was involved in, his death was his own fault. He made somebody mad, which isn't the least bit surprising, considering his personality. He made a lot of enemies."

"Well, one enemy," said Lucy, finding herself in the odd position of defending poor Ev. "But I think most people liked him. Bill knew him pretty well, he helped with the catapult, and he says Ev was a popular guy."

"He was a lazy drunk," said Corney.

"Maybe a drunk, but not lazy," said Lucy. "He was a hard worker, and that gets you respect in a town like Tinker's Cove."

"Well," snorted Corney, standing up. "I see I'm not getting anywhere here, but I warn you, it's in everybody's best interest to present a positive picture of the Giant Pumpkin Fest."

With that, she turned and marched smartly out of the office, muttering to herself and letting the door slam behind her. The little bell jangled furiously, bouncing on its curved metal arm.

"She should know better," said Phyllis.

"Corney's worked so hard on this festival," said Lucy. "She's like a mama bear, determined to protect her little cub."

"She has a point," said Ted, surprising them both. "The festival was a success, despite the gruesome scene at the pumpkin hurl. And the cops say Ev was killed someplace else. He was already dead when he was put in the trunk of that car."

"But why would somebody do that, unless they wanted to discredit the Pumpkin Fest?" asked Lucy.

"Maybe they didn't know the car would be used as a target in the pumpkin hurl," suggested Phyllis.

"Or maybe they did," said Ted in a thoughtful tone.

"It certainly put an end to the events at Jonah's Pond, especially the underwater pumpkin carving. The whole area was roped off as a crime scene," said Lucy.

Just then the fax machine sprang into action, and Phyllis reached across her desk and pulled out a sheet of paper. "Ho, ho," she said, raising the finely penciled lines that served her as eyebrows. "It looks like Ev was into more than just booze. The state police are now investigating Ev's murder as possibly drug related. It seems he was growing marijuana in the basement of his house."

"I heard a rumor he was a dealer," said Lucy, hopping up and grabbing the paper.

"Certainly a producer," said Ted, reading over her shoulder.

She scanned the text quickly, wondering what this latest development meant for Bill. Was he off the hook, or was he going to be implicated in a drug scheme?

Ted was already on the phone with the police chief. "I want my ace reporter to get a photo," he said. After finishing the call, he turned to Lucy. "Tomorrow, first thing," he told her. "I want you to get a photo of Ev's indoor garden."

"Corney's not going to like this," said Phyllis. "Not one bit."

That evening, when Lucy told Bill about the marijuana, he was quick to jump to Ev's defense. "You know, it's perfectly legal to grow six plants for medicinal use," he said, popping the top on a can of beer and sitting down at the kitchen table.

"Did he need medicinal marijuana?" asked Lucy, who was assembling grilled cheese sandwiches for a quick supper before taking Patrick out trick-or-treating.

"He might have," said Bill. "He worked hard all his life, physical stuff. He must've

229

had some serious arthritis pain. He was no spring chicken, you know. Or he might've had something more serious, like cancer. He wasn't the sort to talk about something like that."

"So maybe the drinking was an effort to self-medicate?" mused Lucy, who had recently read an article on that very subject.

"He was an unusual guy," said Bill, taking a long drink. "I had no idea until I started working with him. I thought he'd just be helping me lift and carry those heavy beams for the catapult, but he was full of ideas. He was really a mechanical genius."

Despite her best efforts, Lucy found herself laughing. "Ev was a lot of things, Bill, but I don't think he was a genius."

"Maybe not," admitted Bill, raising his can of beer. "He was a good guy, though. May he rest in peace."

"Amen," said Lucy. If only he would.

Patrick was too excited about trick-or-treating to eat much dinner, and Bill was unable to resist teasing his grandson, who was already dressed in his costume.

"That ninja outfit might be a bit of a problem, though," teased Bill, taking a big bite of his grilled cheese sandwich. "How can people give you anything if they can't see you?"

"Ninjas aren't invisible," declared Patrick. "They're just in disguise."

"Yeah, Dad," said Zoe.

"Everybody knows that," said Elizabeth, chiming in.

"Oh," said Bill, reaching for a second helping of potato chips. "I guess I was misinformed."

Patrick sighed. "When can we go?" he asked, kicking the chair with his foot.

"Don't you mean 'May I be excused?' " teased Bill.

Patrick didn't get it. "May I?" he asked, practically shaking with anticipation.

"Yes, you may," said Lucy, leaving cleanup to the girls and filling a thermal mug with coffee to take with her. "Let's go," she said, watching with amusement as Patrick shot out the kitchen door.

There was only a handful of houses on Prudence Path, and they were all decorated for the holiday and had welcoming lights blazing. All, that is, except the house where Patrick lived with his parents, which was dark. The sight of the darkened house gave Lucy pause, but Patrick took it in stride.

"Mom and Dad will be back at Christmas, right?" he asked.

"Right," said Lucy, quickly changing the subject. "I see some other ninjas," she said.

The little road was filled with small costumed figures, darting from house to house, accompanied by their parents or older siblings. There were princesses and pirates, ninjas and superheroes, and their flashlights danced in the growing darkness.

Reaching Frankie LaChance's house, where a big jack-o'-lantern sat on the porch, grinning a welcome, Patrick rang the doorbell.

"Trick or treat," he said when Frankie opened the door.

"Ah, what have we here?" she asked in her lilting voice, with a charming French accent.

"I'm a ninja," said Patrick.

"So you are," she agreed, offering him a bowl filled with miniature chocolate bars.

"Just a few," cautioned Lucy as Patrick reached into the bowl. Somewhat belatedly she wondered what his parents' policy was on Halloween. Was she even supposed to be taking him out to collect candy from the neighbors? Maybe he was supposed to stay home with a video and a bowl of popcorn.

"Take more than that, and you take some, too," urged Frankie, offering the bowl to Lucy. "If it isn't all gone, I'll eat it, and it's not good for my figure."

"You look as if you've lost weight," said

Lucy, realizing she hadn't actually seen Frankie to talk to in several months.

"I've been dieting," said Frankie, with a little grimace.

"Well, you look great," said Lucy. "It's been a long time. We should get together and catch up over a cup of coffee."

"Great idea," said Frankie.

"Say thank you, Patrick," urged Lucy as he took a few more pieces of candy.

"Thank you!" he sang, then suddenly ran off to join a pack of kids.

Lucy kept an eye on him, watching as Patrick crouched down and ran along a fence in his best imitation of a ninja. He was caught up in make-believe, and he wasn't the only one. The fairies were waving their wands, the pirates were slashing the air with plastic cutlasses, and the superheroes jumped off every porch, their capes billowing behind them.

This was what Halloween was all about, thought Lucy. The night before All Saints' Day was a time to reconnect with neighbors, and an opportunity for children to live out their fantasies. She knew that the Pumpkin Fest was well meant, but maybe it was a mistake to commercialize the holiday. All you needed for a great Halloween was a bag of candy and a little imagination. The simpler the better. The way things were going, Halloween was getting as complicated and stressful as Christmas, and Lucy thought one Christmas a year was more than enough.

The next morning, when Lucy arrived at Ev's place to take photos, she was greeted by Barney Culpepper. "It's a bit of a mess," he told her as he removed the yellow police tape and unlocked the door.

"I'm not surprised," said Lucy, stepping into the ramshackle little house. For all his skills, Ev hadn't taken good care of his property. The porch sagged, the windows were filthy, and the front door opened only partway before it got stuck on the sloping floor. When she stepped inside, she noticed a stale, musty smell, which she assumed came from the dirty clothes that were strewn everywhere. The brown plaid couch wasn't just ugly; Lucy suspected it hosted numerous unpleasant life forms, along with the shaggy orange rug.

"Through here," said Barney, leading her into the kitchen. There the sink and the counters were piled with dirty crockery, and the garbage bin was overflowing. The smell was much worse than in the living room, and Lucy almost gagged.

"Oh, my," she gasped, putting her hand over her nose.

"Yeah," said Barney. "Pretty disgusting, but wait till you see the cellar." He led the way and opened the cellar door, which had a ring of black grime around the knob, and flicked on the light. Lucy descended the stairs and discovered a clean, well-ordered growing room, equipped with bright lights. The room was well ventilated with an industrial fan, which limited the pungent scent given off by dozens of thriving marijuana plants.

"Wow," she said, raising her camera and clicking away. "This is the last thing I expected."

"You and me three," said Barney. "I guess the crummy house and the slovenly appearance were just a disguise. Ev wasn't who we thought he was."

"Bill said he was a kind of mechanical genius, and I laughed," said Lucy. Just then an elaborate irrigation system went into action, distributing a fine spray of water on the plants. "Boy, was I wrong."

"Everybody underestimated him," said Barney. "We thought he was having trouble making ends meet."

This was a new idea to Lucy. "How much is all this worth?" she asked.

"A lot," answered Barney. "This would make him a major player, producing tens of thousands of dollars' worth every eight to twelve weeks."

"How long was he doing it?" asked Lucy.

"The crime-scene guys said it looks like it was going on for years, and one of the neighbors reported a truck coming at night every now and then. It upset her dog, she said."

"Did she complain to him about it?" asked Lucy.

"Yeah, she did. He said he was sorry, but, funny thing, the dog died a few days later."

"A coincidence?" she asked, hopefully.

"I don't think so."

"But Ev wouldn't kill a dog," protested Lucy, remembering how Ev had always been ready to play with Libby, and Patrick, too.

"I'm not saying he did it," said Barney. "But he must've had some serious associates."

"Organized crime?" asked Lucy.

Barney looked around the growing space, which was really a high-tech subterranean greenhouse. "What do you think?" he asked.

Lucy swallowed hard. She really didn't want to think about it at all.

Chapter Fourteen

Tinker's Cove DPW

Press Release

For Immediate Release

Residents Are Advised That the Tinker's Cove DPW Will Be Conducting a Special Curbside Collection of Organic Refuse from the Giant Pumpkin Fest on Monday, November 7, and Tuesday, November 8. Pumpkins, Hay Bales, Leaves, and Other Vegetative Matter Will Be Accepted. Please Do Not Use Plastic Bags, as the Organic Refuse Will Be Taken to the Town's Compost Facility at the Transfer Station.

Residents Are Also Reminded That Dumping in Town Conservation Lands Is Strictly Prohibited and Punishable By Fines up to $500.00.

When Lucy got home that afternoon, she found Bill in the backyard, splitting firewood.

"It will be nice to use the fireplace again," said Lucy, kicking some crinkly brown fallen leaves. The trees bordering the backyard were losing their leaves after a rather disappointing display of muted colors. The experts said it was due to the dry weather they'd had this year.

Bill took a break, resting the heavy maul against his leg and wiping his brow with a bandanna. "Yeah, the forecast is for frost tonight."

Lucy smiled at him and buttoned up her jacket. "What is it they say about firewood? It warms you twice — once when you split it and again when you burn it."

"Yeah, there's a nip in the air today," said Bill, setting a log on the stump he used for splitting wood and bringing down the maul with a practiced swing of his arm. The log split in two with a crack.

"I took those photos of Ev's pot operation today," said Lucy. "Want to see?"

"Sure," he said, taking Lucy's digital camera and peering at the display. "Look at that irrigation system," said Bill. "I told you he was a mechanical genius."

This was not the reaction Lucy had expected. "Bill, this is dozens of plants, a huge operation. Barney says he must have been a major player, involved in organized crime."

Bill shook his head. "He must have been a licensed grower, selling to legal dispensaries."

"There's no evidence of that," said Lucy. "A neighbor said trucks came at night, and when she complained, her dog died."

"Ev loved dogs," said Bill. "He would never hurt a dog."

"I agree, but the people he's selling to might have wanted to send a message to the neighbor to mind her own business."

"Lucy, I think you're going out on a limb here."

Lucy bit her lip. She knew money had been tight since the financial collapse, and Bill hadn't had much work. And on top of that, they'd been paying those exorbitant day-care fees. She also knew that Bill, like a lot of people, had smoked pot in college and didn't think it should be illegal. She had to ask. "Just tell me one thing, Bill. Were you involved with Ev's cash crop?"

"Don't be crazy," he said, looking up as an unmarked police car swung into the driveway. "Damn," he growled, watching as DeGraw and Ferrick got out of the car. "They're back."

"I'm calling Bob Goodman," said Lucy, pulling her phone from her pocket. "Don't you tell them anything except name, rank, and serial number, okay?"

But Bill was already strolling across the lawn, hailing the two state cops with a raised arm. Listening anxiously to the rings of the phone, Lucy watched as the three men formed a little circle in the driveway. *Not voice mail, please,* she prayed and sighed with relief when she heard Bob's voice.

"The cops are here to question Bill again," she began. "Can you come over?"

"I'm on my way," he said. "Tell him to say he wants to cooperate but will answer questions only if his lawyer is present."

"Right," said Lucy, ending the call and hurrying across the yard. Bill, she could see, was already chatting away with the two cops, as if they were old friends.

"Yup, getting ready for winter," he was saying when she joined them.

"Bill, Bob Goodman is on his way over." She turned to the two cops. "He's our lawyer. He wants to be present when you talk to Bill."

"That's not necessary," said Bill. "I was Ev's friend, and I want to do everything I can to help nail whoever did this."

Ferrick and DeGraw exchanged a glance,

and DeGraw pulled out a notebook with a leather cover. "We appreciate your co-operation," he said, flipping the notebook open. "Right now it looks like you were the last person to see Wickes alive."

"Except for the person who killed him," said Bill.

"Uh, right," grunted DeGraw.

"How did you spend Friday night, the night before the catapult hurl?" asked Ferrick, wrinkling his nose and sniffing.

"I worked on some plans upstairs, in my office," said Bill, furrowing his brow. "Then I came downstairs and flipped channels awhile."

Ferrick turned to Lucy. "Can you corroborate that, ma'am?"

Damn, Bill, thought Lucy. Why couldn't he just shut up? "Actually, no," she said. "I was at a Halloween party with our grandson."

"And was your husband home then, when you got home?"

"Of course," said Lucy.

"You saw him?"

Where was Bob? What was taking him so long? "I'd really rather not say any more," said Lucy.

Bill turned to her. "C'mon, Lucy. You know I was home. You must've heard the TV."

"So you were in the family room, watching TV, right?" asked DeGraw.

"Yeah, that's what I told you," replied Bill, sounding tired of repeating himself.

"But you didn't actually see your wife and grandson?" asked Ferrick. "As I recall, there's a hall and a bath between the kitchen and the TV room, right?"

"That's right. I heard them in the kitchen, and then they went upstairs. Lucy had to get Patrick ready for bed."

"And then your wife came down and joined you in the TV room?" continued Ferrick.

"No. I heard the water running. I assumed she was taking a bath. She usually does before she goes to bed."

"And after the bath, she came down and you two shared a snack?" asked DeGraw in a helpful tone.

Playing good cop, thought Lucy as Bill tumbled down the slippery slope. "She must've gone to bed. She goes to bed pretty early, but I stayed up. The Bruins game went into overtime. You can check on it."

"So it was pretty late when you got to bed?" asked DeGraw.

"Yeah, getting on to midnight, I suppose," admitted Bill.

"And all that time you claim you were at

home, nobody actually saw you," said Ferrick. "I mean, the TV could've been on in an empty room. You could've been anywhere, right?"

"In theory, yes," said Bill in a hurt voice. "But why would I want to kill Ev? We were buddies, partners, even. We were both looking forward to the catapult hurl."

"Interesting choice of words," said De-Graw. "So you two were partners?"

Lucy knew where this was going, and she grabbed Bill's arm, attempting to caution him, but he ignored her. "Yeah. The catapult was a joint project. We worked together on it."

"You were aware that Wickes had another project, the marijuana he was growing in the basement?" asked Ferrick.

"I just learned about that today, from my wife. She's a reporter for the local paper."

"So you weren't partners in the pot business?" DeGraw sounded somewhat mournful, as if Bill had missed out on a great opportunity.

"No way!"

"And I suppose you didn't know your partner had nearly seventeen thousand dollars stashed in his mattress," suggested De-Graw.

"No, I didn't. I think I told you yesterday

that I felt sorry for Ev. I thought he needed money, and I insisted on paying him a lousy fifteen dollars an hour. I wanted to help him."

"But if you'd known about the money, that would've been a pretty big, seventeen-thousand-dollar motive for murder," suggested Ferrick.

"I suppose it would," acknowledged Bill, watching as Bob zipped into the driveway in his little BMW. "But I didn't do it, and while you're wasting time questioning me, the real killer is out there, getting away with murder."

"I'm attorney Bob Goodman," said Bob, joining the group. "I'm representing Mr. Stone. And you are?" he asked, indicating the cops.

The two produced their IDs, which Bob took care to photograph with his smartphone. "Saves a lot of time," he explained with a grin. "I used to have to copy all your information by hand."

"We've got plenty of time," said DeGraw.

"Yeah, no problem," added Ferrick.

"Well, I guess if you want to continue interviewing my client, we can go inside and I'll set up a recorder. . . ."

"No, that's okay," said DeGraw.

"Yeah, we're finished," said Ferrick. "For now."

"Right," agreed DeGraw. "But I think you should warn your client here that he'd better not leave town."

"I don't think Mr. Stone has any immediate travel plans, do you, Bill?" coached Bob.

"Uh, no," said Bill.

"Good," said DeGraw.

"Yeah, we'll be seeing you," said Ferrick. The three watched the cops amble to their car, where they took their time getting settled into their seats before finally departing.

"Bill, I could kill you," said Lucy. Her fists were clenched tight, and she pounded them against her thighs. "You should've kept your mouth shut."

"How bad was the damage?" asked Bob.

"They got Bill to admit he doesn't have an alibi for Friday night. He could've been anywhere," said Lucy.

"I was only trying to help," said Bill defensively. "I want them to get whoever killed Ev, that's all."

"Why should they look for anybody else when you're so willing to implicate yourself?" demanded Lucy.

"She's got a point," said Bob, looking serious. "They're looking for somebody with means, motive, and opportunity, and you've got all three."

Bill swallowed hard. "I didn't think . . ."

"Well, from now on let me do the thinking," said Bob. "Whatever you do, don't talk to the cops unless I'm present, okay?"

"Won't that make me look guilty?" asked Bill.

Lucy shook her head in frustration. "Listen to him!" she exclaimed. "Bob wants to protect you."

"That's right," said Bob. "So promise me you won't talk to the cops unless I'm there."

"Okay," agreed Bill.

"Now, where's that grandchild of yours that Rachel is always telling me about?" asked Bob. "I've got some of Richie's old *Star Wars* toys for him."

Lucy glanced at her watch, discovering it was already five minutes to six. "Ohmigod, Little Prodigies closes at six! I've got to get him!"

"Don't break any speed limits," advised Bob as he and Bill headed for his car to get the toys.

Lucy didn't exceed the speed limit, but she went as fast as she legally could, driven by guilt. How could she forget Patrick? Though, to be honest, she had been pretty busy, tied up as she was with the police investigation of Bill. Not exactly something she wanted to share with Heidi, however.

Much to her surprise, Heidi wasn't waiting in the doorway and tapping her foot. Instead, she was on her hands and knees, organizing a low cupboard, while Patrick was busy assembling a puzzle.

"I'm sorry I'm late," began Lucy in an apologetic tone. "Something important came up."

"A breaking story?" suggested Heidi, with a smile, as she rose to her feet.

"I hope not," said Lucy, wondering how she could keep Bill's involvement out of the media spotlight, and realizing that would probably violate journalistic ethics. If there were such things, which she frequently doubted.

Heidi was looking at her with a puzzled expression, and Lucy hastened to come up with an explanation. "Time just got away from me," she said, with an apologetic smile. "Come on, Patrick. It's time to go home."

"I haven't finished the puzzle," he said.

"I'll help," said Lucy, looking over his shoulder. "Just two more pieces. I'll do one, and you do one."

"Okay." With the puzzle completed, and then replaced in its box, Patrick was finally ready to go. "Bye," he said as Lucy helped him into his jacket.

"See you tomorrow," said Heidi, going back to the cupboard, where she turned to Lucy. "You know, I think we may have gotten off on the wrong foot. I wasn't aware of the situation." She shrugged. "I just want to say that Patrick's doing fine, especially when you consider the parental absence. He's coping very well."

Lucy broke into a big smile. "Thanks," she said, giving Patrick's shoulder a squeeze. "I'm rather proud of him myself."

"I know it's not easy, as grandparents, to become full-time caregivers for a grandchild, but you seem to be doing very well."

"Well, I'm trying," said Lucy, taking Patrick by the hand. If she only knew, thought Lucy as they left the building and walked out to the car. The perfect grandparents who did all the right things for their grandson were currently under police investigation. She could see the headline now: GRANDFATHER INDICTED FOR MURDER.

CHAPTER FIFTEEN

Tinker's Cove Food Pantry

Press Release

For Immediate Release

Now That Colder Weather Is Here, the Tinker's Cove Family Pantry Is Seeking Donations of Gently Used Outerwear, Including Coats and Jackets, Hats and Gloves, Socks and Boots. The Need for Such Items Has Grown Dramatically in Recent Years, as the Food Pantry Now Serves Over 120 Families, Up From Only 63 in 2010. All Sizes, From Baby To Extra Large, Will Be Gratefully Accepted. Your Old Coat Could Keep a Neighbor Warm. Donate Today! And Don't Forget, Donations of Cash and Nonperishable Food Items Are Always Appreciated.

When Lucy got to the office on Wednesday morning, deadline day, she found Ted scowling at his computer monitor. "Lucy," he said as she hung her jacket on the coat stand, "I'm surprised at you. This Buck Miller story is nothing but a puff piece."

"Uh-oh," said Phyllis, who was checking the classified ad copy, peering closely at the computer screen through her harlequin reading glasses. "That doesn't sound like our keen investigative reporter."

Lucy reached deep into the recesses of her mind, into the places where things she didn't have to remember were stored, and recalled the story, which she'd written weeks ago. Ted must have been holding it for lack of space due to the Pumpkin Fest coverage.

"You don't need to tell me," she replied, seating herself at her desk, "but it was all I could get with Corney breathing down my neck. She took control of the interview and wouldn't let him say anything."

"Well, I'm not printing this unless they pay for ad space," said Ted.

"Want to hold it a week? I'll call and see if I can get another interview with Buck."

"Good idea," said Ted.

Lucy really didn't expect to be put through to Buck when she dialed the number she'd been given, but much to her surprise, it turned out to be his cell phone. "What can I do for you?" he asked.

"Wow," she replied, somewhat at a loss for words. "I thought I'd have to fight with a receptionist to get to talk to you."

"No way. It's the modern world. I take my own calls."

"Good for you," she said. "The thing is, my editor wants to run a bigger story. . . ."

"Great," replied Buck.

"So I need to talk to you again. Is that okay?"

"Sure. What works for you?"

"This afternoon," suggested Lucy, throwing it out there as a starting point for negotiation.

"Fine. What time?"

Lucy hadn't expected him to agree. The deadline was at noon, but sometimes things ran late at the *Pennysaver.* "How about three?"

"See you then," he said.

"At the store?" she asked. "Like last time?"

"Do you mind coming out here to the main office?" he asked somewhat apologetically. "They're painting the conference room at the store. Corney's idea."

"Not at all," said Lucy, who couldn't be happier at the way things were working out. "Thanks for making time for me."

"No problem. See you at three."

"Must be my lucky day," she said to Ted as she hung up the phone. "I've got an interview with Buck this afternoon."

"Doesn't seem like the kid is very busy," said Ted.

"They're probably not giving him much to do," said Phyllis. "Breaking him in gradually."

"Or maybe Tom Miller isn't keen on sharing," said Ted.

Lucy bit her lip. "I hadn't thought of that," she said. "You think the older generation isn't that happy with the younger generation?"

"It's only natural," said Phyllis. "Lord Grantham certainly wasn't very excited about Matthew's newfangled ideas for the estate."

"Who?" asked Ted, cocking an eyebrow at Phyllis.

"*Downton Abbey*," said Lucy, filling him in. "Lord Grantham ran out of money because the estate was mismanaged, and his son-in-law Matthew wanted to modernize things."

"But his daughter and Matthew's wife, Lady Mary, sided with her father," said Phyllis.

"It was a tense situation," added Lucy,

with a smile.

"You know what's a tense situation?" demanded Ted. "It's coming up on ten o'clock, and I don't have a front-page story!"

"What do you mean?" asked Lucy. "You've got Ev's death at the festival, the cellar full of pot. What more do you need?"

"A confirmation from the state cops, that's what I need," said Ted.

Lucy didn't understand. She'd written the story right after she'd been in Ev's house with Barney. "I was there. I saw the pot," said Lucy.

"I still need official confirmation," said Ted. "Maybe it was oregano."

"I'm pretty sure Lucy knows oregano," said Phyllis.

"I do. I grow it in my garden." Lucy shifted uneasily in her chair, making it squeak. It almost seemed as if Ted was having doubts about her credibility as a reporter. The town's grapevine was notorious, and he might well have heard that the cops had interviewed Bill a second time. "The cops came back yesterday," she said. "They weren't very nice."

"I don't think he's guilty, not for a minute," said Ted quickly, "but maybe you're a bit too close to the case to be impartial."

"This is a community newspaper, and we all live here," said Phyllis, taking off her glasses and rubbing her eyes. "None of us are impartial. It's impossible. I mean, even the classifieds get my goat. That Eugene Simpkins is trying to sell his van for ten thousand dollars, and I know he drove it off a boat ramp last summer — into salt water, no less — and it's not worth two cents."

"I'm not trying to trick anybody into buying a rusty truck," said Lucy. "I know Ev worked for Bill, and the cops have been questioning him, but believe me, that just makes me even more eager to get to the bottom of the story."

"But you have to understand that this is starting to get awkward . . . ," began Ted.

"I understand," said Lucy, getting up and walking over to the coffeepot. She took the empty pot into the bathroom to fill it and found herself blinking back tears while the water ran. This was so unfair! Furious with herself, she brushed the tears away and went back outside to fill the coffeemaker. She sniffed a few times while she counted out the scoops of coffee. "Allergies," she said, by way of explanation.

"So Bill didn't know about the pot?" asked Ted.

"Not a clue," said Lucy. "He thought he

was doing Ev a favor by paying him fifteen dollars an hour."

Ted glanced at his computer. "About time," he said, leaning forward and scrolling through the text on his monitor. "The state cops say the pot in Ev's cellar had a street value of over thirty-five thousand dollars, the equipment was worth sixty thousand, and there's evidence he'd been growing the stuff for some time."

"That's hard to believe, isn't it?" asked Lucy. "You know as well as I do that cops always inflate the value of seized drugs to make themselves look good. And who was he selling it all to?"

"If they know, they're not saying," said Ted. "Just that it was a sizable operation, most likely linked to organized crime."

"It's hard to believe something this big could go on without people noticing," said Phyllis.

"That's a lot of pot. There must've been trucks to pick it up," said Ted. "You'd think the neighbors would've noticed."

"Maybe the neighbors were part of it," suggested Lucy. "The economy's bad. A lot of people in town are unemployed and could use some cash."

"A town-wide conspiracy, and we didn't catch on? We're supposed to know what's going on in Tinker's Cove," said Ted.

"Maybe it's not town wide. Maybe it's company wide," suggested Lucy, voicing a thought that had just popped into her head.

Ted seized on the idea. "Country Cousins?"

"Tell me another one," protested Phyllis. "They're right up there with motherhood, apple pie, and the American way of life."

"Sounds like a terrific front to me," said Lucy, warming to the idea. "They've got trucks and warehouses, and nobody would suspect a thing. And get this, Ev designed their security system."

"How do you know that?" asked Ted, raising an eyebrow.

"He told us. He even gave Bill a bunch of the old stuff so he could set up a system around the pumpkin patch." The wheels were turning fast in Lucy's head. "Think about it, Ted. A security system would be critical if Country Cousins is involved in illegal drugs, and who better to put it in than the guy who's growing the dope?"

"What a story, if it's true," said Ted, shaking his head. "But it's not. Country Cousins doesn't need to go into illegal activity to make money. They make plenty by selling boat shoes and fishing gear."

"You're probably right," said Lucy, but

she wasn't entirely convinced. She thought she might be on to something big. If Country Cousins was peddling pot, along with canoe paddles and polo shirts, it would be a big story, but more than that, it would prove Bill's innocence. But how could she get proof? She could hardly come right out and ask Buck if Country Cousins' exciting new direction included illegal drugs. Or could she?

It was a quarter past three when Lucy arrived at the Country Cousins complex out by Jonah's Pond. There had been a computer glitch sending the paper to the printer, and in the end, Ted had loaded the copy onto a thumb drive and had sent Lucy to deliver it to the print shop outside Camden. She had had to hurry to get back to town by three and was driving a bit too fast when she arrived at the Country Cousins complex and braked so hard at the gatehouse that she was thrown forward against the steering wheel.

"Whoa there," said the guard, a burly man in his fifties.

"Lucy Stone from the *Pennysaver*," she told him, and he produced a computer notebook. Finding her name, he tapped it with a stylus. Whatever happened to clipboards? she wondered as he lifted the bar so she could drive through.

The fenced complex of buildings was bigger than she remembered; a couple of steel buildings had been added since she was last on the site. A large sign directed her to the executive offices, and she followed the arrow, driving past neat, numbered warehouses with concrete loading docks. Many of the docks were occupied by trucks in the process of being loaded or unloaded; some had the Country Cousins logo, while others were clearly from suppliers. It was a busy place, and at one point she had to brake for a forklift that was backing into her path. The driver wheeled about when she tooted her horn, and gave her a friendly wave.

The executive offices were housed in an older, three-story brick building that was located at the rear of the property, overlooking the pond. Lucy guessed from the neat rows of windows that it had been built in the nineteenth century, perhaps as a mill or a factory of some sort. Unlike the gray steel buildings, which were strictly utilitarian, this one had a landscaped patch of greenery by the front door and now featured colorful clumps of chrysanthemums set amid ornamental grasses.

Lucy parked in one of the spaces labeled

for visitors and hurried inside, where a pleasant receptionist directed her to the second floor. She hated being late and ran up the stairs, so she was out of breath when she was showed into Buck's luxurious office.

"I'm so sorry," she said, panting slightly from the exertion. "I'm running late because I had to drive up the coast."

Buck had stood up to greet her and leaned across the broad expanse of teak that served as his desk, now empty except for one of those executive toys comprised of dangling stainless-steel balls that bounce against each other. "No problem," he said. "I was just brainstorming our next campaign."

Lucy could understand why Corney found Buck so attractive. He was tall and slim, and had an engaging way of cocking his head and grinning when he made eye contact.

"Want to give me a scoop?" she invited. "A heads-up?"

"I'm afraid I haven't worked out the details," he said. "Can I offer you something to drink? We have coffee, tea, local apple cider. . . ."

"Water?" asked Lucy, who had worked up quite a thirst.

"Sure." He didn't call his secretary but

instead opened a wooden cabinet that housed a small fridge, with a Keurig machine perched on top. After withdrawing a bottle of water, he twisted the cap off and handed the water to her.

Lucy surveyed the large, high-ceilinged office, which had two enormous windows that overlooked Jonah's pond. From here she could clearly observe the beach area, where, she was interested to see, the yellow police tape was gone. Turning her attention to the room itself, she checked out the seating options, which included a couple of chairs in front of the desk, or the sofa and upholstered chairs on the opposite side of the room.

"Let's sit over there," said Buck, with a nod at the sofa. "It's a lot more comfortable."

Lucy was tempted to sink into the plush sofa but instead chose one of the chairs. She sat down and put her bottle of water on the coffee table. "What a great office," she said, glancing at the framed Wyeth print that hung over the sofa. It pictured an open window with a blowing lace curtain, probably painted at the Olson House in Cushing.

"Sure beats a cubicle," he said, taking the sofa. He leaned back and casually propped an ankle on his knee.

"Well, as I mentioned on the phone," said Lucy, pulling a notebook from her bag and opening it, "my editor wants to enlarge the story. He wants to know how the company is responding to the challenges of the global marketplace. . . ."

Buck furrowed his brow. "Can you be more specific?"

"Well, take your workforce, for example. Country Cousins is one of the county's biggest employers, but labor here in Maine is pretty expensive. Do you have any plans to outsource? Maybe set up overseas call centers?"

"I don't think our customers would like that," said Buck, with a grin. "I don't think they want to hear an Indian accent when they call us." He leaned forward. "That's one of my ideas, you know. I want all our operators to have Maine accents. I'm thinking of bringing in a dialect coach to give some lessons to the folks who aren't native Mainers."

"That's a really interesting idea," said Lucy. "What about maintaining quality? I bought some polo shirts last spring, and I noticed they were made in Bangladesh."

"Did they wear well? Were you satisfied with them?"

"Yeah," admitted Lucy. "They were very nice."

"Listen, I wish we could make everything we sell right here in the USA, but it's not practical, not if we want to be competitive. But we do maintain high standards, as high as we can and still keep our prices in line with our competitors." He was leaning back now, with his arms extended along the top of the sofa. "And we offer free shipping. Always."

"That was my next question," said Lucy. "Any plans to change that?"

"Absolutely not," he said, with a sharp nod of the head. "It's one of the things that make Country Cousins unique. It's a big part of our old-fashioned values campaign."

Lucy was running out of questions, and besides, she really wanted to see what was in some of those windowless, gray steel buildings. "You know," she said, tapping her lip with her pen, "I'd really love a tour. I don't think people realize how much Country Cousins has grown in recent years."

"Great idea," he said, jumping up. "I'll show you around."

Lucy gathered up her things and followed him out the door, and down the hallway, where they encountered Tom Miller. He was coming out of his office, which was on the opposite side of the building. Glancing through the open door, she noticed his desk was piled high with stacks of paper, and even the floor was littered with rolled-up plans and piles of files. It was a marked contrast to Buck's neat and tidy office.

"I'm glad I caught you," said Buck. "Do you know Lucy Stone, from the *Pennysaver*? She's interviewing me for a story."

"Of course I know Lucy," said Tom, with a gracious smile. "Give my regards to Ted. I haven't seen him on the links lately."

A typical CEO put-down, thought Lucy. *Like, you're okay, but I'm best buddies with your boss, so you better watch your step.* "I'll do that," she said, pasting on a grin.

"I'm giving Lucy the grand tour," said Buck.

Tom, who had started off down the long hallway, stopped suddenly and whirled around. "Grand tour?"

"You know, showing her around. The call center, the warehouse, the packing department. The works."

"I'm afraid that's not a good idea," said Tom.

"Really? I was looking forward to seeing your operation," said Lucy. "It would add a lot of color to my story."

"I understand," said Tom in a sympathetic

263

tone. "It's not me, you know. It's the insurance company. Only employees are allowed in the facility, apart from these offices, of course."

"That's too bad," said Lucy, wondering if her guess about the company wasn't as off the mark as she had supposed.

"Well," he added, with an apologetic shrug, "it's just the way things are these days. The insurance companies set the rules."

"They sure do," said Lucy, who didn't believe him for a minute.

"Well, let me walk you to your car," said Buck. "We can finish up while we walk."

"Okay," said Lucy, following him down the stairs. "I noticed you have a great view of the pond from your office."

"It's okay," said Buck in a grudging tone that reminded Lucy of her son Toby's attitude when he was in middle school.

"I saw that the police tape is gone, and I wondered if they've finished investigating out there."

"You mean like divers and stuff like that?"

"I guess so," said Lucy. "Or anything at all."

"Nope. Haven't seen anyone out there." He held the door for her. "Well, it was nice talking to you."

"Thanks for everything," said Lucy, shaking his hand and thinking there really hadn't been much of anything. But, she admitted to herself, even if she had been given a tour, it wouldn't have included the marijuana-processing facility. If it was even there, which was by no means certain.

She was climbing into her car when someone called her name, and she looked up and saw Glory hurrying across the parking lot. She was running awkwardly, hampered by high heels, and was toting several bulging shopping bags. "Ooh, ooh, Lucy! What brings you here?"

"Following up on my interview with Buck," she answered.

"We're all so happy he's joined the company," said Glory. "He's like a breath of fresh air. He's just full of ideas. Like this," she said, indicating the shopping bags. "They're seconds. Buck suggested we donate them to the food pantry."

"And dialect lessons for the operators," said Lucy, "so they'll have distinct Maine accents."

"That's a new one on me," said Glory, biting her bottom lip, painted with shiny coral gloss. "So tell me, were you actually there when they found Ev's body? I couldn't make the pumpkin hurl, so I missed all the excitement."

Lucy nodded. "I was taking photos of the smashed-up car for the paper. A lot of people apparently love this stuff. When it's flying through the air at a high speed, a pumpkin can do a lot of damage to a Hyundai."

"I guess it would." Glory fingered her necklace of oversize South Sea pearls. "Was it terribly gory?"

"I really only got a glimpse of his shirt . . . ," said Lucy.

"Poor man," said Glory. "And at the festival, too."

"It probably means this is the first and last Giant Pumpkin Fest."

"Well, Tom says it's probably for the best. He wasn't all that happy about the festival."

"Do you know why?" asked Lucy, remembering the Conservation Commission meeting. "He didn't want the college kids to use Jonah's Pond for the underwater pumpkin-carving contest, but I didn't understand his objection. The contest seemed so harmless."

"Don't ask me," said Glory, setting the bags on the ground and leaning one hip against Lucy's car. "At first he was a big supporter, but then he changed his mind. He was pretty upset about it all. He even said it made him regret deeding the pond to the town. He thought it was going to be preserved forever as conservation land, and instead they were going to use it for a spectacle and bring a whole lot of people there. He was worried about litter and damage to the plants. There are some very rare endangered species there."

"I guess I thought it was always town land," said Lucy.

Glory shook her head, which made her curls bounce, her big hoop earrings swing, and her décolletage jiggle. "Nope. It was in the family for years, but Tom donated it in return for a tax break. It was back when the company started to take off and they needed to expand. That's when they built all this," she said, indicating the complex with a wave of her bejeweled and manicured hand. "Believe it or not, back then Tom lived over the store with his first wife. Right there on Main Street. And his parents, Old Sam and Emily, lived with them, too. In three or four poky little attic rooms." She put her hands on her hips. "I told him, 'No way, José.' I said I was not going to live in a dinky apartment with Mom and Dad trying to sleep in the next room." She winked at Lucy, a maneuver that Lucy would have thought impossible, considering her heavy application of mascara. "I'm not the sort of girl who keeps quiet when she gets excited!"

Lucy couldn't help laughing. "What did Tom do?"

"What he should have done years ago, honey. He built a house, a little ranch, on Parallel Street. It's still there, but after a few years, when the company really started to take off, I wanted something a little more . . . well, something that reflected his success. I wanted to live on Shore Road and . . ." Glory gave another little bounce. "Well, I usually manage to get my way."

Summer, 1979

It was incredible how things had worked out. Miss Tilley had actually put her in touch with people who wanted to help her. It was like the Underground Railroad back in the days of slavery, she told her. They had a whole network of safe houses and had ways of communicating with signals and stuff. It was just incredible. If you were alone, for example, and it was safe for somebody to call you on the phone, you put a plant on the windowsill.

They told her what to do. She was supposed to begin saving money, which at first she'd thought was impossible, but then she remembered the coins she sometimes found in Tom's pants pockets when she did the wash. So instead of putting it all on his dresser, as she had been doing, she kept some of it for herself. Once she had five dollars, it was enough to open a bank account, which she was supposed to do in her own name only. She also applied for a charge card in her own name when an offer addressed to her came in the mail. In the past she would have thrown the letter away, but this time she filled in the information and mailed it back in the business reply envelope. She didn't even need a stamp!

Some of their advice wasn't all that helpful, however. For one thing, there was no way she could keep gas in the car, because she wasn't allowed to drive, and neither was Emily. Driving was only for men, no two ways about it. And as for getting a set of keys, well, that was a dream. He was crazy about his keys and guarded them carefully. Besides, he had the only key machine in town, and she could hardly ask him to make copies for her. "But not to worry," they told her. They'd figure something out. Meanwhile, she had packed a few clothes in an old duffel bag, which she'd hidden under the bed. If he discovered it, she would tell him it was just stuff she planned to donate to the Salvation Army.

Now she was ready to go, anytime the door was left unlocked. All she had to do was get herself out of the house and go straight to the safe house just a few blocks away. There she would be hidden until a volunteer could pick her up and whisk her away. She imagined what it would be like, speeding through the night in a fast car, leaving it all behind like a bad dream.

That's what kept her going — the thought of escape. It was the hope that enabled her to face each day. If not for that, she knew she'd kill herself — or him.

Chapter Sixteen

Country Cousins

Press Release

For Immediate Release

Country Cousins CEO Tom Miller Announced Yesterday That the Company's Board of Directors Has Voted at Their Quarterly Meeting to Donate Fifteen Thousand Dollars to the Tinker's Cove Police and Fire Association. "The Board Recognizes the Extraordinary Demands Placed on First Responders and Their Families and Wants to Support Them and Express Appreciation for Their Sacrifice in a Concrete Way," Said Miller.

The Police and Fire Association Assists Police and Fire Department Personnel and Their Families With Disability and Medical Expenses, as well as Funeral Expenses.

"This Is a Most Generous Donation," Said Association President Todd Kirwan, "And Will Enable Us to Offer Meaningful Help to Our Members. Country Cousins Is a Good Neighbor, and We're Glad They're Here in Tinker's Cove."

More information than I needed, thought Lucy as she climbed into her car. It was stuffy from sitting in the sun, and she rolled down the window to let the breeze in. So Glory was a noisy lover! She couldn't quite imagine the rather stern and taciturn Tom would enjoy vocal lovemaking, but then again, she didn't know him very well. She had seen him only in his public role, either as a member of the Conservation Commission or representing the company. She'd often taken what journalists called grin and grab photos of Tom, the ones in which generous donors were pictured handing over checks for worthy causes. Thinking back, she had recently snapped Tom giving generous donations to the Hat and Mitten Fund, the Tinker's Cove Cottage Hospital, Westminster College, and the Tinker's Cove Food Pantry. And that was just in the past few months.

Lucy's gaze turned to Glory, who was jiggling her way across the parking lot in her tight capri pants and high heels, and she couldn't help smiling. *Good for Glory and Tom.* It was nice to know that they'd been able to keep the spark alive in their marriage, and maybe she and Bill needed to try a little harder. Although, to be honest, knowing that Patrick was sleeping on the other side of the bedroom wall was somewhat inhibiting.

She shifted into gear and rolled across the parking lot, winding her way through the complex of buildings. As she drove, she wondered if the people who got the Country Cousins catalog, which was carefully written to convey a folksy, old-fashioned vibe, ever imagined what the company was really like. The catalog always featured a photo of the store, with the two benches on the front porch decorated for the season. In spring there was often a litter of Lab puppies on one of the benches, and in summer one of the company's canvas totes brimming with beach or picnic gear; fall inevitably brought a pumpkin or jack-o'-lantern, and winter a pair of the company's signature duck boots holding a holiday arrangement of pine boughs. She very much doubted the average customer had a clue about the company's size or its marketing savvy.

When she reached the gate, the security

guard greeted her with a friendly wave and raised the bar so she could exit. As she drove through the gate, she caught a glimpse of a chain-link fence and took a harder look at the hedge of arborvitae trees that encircled the entire complex. The double row of evergreens was an attractive screen, she realized, that disguised a very serious chain-link fence, as well as a gate that could slide across the entrance, effectively sealing the complex from intruders.

Why on earth did they need that much security out here in Tinker's Cove? It was the sort of fence you'd expect to see at a prison or a military outpost, although there it would be out in the open, not disguised by clever landscaping. But here they'd gone to great lengths, and expense, to construct and hide the fence. It really seemed odd to her, considering that people in Tinker's Cove rarely bothered to lock their doors and often left the keys in the car when they dashed into the Quik-Stop for a gallon of milk.

The road to town took her around Jonah's Pond, and she noticed a flock of Canada geese flying overhead in a *V* formation, headed for warmer climes. *Lucky them,* she thought, watching as the flock circled around and splashed down on the pond.

They would probably spend the night there, then continue on their way after they'd rested. It was a good thing the pond had been preserved as a conservation area, though from what Glory said, the company had profited from the transfer.

That was what you called a win-win situation, she decided. Conservation land was good for the environment, it provided habitat for wildlife, and it helped preserve the rural character of the town. The drive past the pond was certainly picturesque, she thought as a sudden gust of wind sent a shower of rusty brown leaves swirling across the road. Country Cousins was truly a good neighbor and a benefactor to the town, even if they did it to lower the company's tax bill.

Although, she thought, drawing on her knowledge of the town's budgeting process, Tinker's Cove had one of the lowest property tax rates in the state. She'd spent many hours covering finance committee meetings, where every expenditure was carefully scrutinized in excruciating detail. Doing some quick computations in her head, she discovered the conservation designation had probably gotten the company only a small reduction in their overall tax bill. Maybe Tom Miller had done it out of the goodness of his heart or out of personal conviction, or because . . . Here she ran out of ideas.

At the meeting he'd seemed to have a proprietary attitude about the pond, as if he still owned it. She recalled that he'd really wanted to keep the scuba club divers out of the pond, but he'd been outvoted. It was the discovery of Ev's body that had precipitated the cancellation of the underwater pumpkin-carving contest, she realized, with a growing sense of excitement. Was that the motive for Ev's murder? Could it be? Was there something in the pond that Tom, or somebody else, didn't want found? Something important enough to be a motive for murder?

Suddenly Tom Miller seemed like a more complicated person than she'd thought. He'd been married before, according to Glory, and the couple had lived above the store, along with his parents. Glory had refused to continue that arrangement when she married Tom, and who could blame her? A newly married couple didn't want to live with others in cramped quarters; they wanted privacy. And money hadn't been an issue for Tom Miller, not even back then, because Glory had gotten the house she wanted. So why had Tom's first wife put up with such an unsatisfactory living arrangement? And who was this first wife, anyway?

By now Lucy was almost home, but she decided to continue on into town and pay a visit to Miss Tilley. Her old friend knew everything that had happened in Tinker's Cove in her long lifetime, and she knew everybody. She would remember the first Mrs. Miller.

"Her name was Cynthia," said Miss Tilley, who was sitting in her Boston rocker by the fire, with her Siamese cat, Cleopatra, purring in her lap. A small fire was burning brightly, crackling merrily as it warmed the sun-filled parlor.

"What happened to her?" asked Lucy.

"I have no idea," said Miss Tilley as Cleopatra suddenly leaped off her lap and landed on the hooked rug, where she arched her back in a luxurious stretch. She then sat down, raised one rear leg gracefully above her head, and began some intense personal hygiene.

"Cats," snorted Miss Tilley. "So indiscreet."

"Not as bad as dogs," said Lucy.

"Well, dogs." Miss Tilley dismissed the entire species with a flap of her blue-veined hand.

"I didn't realize that Glory is Tom Miller's second wife," said Lucy. "And from what she told me, that first wife lived above the store with Tom and his parents."

"Could be," said Miss Tilley. "I really don't know."

Lucy leveled her gaze at the old woman. "You know. You know everything that's happened in Tinker's Cove in the past hundred years."

"I'm not that old," said Miss Tilley.

"I don't believe for one minute that you didn't know Cynthia and Tom and his parents, too. You were probably invited over for dinner."

"Never," said Miss Tilley, giving her head a little shake. "Poke that fire for me, will you? And add a log."

Lucy obliged, then resumed her seat on the camelback sofa, watching as the fire flared up and began burning a bit more brightly. "I love fall," said Lucy, "all except the short days. Daylight savings ends this Saturday, and it will be dark before five in the afternoon."

"That's why we have the Take Back the Night March then," said Miss Tilley. "Hard to believe, but this is the thirty-fifth march. Rebecca and I are going to carry a banner."

"I had no idea it has been going on for so long. That must be some sort of record," said Lucy.

"A lot of places gave them up after the first few, but we always kept it going," said Miss Tilley, rubbing her knees. "I wouldn't miss it for anything. Not even my arthritis will keep me away."

Lucy was thoughtful. "That's the spirit," she said as the gears in her brain began a slow grind and started to mesh. "You were involved with that network of safe houses, weren't you? The one for abused women, right?"

The old woman leaned forward, her eyes bright. "Do you need help, Lucy? Because there are enough of us left, and we could resurrect the chain of volunteers."

Lucy laughed. "Thanks, but there's no need. Really."

Miss Tilley leaned back in her rocker. "I was just teasing."

"Could you really reestablish the network?" asked Lucy. "If I knew of someone, if I had a friend . . . ?"

Miss Tilley shook her head. "No. That was long ago. And now there's really no need. There are laws in place that protect abused women and children. We didn't have them back then."

"This would make a great story for the *Pennysaver,*" said Lucy.

"Oh, no. My lips are sealed."

"But as you said, it was all a long time ago."

"I took an oath — we all did — to never reveal the names of the women we helped, or the volunteers," said Miss Tilley. "I couldn't break it."

"I see," said Lucy, and she did. "Well, I better go. I've got to feed my family. Is there anything I can do for you before I leave?"

"I wouldn't mind a small glass of sherry," said Miss Tilley. "And some of those Goldfish crackers." She paused. "Better make it a large glass, and don't hold back on those crackers, either."

As Lucy got in her car, she admitted to herself that she hadn't got much information out of Miss Tilley, nothing really except for the name of the first Mrs. Tom Miller. Cynthia. That was something, she decided, starting the car. Now that she knew her name, she could try Google, for one thing.

Of course, Tom and Cynthia's marriage predated Google, and if Cynthia had fled the marriage via Miss Tilley's underground railroad, she would most certainly have changed her name. And how did it happen that Cynthia was an abused wife, while Glory was bouncing along, keeping Tom under her thumb? Did Glory know some sort of tantric sex tricks, like Wallis Simpson was presumed to have used to convince King Edward VIII to give up his throne to marry her?

In this case, she decided, she was better off relying on local people, who probably remembered Cynthia. Her thoughts turned to Bob Goodman, who she knew was Tom Miller's lawyer. She knew he came on the scene too late to know Cynthia, but his law office might have records concerning the couple. She decided to stop in on her way home.

"Any new developments?" he asked when Lucy stuck her head around his door. "Have the police been hounding Bill?"

"No," said Lucy. "Maybe they've figured out he didn't have anything to do with Ev's death."

"It does seem that there are bigger fish to fry, considering Ev's marijuana operation," said Bob.

He was seated at his desk, which was covered with papers, and had dark circles under his eyes. Lucy knew he took his responsibilities to his clients very seriously, and suspected he had been working too hard. "I don't want to burden you," she began.

"Shoot, Lucy," he said, leaning back in

his leather executive chair and folding his arms behind his head. "Unlike most of my clients, you always bring me something interesting."

"This is probably from before your time . . ." she began.

"I came in as a junior partner in nineteen ninety, but the practice was established in eighteen eighty-five, so the files go back a long way."

"That's what I'm hoping. Do you know anything about Tom Miller's first wife, Cynthia?"

"Actually, I do," he said, with a big grin. "I remember because it was one of my first cases. Tom came in and said he wanted to get married but didn't know if he was free, because he'd been married previously to this Cynthia. He said he came home one day and there was no Cynthia. Cynthia had simply disappeared. There was a police investigation. It seemed she had packed a bag and left of her own accord. As I recall, Tom even hired a private investigator, who had no success finding her."

"Was he upset?" asked Lucy. "Did he know why she'd left?"

"I never really got into that. It had all happened quite a few years before, and when Tom approached me, it was long after the three years, which is the legal definition of *desertion.* There was no problem at all about getting a divorce decree. She abandoned the marriage, and Tom made a good faith effort to find her. He had all the paperwork. It was clear that she had simply decided to disappear."

"Did they consider suicide?" asked Lucy.

"There was no body, no sign of emotional distress, at least according to Tom and his parents, who lived with them." Bob cocked his head. "What are you after?" he asked.

"I don't know, really," admitted Lucy. "I'm just curious, I guess. I've been doing this story about Buck Miller coming to Country Cousins, and some things just don't add up." She plunked herself down in a chair. "Do you know they have a very serious security arrangement out there at the complex?"

"I'm not surprised," said Bob. "The insurance company probably insisted. Those warehouses are full of stuff, some of it quite valuable."

"That's what Tom said," admitted Lucy. "He wouldn't let Buck give me a tour."

"Believe me," said Bob, "insurance companies call all the shots these days."

"You know, there used to be an underground network here in Tinker's Cove to help abused women escape."

"And you're thinking Cynthia was an abused wife?" asked Bob, raising his eyebrows.

"Well, it's one explanation for her sudden and complete disappearance. Miss Tilley says that it was like the witness protection program, that these women were given new identities."

"Well, if Cynthia did use the network, she was tricking them into helping her for reasons of her own. I know Tom Miller, I've worked with him for years, and he is not an abuser. He is the nicest guy around. If anything, he's way too easygoing. I simply can't see him as being a wife beater." He paused. "Glory doesn't seem to be suffering, not from what I can see."

"I know," said Lucy, remembering how Tom had walked away rather than insist on his prerogative as CEO of the company when Buck staged his little coup at the candy corn prize ceremony. "That's the problem with my theory."

Bob laughed. "So maybe you better give it up."

"I want to, believe me. But I really think something funny is going on at Country Cousins. Just think about it. Ev's marijuana had to go somewhere to be processed and packaged and distributed, right? And Country Cousins is the ideal facility. They've got trucks and big buildings and a major security fence."

Bob shook his head. "They have an impeccable reputation. They're practically a national landmark. People come to that little country store from all over the country. It's Yankee thrift, baked beans, and brown bread, everything people think of as old New England values."

"Exactly," said Lucy. "Who would ever imagine that Country Cousins is in the illegal drug trade?"

"Except," said Bob, propping his elbows on his desk and tenting his fingers and speaking in a speculative tone, "the truth is that marijuana isn't going to be illegal for much longer — we've already got legal medicinal marijuana — and Country Cousins would be positioned to take over production and distribution for the entire Northeast, maybe the whole country."

"That's what I think," said Lucy.

Bob shook his head. "How could they keep something this big a secret? From what the cops said, Ev was growing a lot of weed, and it would take quite a few people to process it. This is a small town. Everybody knows everything about everybody."

"Not really. Miss Tilley was able to keep her underground network a secret for years and years. We still don't know what happened to Cynthia," said Lucy. "Remember, this is a small town with a lot of unemployment. I bet there are plenty of people who'd be only too happy to keep their mouths shut for a fat paycheck."

Bob nodded. "Okay, I understand where you're coming from, and I'd agree, except for one thing, and that's Tom Miller's personality. I've known him for twenty-five years, and I consider him a friend. A dear, old friend. Rachel and I get together with him and Glory at least once a month. I simply can't imagine him getting involved in anything like this. And as for being abusive to Cynthia, no way. The truth is — and Rachel will agree with me on this — it's Glory who wears the pants in that family. She really picks on him, and he just takes it."

"I'm not disagreeing with you," said Lucy. "But people can change. And there is a theory that some people have personalities that invite abuse. Maybe Cynthia was one of those people."

"No, Lucy, I think you're way off base." He grinned. "In fact, I'm wondering if you've been smoking some of Ev's fine weed."

"Nope, not me," said Lucy, standing up and slipping the strap of her handbag over her shoulder, preparing to leave. "But I bet plenty of folks in town have been."

Bob grimaced. "I suspect you're right about that."

CHAPTER SEVENTEEN

Winchester College

Press Release

For Immediate Release

The Student Government at Winchester College Announces a Series of Free Events Open to the Public as a Holiday Gift to Our Local Community. Planned Offerings Include Theatrical Productions, Music and Dance Concerts, Lectures, and a Film Series.

The Scuba Club Is Kicking Off the Program with a Series of Movie Nights Featuring The Undersea Adventures of Jacques Cousteau. "Savage World of the Coral Jungle" Will Be Shown at 8:00 p.m., Wednesday, in the Frank W. Curtis Science Building, Lecture Hall A. Free Parking Is Available in the Visitor Lot on College Road.

To See the Complete Calendar of Events, Check the Winchester College Web Site: www.winchester.edu.

When Lucy finally got home, along with Patrick, they found Hank's pickup truck parked in the driveway. The discovery pleased Patrick no end.

"Hank's here!" he exclaimed, then ran into the house, eager to see his new pal.

Lucy was also pleased, but for a different reason: she wanted to know if Hank had seen anything unusual in Jonah's Pond when he dove there, preparing for the underwater pumpkin-carving contest.

Hank, however, was a lot more interested in Sara than he was in either Lucy or Patrick. "We were just leaving," he said, twirling his faded and frayed Cinnamon Bay cap in his hands. "The scuba club is having a movie night. We're showing some old Jacques Cousteau TV specials."

"I used to love those," said Lucy. "And Patrick hasn't seen them. What time is the show?"

"Uh, Mom, we're going out to eat first," said Sara. "The show's not until eight, Patrick's bedtime."

Lucy got the message: *Hands off my date!*

"Maybe another time, Mrs. Stone," said Hank, who was on his best behavior and didn't want to offend Lucy. "It's a series."

"Oh," replied Lucy. "Let me know when the next one is, and I can figure something out." She was opening the fridge and pulling out a package of chicken breasts. "Just a quick question," she said, setting the meat on the counter. "When you were diving in Jonah's Pond, did you see anything unusual down there?"

"Like a treasure chest?" asked Hank.

"Yeah!" Patrick was all for it. "Pirate treasure!"

"Sorry. There were some sunfish and some weeds and rocks, and then I was pretty much focused on getting my gear to work, because I really wanted to be able to breathe."

"I can understand that," said Lucy, with a smile.

Hank was clearly intrigued, however. "What do you think is down there?"

Sara rolled her eyes. "Mom is always looking for bodies."

"Sara!" chided Lucy. "That's not true. I was just wondering what might be hidden there. People throw all sorts of things into ponds, you know. There's supposed to be a piano in Gilead Pond."

"A piano!" Patrick thought that was hysterically funny. "In a pond!"

"Maybe we ought to schedule a dive there," suggested Hank.

"Will you be diving in Jonah's Pond again?" asked Lucy.

"I doubt it," said Hank. "The Conservation Commission wasn't very enthusiastic about giving us permission, and I don't want to go through another meeting."

"And there's all that crime-scene tape," said Sara.

"No, the tape's gone." Lucy's mind was busy recalling a recent planning board meeting where a property owner insisted he could build a nonconforming garage because he got permission seventeen years ago. "You know, if there was a problem about diving there, and I doubt there would be, you could say you already got permission. I don't recall that they specified a certain date. You could very well assume it was a blanket permission to dive whenever conditions were best."

Hank cocked his head. "So you really think there's something of interest down there?"

"I'd sure like to know if there is or not."

"I'll ask around tonight, see if anybody wants to check it out," said Hank.

Sara had put on her jacket and was standing by the door, obviously growing impatient. "I'm afraid we're going to be late for our dinner reservation . . . ," she began.

"Right." Hank put on his cap. "It was nice talking to you, Mrs. Stone. Have a good evening." He turned to Patrick, who was dragging a huge bag of dog food out of a cabinet in order to complete his evening chore of filling the dog's dish with kibble. "See you later, buddy."

Zoe came in as they were leaving, fresh from a planning meeting for the Take Back the Night March, along with Libby, who had an unerring internal clock when it came to mealtime. "You missed a good meeting," she told Sara. "Mary Winslow has agreed to come to the march!"

Libby was standing in front of Patrick, tail wagging and tongue dripping on the floor.

"Cool!" said Sara, taking Hank's arm and heading out the door. "You can tell me all about it later."

"Since when are they dating?" asked Zoe, unzipping her jacket as she looked through the window in the kitchen door and watched Hank open the truck door for Sara.

"Since today, I guess," said Lucy, who was dredging the chicken breasts in bread crumbs. "Can you give Patrick a hand with the dog chow? My hands are all gooey."

"Sure thing." Zoe handed Patrick the scoop, and he filled the bowl. Then she helped him replace the bag in the cabinet.

"That's great news about Mary Winslow," said Lucy, who had advanced to browning the chicken in a frying pan. "Miss Tilley will be very happy. She told me this is the thirty-fifth anniversary of the march."

"I guess that's why Mary Winslow agreed," said Zoe, who had unwrapped her scarf from her neck and was adding it to the hook next to the kitchen door that already held her jacket. "Uh, Mom, a cop car just pulled in, along with a tow truck."

"Oh, no!" exclaimed Lucy, turning off the burner and heading out the door. "Hey!" she yelled, recognizing Ferrick and DeGraw as they got out of the cruiser. "What do you think you're doing?"

Before they could reply, Bill drove into the driveway in his pickup truck, braked, and jumped out of the cab. "What do you want?" he demanded.

"Good timing," said Ferrick. "I was afraid we'd made this trip for nothing."

"Yeah," said DeGraw. "We're here to impound your truck."

"You can't do that," said Bill. "Lucy, call Bob, okay?"

Lucy had already dialed Bob on her cell phone and was getting an invitation to leave a message.

"Actually, we can impound your truck. I have a warrant right here," said Ferrick, producing a couple of sheets of paper.

"Let me see that," said Bill, snatching them out of his hand.

Lucy was standing on the porch, where Zoe and Patrick had joined her. She stuck out her free arm, warning them to stay on the porch with her, at the same time she was explaining the situation to Bob's voice mail. "When you get this message, please call us," she finished, grabbing Patrick by the hand.

"What are they doing?" asked Patrick.

"The policemen want to look at Grandpa's truck," Lucy said as the tow truck operator got busy loading Bill's truck.

"Why are they taking it away?"

"They want to examine it very closely," said Lucy, who had a terrible sinking feeling in her middle.

"Why?" asked Patrick.

"For evidence. Maybe it will help them figure out who killed Mr. Wickes."

Lucy thought Patrick was too young to understand the ramifications of the police action, but he was certainly picking up on the tense situation. "Is Grandpa in trouble?" he asked, sounding as if he was going to cry.

"Come with me, Patrick," said Zoe, taking his hand and leading him inside. "Let's watch TV."

"Good idea," said Lucy, giving Zoe a grateful smile.

For once, Patrick sounded reluctant about watching TV. "I don't . . .," he began, but Zoe wasn't taking no for answer. She scooped him up in a big hug and carried him inside. "What's your favorite video? *Frozen*?"

"No!" Patrick was giggling as she set him down. "*The Lego Movie.*"

By now the wrecker was leaving, carrying Bill's truck away, followed by the two cops in their cruiser.

"Mom," called Zoe. "Your chicken's burning."

It was, realized Lucy, catching the smell of burning meat. She ran inside and discovered that she hadn't turned the knob all the way and had succeeded only in raising the heat when she hurried outside. Surveying the charred mess, she found tears pricking her eyes as the smoke alarm began ringing. It was loud enough to wake the dead, and Libby was adding her two cents, barking furiously.

She was hauling the stepladder out of the pantry when Bill came in and took it out of her hands.

"Everything's going to be all right," he said, climbing up to disconnect the alarm.

"No, it's not!" Lucy was flapping a kitchen towel. "The chicken's ruined."

"There's leftover meat loaf," said Bill in a hopeful tone as he opened a window. Meat loaf was his favorite meal, and he couldn't have enough of it.

"We can't eat this," said Lucy, poking at the blackened hunks of meat with a fork.

"I bet Libby will eat it," said Bill.

Libby did seem interested. Her nose was in the air, and she was sniffing the rich aroma of burnt meat, tail wagging.

Lucy sighed and dropped the charred chicken into the dog's bowl, then pulled the Pyrex dish of meat loaf out of the refrigerator. She was mentally reviewing the contents of her pantry, thinking she could boil up some potatoes and Bill could grab some chard from the garden, when he took her in his arms.

"Oh, Bill," she wailed, bursting into tears. "I'm so scared."

"Me too," said Bill, smoothing her hair. "Me too."

"This is just crazy. I can't believe this is happening."

"It is kind of surreal," admitted Bill. "But we've just got to have faith. I'm innocent, and sooner or later they're going to figure that out. They can search as much as they want, but they're not going to find any evidence against me, because there isn't any. There can't be, because I didn't do it. I didn't kill Ev."

"Of course not," said Lucy. She'd had an unpleasant thought that perhaps someone was driving this investigation, fingering Bill to divert attention away from the real guilty party. If that was the case, the police might very well find evidence that had been planted on Bill. It was easy enough to toss something incriminating into the back of a pickup truck. Goodness knows Bill tended to accumulate all sorts of stuff, everything from tools and building materials to freebies he spotted along the road and figured might come in handy one day. "Bill, have you cleaned out the truck lately?" she asked.

"Not really," he said. "It's one of those things I keep meaning to do but never get around to."

Lucy nodded, dumping some potatoes into the sink and scrubbing them. "Is there any arugula left in the garden?" she asked.

"I'll go see," said Bill, grabbing the trug that sat on the floor by the door, underneath the table that collected mail and keys, and held country necessities, like flashlights and bug spray.

They all felt better after eating dinner; Lucy had always believed that there was nothing like a full tummy to give a person a sense of perspective. Of course Bill was right: an innocent man had nothing to fear. He had lived and worked in Tinker's Cove for over twenty years and had built a solid reputation for honesty and integrity. He was well liked and respected, and no one in their right mind would think for a moment that he would be capable of committing a violent crime.

So it was quite a shock when, having just started the dishwasher, she glanced out the kitchen window and saw Ferrick and De-Graw marching up the brick walk. Behind them, in the driveway, there was not one but several police cruisers. Armed officers in bulletproof vests were standing behind each cruiser, ready in case of trouble. But what trouble could they be expecting? She called for Bill, then opened the door.

"What's happening?" she asked. Bill had come from the family room, where he'd been watching the evening news, and was standing behind her.

"Put your hands up!" ordered DeGraw, producing a gun and holding it with both hands inches from Lucy's nose.

Lucy's hands flew up.

"What's going on?" asked Bill.

"Hands up!" screamed DeGraw. Ferrick had also produced his gun and was aiming it at Bill.

"Okay, okay," said Bill, obeying the order.

"On your knees!" yelled DeGraw, causing the dog to materialize suddenly. The noise had disturbed her after-dinner snooze on the family room sectional.

Hearing her growl, Lucy was terrified the cops would shoot her. "It's okay, Libby," she said in what she hoped was a soft, re-assuring voice, but it came out as a terrified squeak. "Can I just put the dog in another room?"

"Don't move," ordered Ferrick. "Don't anybody move."

The dog was moving, keeping an eye on DeGraw and slouching toward him. Behind her, Lucy could hear scuffling and sensed that Zoe and Patrick were coming to see what was happening.

"The kids," she hissed, sending up a prayer. All it would take, she knew, was one wrong move to set off a deadly hail of bullets.

"Look, I'm coming," said Bill. "There's no need for any of this."

The dog, Lucy saw, was primed, ready to go for DeGraw's knee. "Let me grab the dog," she begged.

"Okay," said Ferrick, with a sharp nod.

DeGraw followed her every move with his gun while she dragged the growling dog back through the kitchen and locked her in the powder room. Once the door was securely latched, she raised her arms once again.

"What about the kids?" she asked. "Can they go?" Libby was whining and scratching at the door.

"Everybody, hands up!" snarled DeGraw. "Kids, too."

"Patrick, put your hands in the air, in the air." Lucy sang the nursery school song softly, but the cops were having none of it.

"Shut up!" yelled DeGraw. "And, you, on the floor!"

Lucy watched as Bill stretched out on the floor, his hands still above his head. Two uniformed officers rushed in, and each one grabbed an arm and twisted it behind his back. After they applied handcuffs, they hoisted him to his feet and rushed him out of the kitchen, off the porch, down the walk, and into the back of a cruiser.

"Are you finished?" she demanded, her eyes blazing.

"Not yet," said Ferrick. "We have a warrant to search the premises."

"You have got to be kidding," said Lucy.

Ferrick tilted his head toward the kitchen table. "Why don't you all make yourselves comfortable while we proceed?" he suggested.

Lucy scooped up Patrick and settled him on her lap as she sat down. Zoe took her hand, and they held tightly to each other, making sure their linked hands were in clear sight on the table. It was ridiculous, thought Lucy. Of course the cops had to be careful, she supposed. These days they could encounter anything; some people kept arsenals of automatic weapons in their homes. But not them. She and Bill didn't have guns. They considered guns much too dangerous to keep in their home.

As they sat at the table, they could hear the cops working their way through the house, moving from room to room. She hoped they weren't making a big mess, but it sounded like they were yanking cushions off the furniture and dumping out drawers. It made her furious, and she wanted to yell and scream and slap them, but she knew she couldn't. She couldn't put up any resistance, any sort of fight, or she'd find herself in jail.

Like Bill, she thought, struggling to swallow around the huge lump in her throat. She could feel her heart thudding in her chest, and she buried her nose in Patrick's hair, closing her eyes and concentrating on his sweet, tangy little-boy scent.

"We're done," said Ferrick. "I've got a paper for you to sign. We're taking some evidence."

"Good luck with that," muttered Lucy, scrawling a few initials on the paper he had set on the table in front of her. "My husband is innocent!"

Behind him, DeGraw laughed. "That's what they all say!"

As soon as they were gone, Lucy dialed Bob, but once again she got voice mail. It took a moment for her mind to clear, but when it did, she dialed Rachel and got an immediate answer.

"The cops have arrested Bill, and they searched our house," she wailed. "They had guns. I was terrified they'd shoot us!"

"Ohmigod, Lucy. Bob's out of town, but he must be on his way home by now." She paused. "Are you all right?"

From the bathroom she heard Libby whining and opened the door. The dog charged out and stopped suddenly, finding the cops gone. She gave a good shake and helped herself to a big drink of water. "We're just shaken up. The kids and I are okay. But they took Bill off in handcuffs."

"I'll make sure Bob goes to the lockup as soon as he gets home," said Rachel. "He might be able to post bail." She fell silent; she and Lucy both knew that was not going to happen. "He'll call you as soon as he knows anything," she said. "Just hang tight."

Ending the call, Lucy went through the house, assessing the damage. It wasn't as bad as she'd feared. The cushions were off the couch, but they hadn't been ripped or damaged. The situation was the same in the bedrooms, where the mattresses had been pulled off the beds but had been left intact, and drawers had been rifled. It was worse in Bill's attic office, where files had been dumped on the floor and a bookcase was overturned. It was too much to deal with tonight, she decided, going back downstairs.

"Let's straighten up what we can," she told Zoe. "We'll start with Patrick's room."

An hour later, order had been largely restored and Patrick had been bathed in soothing lavender bubbles, which promised to promote calming sleep. They seemed to work, as he could barely stay awake for his bedtime story, and Lucy decided she would try them herself. Or maybe a shot of scotch. Or maybe a shot of scotch along with the bubbles.

She was pouring herself a jigger full when Bob called, and took a quick gulp, bracing herself for bad news.

"I'm sorry, Lucy, but it doesn't look good," he said. "They're keeping him in jail until he's arraigned — that's tomorrow morning — and I'm afraid that if he gets bail at all, it will be quite high."

"I don't understand," said Lucy. "He doesn't have a record, he's local, he's in business, and he has a family. . . ."

"Oh, believe me, I'm going to make sure the judge knows all that. And bring some nice clothes for him, okay?"

"So he looks respectable," said Lucy.

"You got it," Bob said, then paused to clear his throat. "But you have to be prepared, Lucy. Things don't look good right now. The cops found the murder weapon in Bill's truck. It's a bloody tire iron, and they're confident the blood is Ev's."

CHAPTER EIGHTEEN

Hall and Parris Funeral Home

Funeral Announcement

Evan D. Wickes

Tinker's Cove — A Memorial Service for
Evan D. Wickes Will Take Place at Hall
and Parris Funeral Home, 356 Main Street,
at 11:00 a.m., Thursday.
For Online Condolences and Directions,
Please Visit www.hallandparris.com.

Lucy went straight to Bob's office after
dropping Patrick at Little Prodigies. Patrick
was still upset about the police raid the
night before and clung to her neck when
she bent down to give him his usual good-
bye kiss, but she told him she had to go so
Grandpa could come home, and he finally
allowed Heidi to lead him over to the morn-

ing circle. In her mind, upsetting Patrick was just another mark against the cops, who, she believed, had unfairly and unjustifiably targeted Bill.

That was exactly what she started to explain to Bob, who was hunched over his desk, preparing for the arraignment.

"Great, Lucy. You've brought the clothes," he said, cutting her off and taking the hangers holding Bill's navy blue blazer, tan chinos, paisley tie and light blue button-down shirt. His good loafers and clean underwear were tucked in a recyclable grocery bag, which she also handed over.

"This is all a big mistake, right?" she continued. "You'll be able to get bail, won't you?"

Bob didn't look too hopeful. "Lucy, you've got to prepare yourself. There's going to be a lot of interest in Bill's arrest. . . ."

Somehow the idea that the media would be covering the procedure hadn't occurred to her. Until now she'd been focusing only on her outrage about Bill's arrest and the way the police had terrorized their family. Now she realized their troubles were just beginning, and they would be receiving a lot of unwelcome attention. She was grateful the girls had wanted to stay home, where they were going to spend the day tidying the house and putting all the things the cops had disturbed back in their places. At home they'd be protected from scrutiny, and she wished she had thought to tell them in no uncertain terms not to answer the door and to screen all phone calls.

"Now we're media targets," she said, with a sigh.

He nodded. "I called Ted and explained the situation. . . ." She felt as if she'd been slapped, and seeing her reaction, he quickly added, "I figured you had enough on your plate."

She sank into a chair. "I must be losing my mind. I should have called him right away. I have to resign. This is a huge conflict of interest."

"He doesn't want you to resign. He mentioned a leave of absence, until things settle down."

Lucy was quiet, absorbing this new ramification. She felt as if she was losing everything that mattered to her: her husband, her job, her reputation. And for no reason whatever, because Bill was innocent. It was all so unfair. "I can't believe this is happening," she said, with a sudden spurt of anger. "I wish Bill had never met that Evan Wickes!"

"Please keep that thought to yourself,"

said Bob. "Remember, Ev's death is a tragedy, and you mourn his passing, which your husband had nothing at all to do with. Understand?"

Lucy nodded. "Ev's funeral is today. Bill and I were planning to go, but now I'll have to go alone."

"Not a good idea," said Bob.

Lucy knew he was right. She'd covered funerals where reporters had hounded people considered newsworthy, and she'd even seen one widow viciously attack a woman she suspected had been her husband's lover. Her situation had changed, she realized. Now she was a person of interest, and every move would be scrutinized and discussed. "I understand," said Lucy.

Bob continued. "If anybody asks, remember you have every faith in the American justice system, which will prove your husband's innocence in this sad affair."

"Okay."

"Ready?" he asked, gathering up the papers strewn on his desk and stuffing them in a bulging leather briefcase.

"Do I look okay?" she asked. She hadn't really given much thought to her appearance that morning, but she had chosen the good black pants she always wore when she was covering a trial, along with a gray cashmere turtleneck and a scarf she'd bought in Paris last spring.

"You look fine," said Bob, giving her a thumbs-up.

They took separate cars to the courthouse in Gilead, the next town over, which was the county seat. Lucy was all too familiar with the court complex, which featured several buildings, including the registry of deeds, the probate court, the district and superior courts, as well as the county jail. The forbidding prison, built of gray granite and surrounded with razor wire, was set on a hill and loomed over the other buildings, casting a shadow that never seemed to shift, no matter what the time of day.

Lucy had visited the jail from time to time, when she was covering cases for the *Pennysaver,* and she knew only too well how it smelled of sweat and disinfectant, and how the heavy steel doors clanged when they closed. Bill didn't belong there, and she hated to think of the indignities he had to submit to.

When she arrived at the county complex, she discovered Bob was right to warn her. The parking lot contained several TV trucks, and there weren't any free spaces, so she had to cruise through the entire lot before she found a spot in an overflow lot behind the registry of deeds. Flipping down the sun visor, she checked her face in the mirror and added a slick of lipstick, her version of war paint.

Arraignments took place in the district court, and there was usually a long list of people accused of mostly petty crimes. The lobby was a large, echoing space that contained a couple of stiff wooden benches that usually provided seating for a handful of people, often consulting with a lawyer or anxiously waiting for a loved one. Today, however, it was filled with reporters, many of whom knew her from her work covering various trials. Ted, she noticed, was hanging back, against the wall.

"Lucy! Lucy!" The shout went up, and the mob surged around her, some with notebooks and others shoving microphones in her face. "Have you got a comment?"

Now the shoe was on the other foot, and Lucy had to admit she deserved it; she'd done the same thing to so many people. She was shaking, she realized, and her mind was a blank. Then Bob was beside her, giving her arm a squeeze.

"Mrs. Stone just wants to say that she is mourning the loss of a cherished family friend, Evan Wickes, and she has every confidence in the American justice system that her husband will be cleared of any involvement in his death."

"Is that right, Lucy?"

"Why did they arrest your husband?"

"Did you know about the marijuana?"

"Did your husband know about the pot farm?"

The questions were hurled at her as Bob led her into the courtroom, where, she was appalled to see, several TV cameras had been set up on tripods along the sides of the room. Bob took her to a front-row seat, where Rachel was waiting for her, and she sank gratefully into the place beside her friend, who grasped her hand.

"Thank you for coming," she said.

"Of course I'd come. You shouldn't be alone at a time like this."

Her stomach was in knots, and it was agony sitting there while the judge worked his way through the previous night's arrests. Drunk and disorderly. Driving under the influence. Assault with a deadly weapon, a shoe. Possession of an illegal substance. Possession of an illegal substance. Homicide.

There was Bill, standing behind a thick panel of glass, looking completely out of place in the tie and blazer he wore only to weddings and funerals.

"The accused was involved with the victim, Evan Wickes, who was growing a large amount of marijuana in the basement of his home," began the district attorney, Phil Aucoin, setting out the case against Bill. "Investigators believe that on or about the evening of October twenty-ninth, he became involved in an argument with Wickes that quickly escalated and became violent."

Lucy felt her muscles tense. She wanted to leap to her feet and shout that Aucoin was lying, that none of this was true, but Rachel had placed a hand on her thigh, reminding her to be still. "Just listen," whispered Rachel.

"We have witnesses who report hearing shouts coming from Wickes's home, where a gray Ford F-one-fifty truck was parked. Furthermore, investigators discovered a tire iron in the rear of the accused's truck, a gray Ford F-one-fifty, which they believe was the murder weapon. Because of these factors, we are asking that William Stone be held without bail. . . ."

Shocked to her core, Lucy rested her gaze on Bill, seeking a connection, a shared sense of outrage. But Bill was keeping his emotions tightly checked, refusing to reveal the least hint of fear or anxiety, appearing every bit as calm and composed as an usher passing the plate on Sunday morning in the

Community Church.

Bob was now on his feet, arguing for his friend and client. "Mr. Stone is a longtime resident and property owner in Tinker's Cove, a family man, and a respected businessman. He denies any knowledge of Mr. Wickes's marijuana operation and furthermore denies any involvement in his death. I would like to point out that Mr. Stone has no criminal record. He has never even received a traffic citation.

"I would also like to point out that the alleged murder weapon was found in the uncovered back of Mr. Stone's truck, where it could have been placed by anyone wishing to incriminate him. In addition, I might remind the court that the Ford F-one-fifty is a very popular truck — Country Cousins, for example, has an entire fleet of them — and my client maintains he was home that night, and his Ford F-one-fifty was parked in his own driveway. For these reasons, I respectfully request that my client be released on personal recognizance."

The judge leaned back in his large leather chair and stroked his chin with his hand, considering the arguments. Finally, after what seemed an eternity, he leaned forward. "All right, Mr. Goodman. I'm setting bail at twenty-five thousand dollars — and I hope

I'm not making a mistake. This is a serious charge, but I am mindful of Mr. Stone's reputation. I am also setting the date for a pretrial conference. Will December sixth be agreeable to everyone?"

Lucy didn't hear the rest of the back-and-forth. She just watched as Bill was led away by a bailiff, and then raised her eyes to the ceiling, not seeing the stained acoustic tile that hung there. She wanted to sing and dance and run around, waving her arms, but for now she had to content herself with letting the endorphins flow through her body, erasing the tensions of the past four-teen hours. Bill was coming home. That was all that mattered.

She jumped up, ready to leave, but Rachel yanked her hand. "Stay put, Lucy. The bailiffs won't let the reporters bother you here."

Lucy sat back down, realizing Rachel was right. Out in the lobby she'd be a sitting duck, especially since she wasn't sure what the procedure was for posting bail or where to go to do it. Further complicating mat-ters, she had no idea when or where Bill would be released, and neither did Rachel.

"To tell the truth, Lucy, Bob never thought he'd get bail for Bill. That's why we thought I'd better come to support you."

"This is just a brief reprieve," said Lucy, realizing their troubles were far from over. "There's still the trial, and Bill could be found guilty. He could go to jail. For life."

Rachel grabbed Lucy's hand and squeezed it. "That's not going to happen," she said. "He's innocent."

"Innocent people get sent to jail all the time," said Lucy. "Now that they've got DNA, they're discovering lots of people who shouldn't have been sent to jail."

"That's good for Bill, right?"

"I don't know," said Lucy. "He saw a lot of Ev. They worked together on that darned catapult. I'm sure there were a few scrapes and stuff that would have bled. Bill's DNA is probably all over Ev's tools and stuff, and vice versa." As she spoke, Lucy was thinking that the best way, and probably the only way, to prove Bill's innocence was to find the real murderer.

"Here's Bob," said Rachel as her husband crossed the emptying courtroom to join them.

"It's all set," he said. "We can go round back to meet Bill."

"He's free to go?" asked Lucy. "What about the bail?"

"I posted it. You're good for it, right?" Bob had taken her elbow and was steering her toward the door. A sudden burst of noise, scuffling and voices, indicated the morning session had ended and the pack of media hounds was now free to leave the courtroom. Bob offered words of encouragement as they turned to face the crowd streaming through the double doors. "Head up, Lucy. Look confident."

Until he spoke, she hadn't realized she'd ducked her head and raised her shoulders, as if expecting a blow. She took a deep breath, threw back her shoulders, straightened her back, and tucked in her tummy, adding a toss of the head for good measure. They walked along the concrete path that led to the rear of the courthouse, where prisoners came and went through a solid gray steel door, with a dozen or more reporters following behind.

They waited a few minutes, and then the door opened and Bill walked through, ducking his head and blinking at the sunlight and all the attention. *Not a good look,* decided Lucy, so she rushed to embrace him.

"Look 'em in the eye and smile," she whispered, and he broke into a grin and gave her a squeeze that lifted her right off her feet. That was the shot she hoped would be in the news, rather than the shocked, squinting expression, but only time would tell.

Bob had a sticker that allowed him to park in an area reserved for lawyers, close to the courthouse, so he led them to his car, and they all piled in. It was certainly very weird, thought Lucy, having every move observed and recorded by the media. Part of her wanted to flee, but she was surprised to find that another part rather enjoyed the attention. It was an unsettling discovery, and she could just imagine what her late mother would say, warning her not to get above herself. "Who exactly do you think you are, miss?" was a frequent refrain when Lucy was growing up.

Who exactly did she think she was? she wondered as Bob pulled up beside her car and she and Bill climbed out. She felt as if she'd been playing a role, the strong, faithful wife, rather than revealing the frightened, angry woman she really was. They had finally shaken the press pack, so they took a moment to thank Bob and Rachel for all their help. Then they were alone together in the SUV, and the real Lucy emerged and burst into tears.

"Calm down, Lucy," said Bill, looking over his shoulder and backing out of the parking space, then driving too fast through the lot to the exit. "It's going to be okay. Everything's going to be fine."

"I'm so scared," she blubbered as her cell phone began to ring. She pulled it out of her bag, along with a tissue, and gave her nose a good blow before answering. It was Heidi, from Little Prodigies, and Lucy immediately assumed that Patrick had been having a difficult day.

"We'll come and get him right away," she told Heidi.

"Good. And you understand he can't return until the treatment has been successfully completed?"

"Treatment?" What could she possibly mean? Was he being referred to a psychiatrist or some therapist?

"For the head lice," said Heidi.

"Lice?" screamed Lucy, causing Bill to swerve sharply, nearly running off the road.

"For Pete's sake, Lucy," he growled.

"Are you telling me Patrick has head lice?"

"I'm afraid we've had a bit of an outbreak here," said Heidi, whispering.

Bill was scratching his beard, and Lucy was aware that her head was suddenly very itchy. "What a nightmare," she said, thinking they could stop at the drugstore on their way to the day-care center and pick up the combs and shampoo and disinfectant they would need.

"You can say that again," said Heidi, with a sigh.

Patrick was unfazed, however, when they arrived to take him home. "Heidi says I need to wash my hair with special soap," he said, climbing into his booster seat. "We all do, 'cause we've got little bugs."

"That's right," said Lucy, who was fighting the urge to scratch her head, afraid of what she might find.

Sara and Zoe had rather different reactions, however.

"What's that?" asked Zoe, spotting the bottle of special shampoo sitting on the kitchen table, along with several nit combs.

"Patrick got lice at day care," said Lucy, who was collecting all the hats and scarves belonging to the family, which she was going to take down to the washer in the cellar. Once she got that load going, she was going to strip all the linens off the beds and wash them, too.

"Eeeuw! Yuck!" shrieked Sara.

"That's icky," said Zoe, grimacing. "Poor little guy."

"Poor little us," said Lucy. "We've probably all got them, too. Has your head been itchy?"

"I thought it was dry scalp," said Sara.

"From the chlorine in the dive pool."

Zoe was examining her sister's head, parting her hair with her fingers. "Nope, not chlorine," she said, grimacing.

"I think I'll die," said Sara.

"Shower first," advised Lucy, with a nod at the bottle of shampoo. "And then we can all spend a lovely afternoon picking nits from each other's hair."

"Kinda puts things in perspective, doesn't it?" asked Bill, who was fresh from the shower and had damp hair.

"What do you mean?" asked Lucy, resting the laundry basket on a cocked hip.

"Well, jail was bad, but not as bad as, uh, this."

Lucy gave in to the urge to scratch. "I think it's all pretty disgusting," she said, yanking the cellar door open and clunking down the stairs. "Dis-gus-ting!"

Chapter Nineteen

Tinker's Cove Conservation Commission

Press Release

For Immediate Release

Responding to Several Incidents Involving Minors and the Illegal Consumption of Alcohol, the Commission Voted at Its Last Meeting to Restrict Access to Town Conservation Lands to the Hours between 6:00 a.m. and 6:00 p.m. Groups Using the Conservation Lands Will Be Required to Notify the Commission in Advance, and Forms for That Purpose Are Now Available at Town Hall. Police Have Been Informed of the Change and Will Conduct Regular Patrols.

That evening, after Lucy had checked everyone's heads and had found them nit free, she set out celebratory fixings for make-your-own sundaes on the kitchen table.

"How many scoops can I have?" asked Patrick, greedily eyeing the goodies.

"As many as you want," said Lucy. "We've had a tough day, and we all deserve a treat."

"Five?" he asked, pushing the envelope.

"How about three?" suggested Lucy. "But you can have a different topping on each scoop."

Patrick chose a scoop each of vanilla, chocolate, and cookie dough ice cream, and specified that he wanted chocolate sauce on the cookie dough, strawberry on the vanilla, and marshmallow fluff on the chocolate. On top of all that, he wanted jimmies, whipped cream, and three cherries.

Amused by his certitude, Lucy complied, piling on the sweets.

"What would Molly say?" asked Zoe, who was limiting herself to a single scoop of vanilla with a generous dollop of chocolate sauce.

"I'm sure she'd be appalled," said Lucy, who was helping herself to strawberry ice cream, strawberry topping, and lots of whipped cream. "It's mostly air, not calories," she insisted as she finished off the whipped cream, although they were all too busy eating to pay attention.

The ringtone on Sara's phone — a rap song — broke the quiet, and she reluctantly put down her butterscotch sundae to answer. After a few "Wows" and "That's great" and a heartfelt "Thank you," she ended the call and made an announcement.

"The scuba club is going to dive in Jonah's Pond tomorrow," she said.

"How come?" asked Lucy, licking her spoon. "I thought Hank was dead against it."

"I had a talk with him," said Sara. "I told him about Dad getting arrested and that you suspected there might be something in the pond that would help clear him, and he talked it over with the others, and they're going to do a systematic search of the entire pond. He said it would be a good experience for everyone, anyway."

"This is great," said Lucy. "Isn't it great, Bill?"

Bill was scraping the last bit of chocolate sauce from his bowl. "I don't know what you expect to find, but . . ." He paused to give Sara a big smile. "I sure do appreciate the effort."

"It was nothing, Dad," said Sara, blushing and turning her attention to her sundae.

■ ■ ■ ■

Saturday morning, bright and early, found Lucy and Sara at Jonah's Pond, where members of the scuba club were gathering on the small sandy beach. Most had take-out cups of coffee, and Lucy had brought a box of doughnuts, which they were eagerly consuming. Hank was assigning areas of the pond to various members of the club, who were beginning to put on their wet suits and other gear. They were just about ready to begin the search when Tom Miller roared into the parking area in his company pickup truck. After jumping out, he marched pur-posefully toward the group of divers.

"What do you think you're doing?" he demanded.

"We're going to dive," said Hank, step-ping forward. "It's a practice exercise."

"Well, you can't do that," said Tom. "You need permission."

"We have permission," said Hank, glanc-ing at Lucy. "We got permission at the Conservation Commission meeting."

"That was for the contest, that underwater pumpkin-carving thing," said Tom.

"Actually, it doesn't say anything here about the contest, and no date is specified," said Hank, producing a folded piece of paper.

Tom took the paper, glanced at it, and tore it in half. "I don't care what this paper says. It's not correct. I'm on the commission, and I say you can't dive here."

"I think you're overstepping your authority," said Lucy. "You don't own the pond anymore. It's conservation land, and the Conservation Commission gets to decide what happens here."

"And what exactly are you doing here?" demanded Tom, turning on Lucy. "Are you a member of the club?" Tom was quite red in the face, and his body was rigid. He kept flexing his hands, as if he wanted to punch somebody.

"I'm a citizen, and I have every right to be here," said Lucy, refusing to be intimidated. "This is town-owned conservation land open to the public."

"I'm warning you," snarled Tom, "if you persist in this dive, there will be trouble. Mark my words."

"Yeah, Hank," said one of the divers. "We don't want any trouble."

Sensing that dissent was brewing among the ranks, Tom pressed his advantage. "I'm calling the police," he said, reaching for his cell phone.

"C'mon," said another diver, a girl. "We can dive someplace else. It's clouding up, anyway."

Lucy glanced at the sky, which was quickly filling with storm clouds, and noticed a stiff breeze had blown up. There was no sense continuing a losing battle, she decided.

"Better not," she said to Hank, with a shrug of her shoulders.

"Okay, we'll cancel the dive," he said, hoisting his tanks and carrying them toward his truck. Then he stopped and turned, facing Tom. "But I think Mrs. Stone is right. This is public land. Maybe the permit has expired, but the commission did vote to let us dive here, and we're going to follow up on this at the next meeting."

"Good luck with that," snarled Tom, who had placed himself between the straggling group and the pond, as if he was prepared to fight anyone who tried to enter the water.

"Weird," said Sara, trudging up the path to the parking area, loaded with her heavy equipment.

"There's something in there that he doesn't want found. I'm sure of it," said Lucy.

"I think you're right," said Sara.

By now they'd reached Lucy's SUV, and Sara was loading her diving stuff in the rear.

When she lowered the rear door, she suddenly laughed. "I guess Tom Miller's not going anywhere soon." She pointed to his Country Cousins truck, which had a very low rear tire.

"Interesting," said Lucy, climbing behind the wheel of her car and reaching for her cell phone. "I think I'll do the neighborly thing and get some help for him."

"Are you crazy?" asked Sara.

But Lucy wasn't calling for a tow. She was calling the state cops, asking for DeGraw. He was out, she was told, but she could leave a message on his voice mail.

"I think I may have a lead on the tire iron," she said, giving Tom's name and license plate number. "It's worth checking out."

"Do you really think Tom killed Ev?" asked Sara. "Why would he do that?"

"I don't know," said Lucy as she drove out of the parking area, "but I do think something suspicious is going on at Country Cousins."

"There sure is!" exclaimed Sara a few moments later, when they were approaching the company complex. "It's a raid or something."

A uniformed cop was standing in the road, holding up traffic, as a long line of police vehicles, lights flashing, was proceeding onto the property. Some of the vehicles had the state police logo; others were unmarked but had federal license plates.

Lucy immediately pulled off to the side of the road and started snapping away on her camera, at the same time ordering Sara to call Ted and tell him about the raid. Her view was largely blocked by the arborvitae hedge, and she was considering trying to sneak onto the property to get an eyewitness account when the cop in the road approached, waving her on. She put the camera down and asked what was happening, but he wasn't about to talk. "Nothing to see here. Move along," was all he had to say.

Lucy had no choice but to obey, but Ted called her with an update later, when she was having a bite of lunch. She was alone. Bill and the kids were out, busy with Saturday activities.

"Buck Miller's been arrested," he said. "He was using Country Cousins trucks to distribute marijuana. It was a huge operation. Cops say it's their biggest bust ever. And he was crossing state lines, so he's facing federal charges. This is huge, Lucy."

Lucy swallowed the bite of tuna fish sandwich she was eating. "What about Tom

Miller? Did he know? Was he involved?"

"Doesn't seem so," said Ted, "but it's early days. Who knows what they'll find. They're going over that complex with a fine-tooth comb."

Thinking of her recent experience with the nits, Lucy wished he'd chosen a different metaphor. "What I hope they'll find is proof that somebody there killed Ev," declared Lucy. "I think it might've been Tom Miller. I noticed his truck, his silver Ford F-one-fifty, has a really flat tire."

"And you think he's missing his tire iron, or he'd change his tire?" asked Ted.

"Could be," said Lucy.

That evening, Lucy and Bill were in their room, getting ready to catch the late movie at the newly restored downtown theater. Patrick was asleep in his father's old room, and Zoe had agreed to stay home with him because she had to finish a term paper. Sara was out with Hank. Lucy was applying a quick slick of lipstick when Bill's cell phone rang. It was Bob, telling him that all charges against him had been dropped. Instead, he said, Buck Miller was now charged with Ev's murder.

Shocked, Lucy grabbed the phone. "Buck? What about Tom?"

"I don't know anything about Tom," said Bob, sounding puzzled. "What the DA told me is that some Country Cousins employees who were involved in the marijuana operation actually came to him, asking for immunity in exchange for their cooperation. A couple of them say they witnessed a heated argument between Buck and Ev. The two came to blows at the warehouse, and then they went outside and nobody saw Ev after that. The presumption is that they continued the fight elsewhere and Ev was killed. Police investigators found traces of Ev's blood in a company truck."

Lucy was finding it hard to reconcile her image of Buck as a clean-cut, ambitious young striver with this new development. "The employees ratted him out?" she asked. "Who were they?"

"I don't know. The DA wouldn't tell me." He paused, and his tone changed to a gentle reprimand. "Not that it matters, Lucy. The important thing is that Bill is free and clear."

"Absolutely," said Lucy, knowing she deserved a scolding. Bob was right, and she was a horrible wife, more interested in the unfolding story than in her husband's release from a murder charge. "Of course," she added in her own defense, "I always knew Bill was innocent. But thank you for all your help. You've been wonderful, and we're really grateful."

"No big deal," said Bob, sounding embarrassed. "I'm just glad Bill is off the hook." Then Bill was taking the cell phone out of her hand and wrapping her in his arms, kissing her, and drawing her toward the bed.

"What about the movie?" she asked, but he overrode her objections with another kiss. "And the kids?"

"We'll be quiet," he said, covering her lips with a finger before moving on to undo her bra.

Next morning, however, Lucy's curiosity got the better of her. Bill was busy cooking waffles for everyone, so she took a moment to slip into the family room and call Barney Culpepper.

"I heard they arrested Buck," she said, then took a sip from the mug of coffee she'd carried with her.

"Yeah," replied Barney. "Good news for Bill, eh?"

"Sure is. A huge relief," admitted Lucy. "Bob told us some Country Cousins employees actually turned him in."

"I guess Buck didn't inspire a lot of loyalty," said Barney. "Too ambitious."

"Maybe they just felt they were getting in too deep, especially if they knew he'd killed

Ev. Pot's one thing. Murder is another," said Lucy.

"He denies it, of course," said Barney. "Claims he spent the entire night Ev was killed with Corney Clark. What do you think of that?"

"I guess I should be surprised, but I'm not," she said, recalling how Corney had been all over Buck at the first interview. "What does Corney say? Is she sticking by her man?"

"Not exactly," said Barney. "So far we haven't been able to locate Corney."

"Ohmigod!" exclaimed Lucy, terrified for her friend. "You don't think he killed her, too?"

"Hold your horses, Lucy. Corney's a big girl. She could be anywhere. Maybe she went to visit her mom. Or snuck off to some spa somewhere."

Once again, Lucy's thoughts turned to Jonah's Pond, and she wondered what secrets it might hold. "I suppose you guys are looking for her," said Lucy.

"Well, you know our resources are pretty limited," said Barney. "We did check out her place. There was no sign of any trouble there. It was neat as a pin. Truth is, Buck's legal team is on it. They've hired a private investigator."

"So the department isn't looking for her?" asked Lucy, appalled. "The man's accused of murder and his girlfriend disappears, and you're not following up?"

"We're following procedure," said Barney, sounding a bit huffy.

"Procedure," said Lucy sarcastically. In her opinion *procedure* was one of those terms, like *zero tolerance,* that substituted all too often for clear thinking and common sense.

"Well, it's been nice chatting," said Barney, "but I gotta go. Dispatch is calling."

"Take care, Barney," said Lucy, ending the call. She followed the delicious smell of bacon and pumpkin waffles into the kitchen, where she joined the rest of the family at the big round table.

"This calls for a toast," she said, raising her glass of orange juice. "Here's to Dad!"

Patrick chimed in, lifting his mug of cocoa. "To Grandpa!"

"Three cheers," demanded Sara, and they all joined in heartily.

"I don't know if it's my waffles or my innocence that you're all cheering about," said Bill.

"Both," said Lucy, pouring on the maple syrup.

She had just finished loading the dishwasher with the breakfast dishes when Sue called. "Guess who I saw this morning?"

"Corney Clark?" guessed Lucy, hoping she was right.

"No. Not Corney. Marcia Miller!"

"Of course!" said Lucy. "She's a mama bear come to help her son. You know Buck's accused —"

"Yeah, yeah," said Sue. "Old news. Marcia is new news."

Lucy had to agree. "What does she look like? She must be pretty old now?"

"She doesn't look old. She's been living in France. They have ways of dealing with aging. And she has a new husband and a new name. She's Marcia d'Aubigny now."

"Would I recognize her if I saw her?"

"Absolutely. For one thing, she's better dressed than everyone in Tinker's Cove except me. And her color job is fantastic. And she's quite slim. She was riding a bike when I saw her."

"Riding a bike?"

"Yeah, she said it was for exercise."

"So you spoke to her?"

"I did. She said she was struck by how nothing much had changed in Tinker's Cove since she left, and she was here because of all this nonsense with Buck, which is absolutely ridiculous, since he is the sweetest, best son a woman could have, but she really wished there was a decent bakery in town, because the French bread at the IGA is not really bread at all."

"Interesting," said Lucy.

"And then she really let it rip," continued Sue. "She kind of leaned close, like she was telling me a secret, and she said she had never wanted Buck to come back to Country Cousins, because she doesn't think much of Tom Miller. 'He's the one they ought to be investigating,' she said. 'Everybody thinks he's Mr. Nice Guy, but he's not. He hides his true nature, so nobody knows what he's really capable of.' "

When Lucy heard this her eyes widened. "She really said that?"

"She did. But I think it's just sour grapes or jealousy. In my opinion, Tom's a great guy with a generous heart, and it's unfortunate he got stuck with such a horrible family."

"I'm not so sure," said Lucy, thinking of his missing first wife. "I think Marcia may be right. I think there's a side to Tom Miller that we don't know anything about."

"Give it up, Lucy," said Sue. "And great news about Bill. I hope you're celebrating today."

"We already did," said Lucy, patting her

full tummy. "Waffles."

"You wild and crazy kids," said Sue, laughing.

Halloween, 1979

She felt as if her head would explode. Her vision was wonky, a kaleidoscopic assault of flashing lights and sharp angles that whirled every which way. She was flat on her back on the wood floor, rough with wear, and he was on top of her. She could feel his weight pressing on her chest and hips, and she could smell the bleach and starch Emily used on his white shirt, and his old man's breath, foul from the pipe that was always in his mouth. She couldn't get any air, so she tried to push him away, tried to wiggle and squirm out from under him.

She tried to call for help, to call Tom, but could manage only a feeble croak, a mere mouse squeak of a cry.

"You'll never get away now," he whispered, his voice hoarse. Then she felt his hands around her throat. He was gentle at first, stroking her neck and pressing himself rhythmically against her groin, but then his hands tightened and she heard his dentures clicking as he groaned and grunted with pleasure. The bright, jangly lights faded, coalescing into a single soft light. *Like the moon on a hazy night,* she thought, with a sense of wonder. Then it was gone.

CHAPTER TWENTY

Tinker's Cove Women's Club

Press Release

For Immediate Release

The Women's Club Announces Its Annual Thanksgiving Pie Sale, to Be Held at 10:00 a.m., Wednesday, November 24, in the Community Church Fellowship Hall, Main Street. All Pies Are Homemade and Will Go Fast! Proceeds Support the Club's Scholarship Program.

Lucy was at work on Monday, reading the hundreds of e-mails that she had received over the weekend and deleting most of them. There were sales at the Kittery and Freeport outlets, hardly news, despite the hyperbolic prose claiming "rock bottom prices you won't believe" and "70, 80, even

90 percent off." Dancing Deer Baking Co. and Stonewall Kitchen had special Thanksgiving offers, which gave her pause. *Thanksgiving?* That meant Christmas was just around the corner. Usually a truly depressing thought, but this year it meant Toby and Molly would be coming home soon. And there were the usual announcements for the "Cove Calendar" listings of bake sales, community theater productions, club meetings, and holiday bazaars, all of which she forwarded to Phyllis. It was only by chance that she noticed that Detective Lieutenant Horowitz had sent the announcement that the state police were holding an unclaimed property auction. That meant, she realized with a sense of growing excitement, that Horowitz was back on the job, and she reached for her phone.

"Did you have a nice vacation?" she asked when he answered her call.

Horowitz was not one for social niceties and ignored her polite inquiry, getting right down to business. "Lucy Stone, it seems you were busy while I was gone." He chuckled. "And some people say there's no God."

"Ha-ha," said Lucy, who suspected that the state police lieutenant had actually grown fond of her through the years but didn't want to admit it to her and maybe

339

not even to himself. "If you'd been here, I'm pretty sure Bill would never have been arrested. Your colleagues Ferrick and De-Graw were awfully quick to pin Ev's murder on him."

"Well, it all worked out in the end, right?"

"There were some awfully tense moments. I wouldn't want to go through it again," said Lucy.

"Do you want to file a complaint?" he asked.

"No, no," said Lucy, who figured that was asking for trouble. "But I do have some information. . . ."

"Here we go again," groaned Horowitz.

Lucy chuckled. "This is important," insisted Lucy. "I think you may have the wrong guy. Again."

Horowitz sighed. "Shoot."

"Well," she began, "you know how the case against Bill hinged on that tire iron they found in his truck? Well, on Saturday morning, Tom Miller was driving around on a practically flat tire, which makes me wonder if maybe his tire iron was used for something other than changing a tire."

"An interesting idea, Lucy, but don't you think somebody as rich as Tom Miller would just drive into an auto repair place and get his tire changed? Or get one of his employees to do it? It's most probably a company vehicle, right?"

"Not if his tire iron was missing," insisted Lucy. "It would be bound to raise suspicion since Ev was killed with one."

"Lucy, why don't you fix yourself a nice, calming cup of chamomile tea?" suggested Horowitz. "I started drinking the stuff when I was on vacation in Italy, and I found it was very relaxing."

Lucy was dismayed. "Aren't you going to follow up with Tom Miller?"

"I'll think about it," said Horowitz. "And in the meantime I don't want you doing anything foolish, understand?"

"Of course not," said Lucy. Ted had come in, whistling cheerily, and she had to end the call.

"What are you so chipper about?" demanded Phyllis, who was right behind him, carrying a couple of recyclable grocery bags.

"It's a beautiful fall day, and I've got a big story right here in town. . . ."

"Well, I'm glad you're so happy, because I've got a petty cash voucher right here for you to sign. . . ."

"What is this?" he demanded, taking the slip of paper and examining it closely. "Ninety-eight dollars for coffee?"

"Coffee's going up, but it was buy one,

get one free, so I stocked up and bought the limit, which was eight big cans. And, of course, there's that fake creamer stuff you use, which is nothing but a lot of chemicals, but you don't like the store brand, though how you tell the diff, I'll never know, and then I had to get the sugar, which is going to give you diabetes. Well, it all adds up." She dropped the bags on her desk with a clunk. "Do you want to see the receipt?"

Ted raised his hands in surrender. "No, no, that's okay. I'm sorry I asked." He turned to Lucy. "Sometimes I wonder if I'm really the boss around here, you know?"

She smiled sweetly. "Your wish is my command, master."

"Ah, since you're so agreeable this morning, I wonder if you'd like to go around town and snap some photos of Country Cousins and the Millers' house. You might even lurk a bit and see if you can catch some candids of the Millers themselves, if they happen to be out and about."

"Tabloid stuff?" asked Lucy, surprised by his request, and a bit repelled, too. She was still smarting from her own recent experience with the press and wasn't comfortable about harassing Tom and Glory. "We don't do that. Besides, everybody here in Tinker's Cove knows what the Millers look like and where they live and what they own."

"So they do," said Ted. "But this is a story with regional, even national appeal, and I can sell those photos." He was pouring himself a mug of coffee, then stirring in the creamer that Phyllis so despised. "You could even get some video on that camera of yours, right?"

"Okay," agreed Lucy. While she didn't much like the assignment, she wasn't about to jeopardize her job. And, she had to admit, it was preferable to being stuck in the office all day and writing a boring story on the proposed new zoning regulations. She slipped on her Country Cousins barn coat, grabbed her camera, and stepped through the door, glad to be out in the sunshine and fresh air.

She decided to begin with the Country Cousins store a few doors down on Main Street, which was closed and had yellow police tape wrapped across the porch. It was one of those pictures worth a thousand words, when you considered that Country Cousins was famously open for business 365 days a year, 366 in a leap year. She was in luck. She even got a short video interview with Dottie Halmstad, a longtime employee, who had arrived for work and realized she wasn't needed.

"I can't believe it," said Dottie, whose gray hair was styled in an easy-care cut. "In all my years the store has never been closed. Not even for blizzards and hurricanes. We always had to come in, no matter what."

Lucy's next stop was the headquarters complex, where she got a photo of the state trooper who barred her entrance. She parked the car on the side of the road and walked back to the gate, where she was able to get pictures of the many police vehicles parked inside the complex, as well as a short clip of a jumpsuited crime-scene investigator carrying a paper bag out of one of the buildings and carefully stowing it in a van.

She knew that Tom and Glory Miller's house was just a little ways down the road, and headed there, promising herself that she would simply snap a photo of the big mansion, and would make it quick, so as not to attract any unwelcome attention from the residents. She was mentally composing the shot as she drove down the country road, picturing a scene with the huge house in the background and the mailbox bearing the Miller name in the foreground. Once again, it would be a picture that told a story. The oversize house was a symbol of achievement and success that anyone could understand, and the fancy custom-made mailbox was a far cry from the cheap, battered boxes most rural mail customers had in front of their houses. And Country Cousins was a mail-order business, to boot.

Lucy was pretty pleased with herself as she pulled over to the side of the road and parked a car length away from the fancy mailbox. The Millers' property wasn't fenced, but there was a low rose hedge, now dotted with crimson hips, which she hoped would conceal her if she crouched while she snapped a few photos. She had been careful to park the SUV next to a bushy evergreen, thinking it would hide the car from anyone looking out of the house.

It took a bit of creeping around and peeking before she had the picture she wanted in the viewfinder, and she was just about to snap it when the front door to the house opened and Marcia stepped into view.

Just as Sue had told her, Buck's mother, who was dressed in black leggings and a bulky designer sweater, looked as if she'd stepped right out of the pages of the French edition of *Vogue.* She was pulling on gloves as she crossed the white oyster-shell driveway to a Cadillac Escalade with a small Hertz sticker on the side window, stepping lightly in her ankle boots.

She was opening the car door when the

door to the house opened once again and Tom Miller came out. He stood on the porch, arms akimbo, and yelled at her. "You're making a big mistake!" he bellowed.

Marcia merely looked at him, then calmly proceeded to settle herself behind the wheel of her rental car.

That angered Tom, who charged across the driveway and attempted to open the car door, but found it was locked. That infuriated him, and he grabbed one of the decorative stone blocks that edged the driveway. Marcia's car was rolling and she was picking up speed when Tom threw the chunky block, shattering the driver-side window. The block bounced off without hitting Marcia, but she was shocked and too stunned to drive and merely sat, clinging to the steering wheel and shaking her head.

Lucy was dialing 911, unsure whether to remain in hiding or to risk attempting to intervene between the two. When she saw that Tom had the door open and was pulling Marcia from the car, she decided she had to act.

"Stop! I've got this all on tape!" she screamed, holding up the camera.

The camera was like a red flag to a bull, and Tom charged at her.

"I've called the cops," she yelled, stopping

him in his tracks.

"Well, call them back and tell them it's a big mistake," he ordered her in his CEO voice. "And, by the way, I'm tired of your snooping around. This is a private family matter, and I'll thank you to leave us in peace."

Lucy looked at Marcia, who was brushing bits of glass off the complicated folds of her beautiful russet sweater. "Are you all right?" she asked.

"Let the police come," Marcia said. She was slightly out of breath, and Lucy noticed that she'd picked up a bit of a French accent. "You saw what he did to me. He wants to kill me. It is time that the truth should come out."

"That's fine. Let the police come," said Tom, resorting to negotiation. "But she," he said, pointing at Lucy, "has to go. She's from the newspaper. She'll have our faces plastered on every front page from here to, to . . ."

"To Paris?" asked Marcia, raising a dubious eyebrow.

"You're part of this family, too," muttered Tom. "Maybe it's time you started to face up to your responsibilities. You can't run away this time. It's your kid who's in trouble, and maybe you ought to think about starting some damage control." He turned to Lucy. "And, you, if you'll just mind your own business for once . . ."

"Mind my own business! That's ripe," exclaimed Lucy. "This *is* my business. You're the one who put the tire iron in my husband's truck. You tried to stick him with murder when you knew all along it was Buck!"

"Oh, no. He wouldn't do the least little thing for Buck. Not anything at all," said Marcia, stepping out of the Cadillac. "Oh, no. Tom was protecting himself and his big secret." She tilted her head in the direction of the Country Cousins complex, visible in the distance on the hill above Jonah's Pond. "Why do you think I left? I was afraid, terrified, after what happened to my husband. When he died, there was no one to protect me, but I'm not afraid anymore. It's all going to come out, finally. Isn't that right, Tom? The big family secret."

"You don't know what you're talking about," scoffed Tom. "There's no secret."

"But there is," said Lucy. "I suspected it all along. There's something in the pond that you don't want found, right? That's why you wouldn't let the kids dive. . . . Somebody could have died, you know, because you tampered with their equipment."

"Somebody did die," said Marcia. "Tom's first wife, Cynthia."

"I didn't kill Cynthia!" declared Tom. "She deserted me. She ran away."

"Enough with the lies, Tom," said Marcia. "I know what happened to Cynthia. My husband, Sam, said he saw you and your father loading her body into a trunk when he was just a kid. He had nightmares about it his whole life."

"He saw?" asked Tom, with a little start. "I didn't know that. He never said."

"Why would he say?" demanded Marcia. "So you could kill him, too?" She shook her head. "No. He knew the family way. Secrets. Always secrets."

Tom stared at the ground; then he looked up and straightened his shoulders. "You're right. Too many secrets. But I'm telling the truth. I didn't kill Cynthia. It was my father. He killed Cynthia when she tried to leave. He had us all under his thumb with his locks and control. We had to account for every minute. I grew up that way, and I thought all families were like that. It wasn't until Glory came along that I realized how nutty it was. . . ."

"Nutty!" exclaimed Marcia, not convinced. "That's a funny word. Like it was nothing but a little eccentricity? A teeny little awkwardness? A little quirk? No, no, no. It was murder. You took a life. You killed your wife."

"It wasn't me," said Tom, speaking with a clenched jaw. "I didn't kill Cynthia. I loved her. I would never hurt her."

"Oh, Tom," sighed Marcia. "You always do this. You have to put the blame on someone else. You can't face the truth. You say you loved her, but you let your father abuse her. He was always at her, Sam says, forcing himself on her, making her —"

"Shut up!" snarled Tom. Lucy had never seen Tom Miller like this. She'd always seen the affable, handsome, friendly Tom, but this Tom was behaving like a cornered dog, with his curling lips and his eyes that darted nervously back and forth.

"I will not shut up," declared Marcia. "This has gone on too long. I didn't want Buck to come back here, and I was right. You've gotten him involved in drugs, and now you're trying to pin that murder on him."

"Now who's the one trying to pin blame on someone else!" said Tom.

"It was you, wasn't it?" said Lucy, wondering what was taking the cops so long.

"Buck is young and foolish and greedy, but he would never kill anyone," said Marcia. "But you, Tom, you would do anything to protect your precious secret."

"You killed Ev," said Lucy as the puzzle pieces fell into place. The pumpkin maulings, the vandalism, the bureaucratic red tape were all efforts to stop the Giant Pumpkin Fest. "The fest was too risky for you. All the outsiders coming to town, the media . . . All it would take was one slip and Tinker's Cove isn't the pumpkin capital. It's the pot capital. You had to stop it. . . ."

"I had to stop the pot. That much is true," said Tom, jutting his chin out defensively. "It was all getting out of control. Ev wanted more and more space, more workers, more trucks, and Buck thought it was great. He was convinced marijuana was going to be legal soon and we'd be in position to control the Northeast market, maybe the world. The kid was so high most of the time, he thought he was king of the world."

That was too much for Marcia, who suddenly threw herself at Tom, shrieking, "Liar! Liar!" and beating his chest with her fists. Tom tried to subdue her and succeeded in grabbing her wrists, causing Marcia to kick at his shins with her pointy-toe boots. In the distance, finally, Lucy heard the faint wail of a siren, but time seemed to stop while the two struggled. Marcia had the advantage of surprise, at first, but Tom was bigger and stronger and was soon able to subdue her. She had given up the fight and was holding her arms up defensively, but Tom didn't stop, couldn't stop. Lucy watched, horrified, as he wrapped his hands around Marcia's neck and began to choke her. Marcia was making awful sounds as she struggled for air, and Lucy looked desperately for something she could use to stop him.

Then, suddenly, Glory was there, raising the canister of candy corn and smashing it down on Tom's head, momentarily stunning him. Marcia staggered backward and collapsed on the oyster-shell driveway, her hands at her neck, chest heaving. Tom fell to the ground, and Glory was on her knees, crying and cradling his bleeding head. The heavy cut glass canister lay where it had fallen, amid the scattered candy corn.

"So tell me all about what happened while I was gone," said Corney, fresh from an island vacation and sporting a fabulous Caribbean tan.

Where to begin? wondered Lucy. They were standing among the crowd gathered for the Take Back the Night March, watching the sun set from the town pier. Then, as darkness fell, they would climb the hill to Main Street to march to the Community Church, where a program would take place featuring the much-anticipated appearance of Mary Winslow.

"Marcia and Glory are taking over at Country Cousins. Buck is facing charges for distributing marijuana, and Tom is accused of murdering Ev Wickes. That's it in a nutshell."

"That much I know, Lucy. Why did Tom kill Ev?"

"To stop the marijuana operation. And he also wanted to throw a monkey wrench in the Giant Pumpkin Fest, because he was afraid the underwater pumpkin-carving contest would uncover the big family secret, the body of Tom's first wife, Cynthia, which was hidden in the pond."

"Tom killed his first wife?"

"He says not. He insists it was his father, Old Sam, who had been sexually abusing her. Old Sam was a kook. He kept every room in the house locked. He was a lot like Lizzie Borden's father. A real control freak."

"But Lizzie killed her father, or so they say," said Corney.

"Cynthia only tried to run away, but Old

Sam caught her and killed her and made Tom help him bundle her body in a trunk and drop it in the pond. Marcia says Sam saw the whole thing as a child and was haunted by it."

"And Buck?"

"Well, you were right that he is a real go-getter. It seems he was positive marijuana would soon be legal here in Maine, like in Colorado, and he wanted Country Cousins to be in position to dominate the market."

"Will he go to jail?" asked Corney as the crowd began moving up the hill, led by Miss Tilley and her friend Rebecca Wardwell. Seth Lesinski was there, too, along with a big contingent from the college that included a surprising number of male students.

"I don't know. He's got Bill Braxton representing him."

"The state rep?"

"Former state rep," said Lucy. "He's now CEO of a legal medical marijuana dispensary."

"Is it just me, or does that seem a bit dodgy?" asked Corney.

Lucy shrugged, striding along as the group reached the top of the hill and the pace picked up. "It's all about who you know. You know that. You're the one who's always talking about networking."

"I think I left town at a good time," said Corney. "Buck might've tried to get me involved."

"For a while there I was worried you might be at the bottom of the pond, too," said Lucy.

"They did have a total immersion treatment at the resort's spa, but I passed on it," said Corney, with a grin.

"Sounds like a smart decision," said Lucy as the group gathered in front of the Community Church. Mary Winslow was already there, waiting in her wheelchair on the paved terrace in front of the church doors.

"Thank you all for coming," said Miss Tilley, speaking into a microphone. "This is a wonderful night, the thirty-fifth anniversary of our first Take Back the Night March." She paused while the crowd applauded. "In these years we've made some great strides to stop violence against women, but sadly, we know that it still continues. Here tonight we have a survivor of abuse, Mary Winslow."

Rebecca wheeled Mary forward to the mike, which she removed from its stand and passed to her.

"Tonight I want to say only that violence against women must end, and I want to dedicate this march to the memory of Cynthia Miller and all the other women who have suffered and died at the hands of people who claimed to love them."

Mary then lit a candle. Miss Tilley used it to light her candle, then passed the light on to Rebecca. Rebecca carried her candle to the edge of the terrace, where Sara was standing, and gave the light to her. Sara passed it to Zoe, who passed it to Renee, who passed it to Amy, and on and on it went, until everyone was holding a lighted candle. Then, at a signal from Mary, they raised their candles high above their heads, lighting the night with the glow of hundreds of candles.

ABOUT THE AUTHOR

Leslie Meier is the acclaimed author of over twenty Lucy Stone mysteries and has also written for *Ellery Queen's Mystery Magazine.* She is currently at work on the next Lucy Stone mystery. Readers can visit her website at www.LeslieMeier.com.